THE REMINGTON FACTOR

RAYMOND OBSTFELD

CHARTER BOOKS, NEW YORK

THE REMINGTON FACTOR

A Charter Book / published by arrangement with
the author

PRINTING HISTORY
Charter Original / January 1985

All rights reserved.
Copyright © 1985 by Raymond Obstfeld
This book may not be reproduced in whole
or in part, by mimeograph or any other means,
without permission. For information address:
The Berkley Publishing Group,
200 Madison Avenue, New York, New York 10016.

ISBN: 0-441-71344-0

Charter Books are published by The Berkley Publishing Group,
200 Madison Avenue, New York, New York 10016.
PRINTED IN THE UNITED STATES OF AMERICA

Beginnings

Thursday

TWO MIDDLE-AGED MEN staggered down the corridor of the twenty-first floor of the Commodore Hotel.

"I've got a question for ya."

"Shoot, Buddy."

Buddy stumbled forward into the elevator door, bounced back, then stabbed his finger at the button a few times before hitting it. "I've got a question for ya. It's important."

"Well, goddamn it, ask it, then."

"Don't get sore, Kevin, for chrissake."

Kevin sighed, pounding an impatient fist on the elevator door. He was eight years younger and thirty pounds lighter than Buddy, and when the two of them drank together, Kevin always wanted to poke Buddy in his fat gut. "I'm not goddamn sore, Buddy. Just ask your goddamn question."

"Right." Buddy reeled for a few seconds, trying to remember what his question was, then grinned wickedly when it came back to him. "Oh, yeah, I remember."

"Well, ask it, then!"

Buddy snickered. "How come blond pussy is softer than other kinds of pussy?"

The door slid open on an elevator occupied by one elderly woman wearing a pastel green trench coat and carrying a matching umbrella.

The woman frowned at Kevin and Buddy as they

3

lurched into the tiny elevator, giggling like schoolboys, their breath stinking of stale booze and foul cigars. She stepped back until her shoulders pressed against the back of the elevator.

"Well?" Buddy continued. "Answer me that one, smart-ass."

"I can't."

"Why the fuck—oops, pardon me, lady. Why not?"

Kevin lowered his voice and looked embarrassed. "I ain't never seen *real* blond pussy."

"Never?" Buddy was incredulous.

Instinctively both men turned to look at the woman's hair, which was mostly gray. They burst into laughter. "No point askin' her," Buddy roared. They slapped each other on the back a few times.

"Say, Kevin," Buddy said in a low, hoarse voice.

"Speak up, son. I can't hear ya when ya mumble."

"I . . . I feel . . . funny," he gasped, and then dropped to his knees with a dull thud that rocked the elevator.

"Come off it, Buddy," Kevin said, slapping him playfully on the back, but there was a high-pitched note of panic in his voice. For indeed Buddy did look funny. His face had turned a sickly gray, and his lips were dark blue. He was reeling, not drunkenly now, but like a man teetering on the edge of a cliff a second before falling. His suddenly swollen tongue flopped out of his mouth like a thick black fish.

"Christ, Buddy—"

Without warning, Buddy screamed and then clamped his mouth shut, biting through the end of his tongue. Blood spurted up into Buddy's face and across Kevin's khaki pants. A small hunk of tongue rolled down the front of Buddy's shirt before dropping onto the elevator carpet.

"Jeez, Buddy!" Kevin cried, flailing his arms helplessly as Buddy fell backward, clunking his head against the wall, his body jerking as if he were being electrocuted.

The elderly woman dropped her umbrella and bent over Buddy, pushing Kevin out of the way. She dropped to her knees and tore open the collar of Buddy's shirt, then forced his head up and pried open his mouth to keep him from swallowing what was left of his mangled tongue.

"Buddy! For chrissake, Buddy," Kevin moaned, hugging his own chest and unconsciously rocking himself.

"Shut up and help me hold him still!" she shouted.

Kevin hesitated a moment before stooping down and pinning Buddy's convulsing shoulders to the floor. Blood seeped out the sides of his mouth and Kevin had to keep himself from giggling because it reminded him of Christopher Lee in all those horror movies. He almost expected Buddy to start growling and baring a new pair of size eleven incisors. Buddy's head just kept flopping from side to side like the rest of his body, as if he were sizzling in an invisible frying pan. The old woman kept digging into his mouth for his tongue, not even minding that his head-shaking had sprayed blood all over her coat.

Finally the elevator slid to a stop with a little kick and the doors whooshed open onto the crowded lobby. Two well-dressed couples who'd been waiting for the elevator pressed in without looking, then realized what was going on. The two women took one look at Buddy's thrashing body and the blood gurgling out of his mouth, and began to scream. The men with them quickly hustled them out of the elevator as a bellman hurried to hold the elevator door open.

"Get help, for God's sake!" the woman in the elevator yelled at them, and one of the men pushed his way through the gathering crowd. She heard his shouts for help in the distance, but she didn't relax. She couldn't. Her hands were full just holding Buddy still enough to keep him from hurting himself. Kevin continued to whimper next to her. "Jeez, Buddy. My God, Buddy."

"It's okay, mister," she said soothingly to Buddy. "Everything's okay. They've gone for help."

Buddy jumped and bucked as if all his internal organs were fighting to escape his body and would burst right through the skin like shrapnel. The woman looked over her shoulder at the crowd of staring people. "Where's the doctor? Find a doctor!" she demanded.

"Oh, jeez!" Kevin yelled suddenly, jumping to his feet and backing away. "Oh, my God!" He covered his mouth as if to muffle a scream.

The woman turned back to look at Buddy. He was still alive, but his body was no longer flailing and bucking. It was still, though it vibrated slightly as if the blood were boiling swiftly through his veins. She looked at his face and gasped, pulling her hands away in horror.

"Lord!" she gasped.

Buddy's eyes were open wide and staring fixedly at the ceiling. But something was wrong.

"His eyes," she whispered. "His eyes."

A small drop of blood was oozing up out of the white of one of his eyes. When enough blood had gathered to form a large drop, the weight caused it to roll down into the corner of his eye where it puddled until it was joined by another thick drop. And another. And yet another. Finally it spilled out of the eye and ran down his cheek like a dark tear, leaving a thin pink streak behind. Then the same thing happened to the other eye. Buddy's expression was no longer one of pain; his face was paralyzed into a mask of indifference, making the scene all the more horrible. He looked almost amused.

The woman inched a finger forward, slowly moving it toward his face, toward the cheek, toward the blood. Ever so carefully, like a child approaching an open flame, she brushed her fingertip lightly over Buddy's gray cheek.

Immediately the skin on his cheek burst open like an overripe peach, forming a wide split that ran from his cheekbone to the corner of his mouth. Beneath the skin she could see exposed muscle and even a few of his teeth. Fresh blood pumped up and spilled out of the wound as if his cheek had been slashed with a dagger. The woman recoiled with an involuntary shout, falling back hard on her buttocks. The elevator swayed with the shock.

The blood seemed to be everywhere, and Buddy

began to choke as it poured along the split skin and into his open mouth.

The woman leaned forward on her knees again and held Buddy's head up to keep him from drowning in his own blood. She turned him to allow the blood to drain out of his mouth, but as she did so, her left hand rubbed against his right ear. It came off in her hand.

"Jeez, Buddy!" Kevin screamed and bolted out of the elevator, knocking people aside as he ran.

The gray-haired woman stared at the ragged ear in her hand, then dropped it when she heard shouts.

"Coming through. Move away, please. I'm a doctor."

A baby-faced, slightly potbellied man in his early thirties edged through the crowd and took in the situation.

The woman turned to him and tried to speak but was unable. She was crying, with great sobs wracking her body. The doctor helped her to her feet and handed her over to the crowd. They were solicitous and sympathetic, but no one wanted to touch her. Her hands still dripped blood.

The doctor looked at Buddy and seemed to choke. "I'm a doctor," he said again to no one in particular. He got down on one knee and began to examine Buddy.

The crowd stared in hushed fascination as the doctor began tending to the bloody body on the floor of the elevator. He reached out and took hold of the top of Buddy's head to tilt him sideways, as the woman had tried to do. But when his hand touched Buddy's hair, a large chunk of scalp peeled away as if it had been hacked off with a hatchet.

"Shit!" the doctor yelped and jumped back, flinging the scalp out of his hand. Several strands of bloody hair stuck to his palm, and he rubbed it frantically against his tweed jacket. He turned quickly to the crowd behind him. "Everybody get the hell out of here. *Now!"*

The crowd caught the urgency in his voice and backed off a few feet, but did not disperse. They huddled together as if under a hypnotic spell.

As soon as the bellman and the rest of the crowd backed away from the elevator, the doors suddenly closed with a hollow thud. The doctor spun around in a wild panic and began pounding on the doors. The muffled booms echoed through the small elevator like marching troops. Just as suddenly, the doors opened again, and he pulled the emergency stop knob to keep them open. The crowd was still there, watching and waiting. Somewhere in the distance, a siren wailed.

The doctor's breathing was shallow when he turned back to Buddy. But it was too late. Buddy choked a few times, then his breathing stopped. The doctor had a vague feeling that he should try to resuscitate the patient, but he was afraid to touch any part of the body.

A loud murmur of approval ran through the crowd as two paramedics ran through the lobby carrying a stretcher, the hotel manager pointing the way. The doctor wiped the sweat from his eyes and stared at the hunk of scalp he'd thrown down. Blood seeped out of the bald patch at the back of Buddy's head.

"What the hell? Christ, Rod, look at this," the first paramedic said.

"Looks like he drowned in his own blood, Bill," Rod said. "Start the CPR."

Bill hesitated a fraction of a second, then shrugged and bent over Buddy to probe his neck in search of a pulse. When he touched the throat, his fingers sank into the flesh as if it were fresh dough. "God," he said, jerking his hand back. As he pulled his fingers out, Buddy's neck made a slushy, sucking noise. Now there were three holes in the neck, each filling up with blood that then spilled downward.

"Now what?" Bill asked.

Rod shook his head.

The crowd remained horrified at the bloody spectacle before them. All except one man. He had left his seat in the lobby to investigate the commotion, but he had not joined in the crowd's collective muttering and head shaking. Instead, he used his battered violin case as a wedge to push himself closer to the open elevator.

He was at least six inches taller than anyone else in the

crowd, and no one argued with him as he pushed forward. But his height wasn't the only thing that kept those he'd edged aside silent. One look at his face was enough. Like his body, it was long and bony, with circles under his eyes so dark they looked like tattoos. Over his right eyebrow was a large, circular green and yellow bruise.

He squeezed past a thick-waisted woman at the front of the crowd. Next to him, an old couple clutched each other's blue-veined hands.

"My God," the old man sighed, a tear trickling down one wrinkled cheek. "Terrible, isn't it?"

"Terrible," the tall man nodded, but his face belied his speech. Unlike the pitying frowns of the others, he wore a thin but unmistakable smile.

Dr. Jeremy Feld rolled over onto his left side and tugged the covers up. He couldn't sleep unless his shoulder was completely covered. But not his neck; the bedclothes couldn't even touch his neck. It was a compulsive habit that alternately amused and annoyed his wife. Not that he was going to get any sleep tonight anyway. He'd been up half the night talking with authorities from the hospital, the hotel, the police, and God knows who else. He'd repeated the story so many times it didn't sound real to him anymore. But it had been real. The queasiness of his stomach and the film of cool sweat on his body told him that much.

After putting their four-year-old daughter Claudia to bed in the next room, Sheryl had done her best to comfort her husband, but it had been no use. He'd tried to explain to her what had happened, but she knew very little about medicine. All deaths were equally horrible to her, and so when he'd described what had happened in the hotel elevator, she hadn't been any more surprised than if he'd described a heart attack.

But this death was different. Very different. Even the paramedics, who were used to seeing the worst that can happen to people, were shaken by this one. But no one would talk to Jeremy about it. Two doctors from the

hospital had questioned him in the presence of three
men in rumpled business suits—cops, he guessed—who
stared but said nothing. Why the silence?

Afterward he'd cornered one of the doctors and
asked him for a diagnosis, but the doctor had merely
shrugged, sucked on an unlit pipe, and walked away.

Jeremy sighed and tugged the covers a little higher.
The blanket was soft, the sheets clean and cool. It was a
nice room. The Prince Barnes Suite. A hundred and
forty-three dollars a night. The auto club book had said
it would cost a hundred and twenty-five dollars, but it
was last year's book. Besides, the Commodore had a
wonderful restaurant. Four stars from the auto club.

What a night. What a goddamn night. With only two
days left of the week's vacation, this kind of thing had
to happen. Why couldn't Sheryl have listened to him
this one time and agreed to go to Hawaii for the week?

He shifted in bed again, careful not to disturb Sheryl.
He fanned his face with his hand. He was still sweating
despite the air conditioner. Sheryl had told him to take
the blanket off, but he reminded her that he couldn't
sleep without a blanket covering his shoulders. She'd
shaken her head and laughed. Tonight his obsession had
amused her.

He felt a drop of sweat roll lazily across his thigh.
Christ, every part of his body ached. His insides were
tender, his muscles sore, as if he'd been riding a wild
horse all day. Tension, he decided.

He looked at the digital clock on the bedside table:
3:45 A.M. He'd never get to sleep.

He lifted his head to look at Sheryl, but she was
curled up with her back to him, her face sandwiched between two pillows. She'd stolen his pillow while he was
in the bathroom scrubbing his hands for the eighteenth
time. His skin was almost raw now, but he couldn't help
himself. He had to wash away the memory of the
bloody scalp sticking to his palm.

Maybe he should try to read. He climbed gently out
of bed, anxious not to awaken his wife. He tiptoed to
the dresser, and picked up the Ross Thomas novel he'd
left there, *Chinaman's Chance*. Just the thing to get his

mind off of what had happened earlier. He couldn't stand to think about it. Every time he recalled the torn ear, the bloody scalp, the bleeding eyes, the punctured throat, the memory slammed into his stomach like a fist. It had already sent him to the bathroom three times tonight to vomit. His stomach couldn't take another bout. Still, he'd done better than the other two—the elderly woman who'd tried so hard to help the victim, and the dead man's lodge brother. Both had to be sedated, and the lodge brother had been kept overnight in the hospital for observation.

Jeremy wished he knew exactly what had happened, what had caused such horrible symptoms. But he didn't have a clue. In his pediatric practice he'd seen nothing to compare with this case.

He took a few steps toward the door that separated their bedroom from the one where their four-year-old daughter slept. A two-bedroom suite was an extravagance, but it had delighted Claudia so much it had been worth it. Besides, this was a vacation, and he and Sheryl had planned to catch up on some serious lovemaking.

He turned the knob slowly, quietly, opening the door only far enough so that he could squeeze through. The hinges squealed a little. He looked back at Sheryl, but she didn't stir. He slipped through the door and over to his daughter's bed. The floor was carpeted, but the wood underneath moaned occasionally.

He stood next to Claudia's bed and looked down at her quiet, peaceful face. She looked exactly like Sheryl. Not one damn thing from him. Her aristocratic brow, her sandy hair, the slight overbite that would someday become sexy instead of cute. God, he thought, don't let that day come too soon. He leaned over, his nose a few inches from her face, and inhaled. Jesus, how he loved her smell. When is it, he wondered, that children lose that smell and start waking with a sour taste? He brushed a lock of wispy hair from her forehead, and Claudia frowned and turned onto her side in that curled position her mother favored. He crept back out the room and closed the door.

The images of Buddy Zane were almost gone now—

not forgotten, but overpowered by other images. Images of Claudia peacefully asleep. Memories of last Christmas, his wife giggling in the bathtub as they'd washed off the body paint she'd bought on a whim. And there was his medical practice, not large enough yet to make them wealthy, but sound enough to keep them comfortable. *Comfortable*. That was a nice word. Sounded good. Felt good in the mouth. Especially after tonight.

He hitched his drooping pajama bottoms and walked around the bed to look at Sheryl. The pillow on top of her head covered her face. This room was darker than Claudia's, and he had to walk more slowly and carefully so as not to bump into anything. His foot touched something wet in the carpet, and he fought a stab of anger that threatened his loving mood. He'd told Sheryl a hundred times not to leave her glass of water on the floor next to the bed. She'd knocked it over half a dozen times, and he'd toppled it on two different occasions.

He inched another step forward, trying to recapture his loving mood. He remembered the surprise birthday party she threw when he turned thirty. They danced to old rock 'n' roll songs all night. The Beach Boys, Jan and Dean, and Freddy and the Dreamers. He smiled. He reached down and gently lifted the pillow from her head, but it was too dark to see her face. He chuckled to himself as he reached for the table lamp. He wanted to see Sheryl's face. It was a three-way bulb and the low setting shouldn't disturb her. As his right hand felt along the lamp base for the switch, his left hand moved toward the outline of her hair to brush the wispy lock he knew was hanging there like a question mark. His hand softly swept the hair from her forehead and became tangled in her curls. He carefully pulled his hand away, but it seemed to remain tangled. A cold bullet of adrenaline shot through his stomach. She was going to be angry if he awakened her by pulling on her hair.

His right hand found the light switch, and he clicked the bedside lamp on—and jumped back in terror.

His wife's face was crazily split into crisscrosses, the skin gashed and torn as if it had been slashed with a razor. Her eyes hung out of their sockets, attached only by the thinnest thread of muscle. Dark blood soaked the pillows and sheets around her face and had seeped over the side of the bed into the carpet where it was staining his feet. Half of her lower lip flapped against her chin as if it had been ripped off with pliers. Several of her teeth lay in a line on the pillow where they had fallen. A ten-inch strip of hair was gone from the top of her head. Tiny pinpricks of blood were starting to bubble up through the missing scalp. Tangled in his trembling hand was the missing hair from his wife's head.

Dr. Jeremy Feld stumbled backward into the bedside table, knocking the lamp over. The light bulb popped out, throwing the room into thick, cloying darkness.

Then he screamed and screamed and screamed.

The tall man carried the violin case through the hotel lobby, past the bored cops standing around checking their watches and sipping black coffee. Reporters wandered around interviewing anyone who stood still for more than two seconds. The hotel manager, the medical examiner, and the hotel doctor conferred behind the reservations desk where dozens of hotel guests were lined up, anxious to check out. It was five in the morning, and all of them looked as if they could use about two days of sleep.

The violin case was much lighter now that it was empty, and he raised it slightly in a half-salute as he passed the doorman.

"Cab, sir?" the doorman shouted above the wail of approaching ambulances.

The tall man looked at his watch. "No, thanks," he smiled. "It's a perfect morning for a walk. Perfect."

Friday

"DEEP SHIT, GENTLEMEN," she said, swiveling about to face the three men sitting around her desk. "That's what we're in now. And I mean neck deep."

The stony expressions on the men's faces clearly showed that they agreed with her assessment. But she knew that their minds were also occupied in figuring out how best to avoid being blamed for what had happened. Or better, how to shift blame to one of the others sitting in this room. She liked that about them. It proved they were the right men for the job.

"Any questions so far?"

The three men said nothing.

Celia Bedford smiled. At fifty-eight, she still looked like a glamorous woman in her mid-forties, with her long, thick black hair and high sloping cheekbones. A lot of people thought she looked like Jackie Onassis, and more than once had she been asked to sign autographs while lunching at Ciro's. Certainly the resemblance hadn't hurt her career in Washington. But aside from the pretty face, she also had an exceptionally attractive figure, the result of rigorous daily workouts on the trampoline in her living room. Half an hour in the morning during the "Today Show" and an hour in the evening to Donna Summer records. Her looks, like her career, hadn't come easily, and she was proud of both.

She pushed herself out of her chair and walked slowly

14

around her desk. With a simple, graceful motion, she hopped up onto the edge of the mahogany desk and crossed her legs. There was a faint rustle of nylon brushing nylon, and it pleased her to see all three of the men, even Morley who was a homosexual, shift their eyes to glance at her legs. She pulled the hem of her skirt down over her knee and pretended to look for loose threads. She would let the men worry a little, let them sweat it out. Their minds worked much better under pressure. Fear made them more devious.

"Well, since you have no questions, are there any suggestions?"

Still, the three men said nothing.

She looked around the room and shook her head. Like many other rooms in Washington, this one had been done by a decorator who was commissioned to do a hundred rooms at once and had therefore bought a hundred identical lamps, tables, desks, chairs, and whatever other items the wholesalers were trying to unload that month. This office also had the best in electronic anti-bugging devices built into the furniture and the walls. Aside from the standard-issue devices, Celia Bedford had had a more powerful anti-bugging device secretly installed after she'd found a microphone attached to one of the original mechanisms. She knew it had been planted by one of the men in this room, but that didn't bother her. She liked initiative.

She stared at each one in turn and smiled. Her teeth were perfect since she'd had the front ones capped, and she knew that when she smiled she looked at least fifteen years younger. So she smiled a lot. Even at times when others found a smile inappropriate. Like now. But Celia Bedford knew what she was doing. She was the head of this tiny group, the existence of which was one of the few remaining secrets in this town. The group had a name, of course, but it never appeared on stationery, government budget requests, or mailing lists. They had no staff, nor did they send any memos to one another. All meetings were conducted in this office while the electronic jamming devices were on. Outside this room the three of them exchanged only the most casual pleasantries about weather and traffic. They never met socially; in fact they didn't even like one another very much. But unlike most other government operatives, they were very good at their job.

Those who had a need to know called them I-COOP, a shortened form of Intelligence Cooperative. I-COOP consisted only of the four people sitting in Celia Bedford's office, and each represented a different intelligence community. Morley was from the FBI; Hawkins, the model train freak, was from the CIA; and General Steve Gerrard, who was fighting his ex-wife for custody of their three daughters because she had allowed a man to move in with them, was the Pentagon's military intelligence liaison. Celia Bedford had been their chief since the group's formation twelve years earlier. She reported only to the President or his council. She never freely offered information, however, and no President had ever been foolish enough to want to know about things he would be politically better off not knowing.

The group's alliance was an uneasy one, formed only out of necessity. Each felt a loyalty to the agency he represented, and each member of I-COOP had the power to issue orders, request equipment, demand unlimited manpower for his own agency without asking anyone else's permission or going through the usual channels. This staggering power had been the main stumbling block to I-COOP's creation, despite the fact that every administration since Roosevelt had tried to organize a similar group. One man had always stood in its way: J. Edgar Hoover. The angry bulldog had refused to permit anyone but himself to have power over the FBI. Besides, he'd never liked any of the other intelligence outfits anyway. They'd lacked his brand of discipline. But after his death in 1972, I-COOP had been established and had later been responsible for many of this country's most dramatic and vital intelligence successes.

And some of its most devastating failures.

Including this one.

Celia Bedford reached around and snatched a piece of

paper from her desk. "According to this report, eight
people have died so far."

Hawkins from the CIA cleared his throat. "When
was the last death?"

"Ten o'clock this morning."

Hawkins cleared his throat again. He invariably
cleared his throat before speaking, which drove everyone else mad with impatience.

"For chrissake, spit it out, Tom," Eric Morley said.

Hawkins ignored the interruption, cleared his throat
again, and said, "Is there a chance that other deaths
have gone unreported?"

"Eric?" Celia nodded at Morley.

"That's possible but unlikely. We have agents covering everyone who was anywhere near the hotel at the
time."

Hawkins cleared his throat. "What about the people
they come in contact with who weren't near the hotel?"

Morley shrugged. "We have limited manpower,
Tom. I can't goddamn cover everyone in this country."

"Besides," Celia said, "secondary exposure is not a
serious consideration due to the material's age. Even
primary exposure was limited. Those who are going to
die are already dead. There's nothing we can do for
them. Our job is to make sure this doesn't happen
again."

General Gerrard tugged nervously on his wispy
mustache. He'd worn the mustache for nearly nineteen
years, yet he still behaved as if he'd started growing it
last week. "What do we have to go on?"

Celia took a deep breath and uncrossed her legs.
"Well, we know it was a deliberate act."

"No chance at all of an accident?" Morley asked. He
grinned slightly to show that he was goading her. Apparently he'd found the person he was going to lay the
blame on if things didn't work out. Well, like the other
two men, he'd been hungering for her job for several
years now, and Celia realized he was the best qualified
contender.

She assessed his youthful, rugged good looks and

smiled. "God, you're gorgeous, Eric. Too bad you like to take it in the ass."

Hawkins cleared his throat, and General Gerrard shifted uncomfortably in his chair.

Morley just kept grinning at her. They'd played this game for years, and he didn't mind. In fact, it had been Celia who'd kept him from being thrown out of the FBI after someone told the director about his sexual preference.

Celia returned his grin. She remembered her meeting with the director of the FBI after he found out Morley was gay. She'd twisted some beefy arms and bruised some delicate male egos to make sure Morley kept his job. Of course, she didn't tell them that she was the one who'd anonymously leaked the information to them in the first place. Now Morley owed her one. And she would know the right time to collect.

Hawkins cleared his throat. "I think we can safely assume that this was a deliberate act."

"By whom?" General Gerrard asked.

"Only a few people could have done it," Hawkins said.

"Four people," Celia said.

"Eight people," Morley smiled. "If you count us."

"For the time being I won't count us. That leaves the other four."

"But it can't be one of them," General Gerrard said. Now he was chewing on one end of his mustache.

"That's right," Hawkins said. "We've taken care of them."

"Apparently not thoroughly enough. If we assume that it is none of us"—she nodded politely at Morley— "then the only other possibility is one of the other four people who knew about Moonshadow."

Morley crossed his legs in a conscious parody of Celia, tugging at the knees of his pants. "Including Clifford Remington?"

At the mention of that name Celia frowned and Hawkins and Gerrard shifted in their chairs. They knew Clifford Remington had always been the toughest part of the whole operation. Not only because of the special status he'd had with the project, but because they'd always considered him the most dangerous of the four men involved with Moonshadow. The one they had to fear most.

"Especially Clifford Remington," Celia said.

"How can we be so certain that it's not one of us?"

"I've had all of your movements checked out thoroughly for the past month. So far you're all clean." No one protested this; they looked more relieved than angry. "Of course, that still leaves me." Celia smiled, showing her perfect, capped smile. "But that's a chance you'll have to take. For now."

General Gerrard picked a mustache whisker off his tongue. "So what's our plan of action going to be?"

"Good question. Obviously whoever caused these incidents is capable of causing others, many others, any time or any place. Our objective is to stop him, for two reasons: first, because his actions could cost thousands of lives; and second, because the trouble he causes could eventually lead some people to ask questions about Moonshadow and about our involvement in it. Needless to say, if anyone finds out what we did, that will be the end of I-COOP."

"And the four of us as well," Eric Morley added.

Hawkins cleared his throat. "The media are calling it the Brotherhood Disease because six of the eight dead were members of the Brotherhood of Granite convention."

"Good," Celia said. "Let them concentrate on that angle for a while. They'll check out the food, the laundry detergent, and everything else in that hotel. That will give us the time we need."

"The time to do what?" Morley asked.

She shrugged. "There's only one thing we can do, and it's already being done." Then she crossed her legs again and smiled. "Anyone know what time it is in Dallas?"

Saturday

"HOW ABOUT A train accident?"

"What kind?"

"Pushed in front of a subway train. Splat!" He slapped his beefy hands together to demonstrate.

"They don't have subways here."

"Well, they've got goddamn trains, don't they?"

"Sure."

"Well, then?"

He thought about it a second then shook his head. "Nope. Too messy."

"Car accident?"

He shook his head again. "Uh-uh."

Edge Connors clucked his tongue while he thought. "How about strangulation? Piano wire around the neck, a quick jerk, it's all over in seconds." He made a choking noise.

Tyrone Willis shrugged. "Possible."

"Okay," Edge said, "let's keep it on the back burner." He clucked his tongue a few more times and sighed. "Mugging's pretty good in this situation."

"Yeah," Tyrone nodded. "I was just thinking the same thing."

Edge grinned. " 'The greatest minds are capable of the greatest vices as well as of the greatest virtues.' "

"Who said that?"

"Descartes, the philosopher."

Tyrone shook his head and grinned. "Where do you come up with that stuff, man?"

"Reading. Like the commercial says, 'Reading is fundamental.' I'm telling you, the son of a bitch who stole our TV last spring did Jenny and me a favor. Since then we've had more time to read and talk and even screw. It's been great. I wish the punks had left the stereo, though. I built it myself."

Tyrone shook his head again. "You're nuts, man." He shifted uncomfortably in the driver's seat of the Honda Accord. He'd moved the seat as far back as it would go, but his legs still felt cramped. Hell, it wasn't easy being six feet five and always driving rented cars. Especially the kind their budget allowed.

"So, it's a mugging, then," Edge said from the back seat. He was four inches shorter than his partner, but painfully cramped nonetheless. "Agreed?"

"Okay. How?"

"Gun?" Edge patted the lump under his corduroy sports jacket.

"Too noisy."

"We can always go back to the piano wire. That's quiet."

"Yeah, but not a very popular M.O. with muggers. Too professional. It's got to look like a real mugging. Amateur stuff, you know?"

"Right." Edge clucked his tongue again. The sound used to annoy Tyrone, but now he found it helped him think. "We could crush his windpipe, I guess."

Tyrone shook his head. "Same problem as the piano wire. Too specific, too professional."

"Well, shit."

"Let's just keep it simple."

Edge reached into his pants pocket and pulled out a Boy Scout knife he'd carried since he was a kid growing up in Fargo, North Dakota. He'd carried it through two years in Vietnam, and he'd been carrying it ever since.

"I guess it's Howdy Doody time." He'd called his knife that ever since he swapped his Howdy Doody lunch box for it with Timmy Jenkins.

"Doesn't look like much."

Edge opened the blade. It was barely three inches long, but shiny as new chrome, sharp as a blade of wild grass. "It'll do," he said with a shrug.

"Okay, but keep it simple. A minimum of blood."

"I was just thinking the same thing."

"Great minds . . ." Tyrone winked and turned to continue his watch on the building that housed Dr. Yuri Hermann's office.

Jim Talon sat on his psychiatrist's sofa and sipped the coffee the doctor's secretary had brought in. She'd apologized for serving it in a paper cup, but she'd broken the last of the porcelain cups earlier that morning.

"Would you believe it?" Dr. Hermann said. "Last week I bought two dozen brand-new mugs, and she's managed to break all of them already?"

Jim said nothing.

"I think she does it on purpose," Dr. Hermann continued, warming to the subject. "I think she subconsciously resents serving coffee as part of her job. It threatens her identity, forces her into the traditional role of a woman as servant."

"Maybe she's right," Jim said, just to say something.

Dr. Hermann squinted at Jim, then smiled. "Maybe."

The two men stared at each other a few moments.

Jim glanced at his watch, realizing that his time was about up. "Well?"

"Well, what, Jim?"

"What do you think?"

"About?"

Jim sighed. He hated these games. "Look, Dr. Hermann, I've been coming to you for a couple months now, and I still have the same problem. Sure, today I'm fine. But last week I was out of it for almost a whole day. That's the longest time yet."

Dr. Hermann leaned forward and squeezed Jim's shoulder. "These things take time, Jim."

"Yeah, so you've said. But in the meantime, it's driving me crazy. Not to mention what it's doing to Alice. Sometimes I think I must be crazy."

Dr. Hermann pursed his rubbery lips and frowned. " 'Crazy' is a layman's term, Jim," he said. "We in the profession prefer the term 'loony.' "

Jim Talon laughed involuntarily. "I'll try to get in touch with my feelings about that, Doctor."

Dr. Hermann chuckled. "Seriously, Jim, I wouldn't worry about this too much. Temporary memory loss, sense of displacement—these things just happen sometimes. It doesn't mean you're going off the deep end."

"What causes it?"

Dr. Hermann took off his glasses and rubbed the bridge of his nose. "Could be a hundred different things. Your time in the service, for example."

"But I never saw action. I was in San Diego the whole time."

"Guilt, then, over not having fought. I see it all the time, especially in men who had a college deferment or who went to Canada, particularly if a close friend or relative was killed in Vietnam. As I said, it could be caused by any one of a hundred different things. That's why we'll need some time to pinpoint it."

Jim sighed. "Could it be medical? A tumor or something?"

"Not in your case, Jim. I've gone over all the test results from the hospital with several other doctors. You're in fine physical health. I think you just have to be patient, that's all."

"Sure. That's all."

Like many psychiatrists' offices, this one had a rear exit that allowed patients to leave discreetly. Dr. Hermann shook Jim Talon's hand as always and ushered him to the private exit. "See you next week, Jim." He waved.

Jim Talon walked down the corridor listening to a Hundred and One Strings playing "You Light Up My Life" over the intercom. He walked one flight down to the lobby and pushed his way out the air-conditioned building into the steamy Dallas heat. Sweat beads immediately popped out across his forehead.

Another seventy bucks down the toilet, and he didn't feel any better or know any more about why his perfectly happy life had suddenly turned to shit. He wiped his forehead with the sleeve of his jacket and tried to decide whether to go back to work or take the rest of the day off. Working might get his mind off his problems, but he didn't feel much like hanging around the restaurant paying bills and checking the stock. Hell, what good was it to be boss if you couldn't take the day off once in a while. Talon's Steaks and Ribs Ranch could do without him tonight.

He decided to call his bartender, Nancy, and tell her to run things tonight. Then maybe he would call Alice. They'd go out to dinner at someone else's restaurant and put up with the usual joke from the owner: "What's the matter, Jim, don't you like your own food anymore?" No, he wouldn't call Alice. He'd surprise her. She was due for a happy surprise. Lord knows she'd sure had her share of the other kind lately. He shaded his eyes with his right hand and kept looking for a phone booth from which to call Alice. He didn't see any.

But he did see something odd. Across the street a green Honda Accord was parked against the curb with two men in it—one in the front seat and the other in the back. Why? Maybe one was a chauffeur. But in a Honda?

He shook his head and grinned. Obviously they weren't locals. In Texas, if you have money, you're allowed to flaunt it. Still, there was something vaguely disturbing about that car, almost familiar. He felt a tightening of his scrotum and a tingling at the back of his neck. He picked up his pace and rounded the corner in search of a phone.

He didn't see the Honda pull away from the curb.

There was a booth on the sidewalk in front of a bookstore that specialized in science fiction. He called Nancy and gave her a few instructions, then decided to call Alice after all. She was delighted. He'd be home in twenty minutes. She'd be dressed and ready to go.

His Ford Fiesta was making a grumbling noise as he drove, and he decided to spend Sunday tinkering with the carburetor. Jim drove a few miles over the speed limit as he wound along Turtle Creek Park toward home. Fifteen minutes later he pulled into the shady residential street and headed for the house he'd lived in ever since he married Alice five years earlier. The house originally belonged to Alice and her first husband, who died in an auto crash coming home from Six Flags over Texas Amusement Park at Arlington. At first, living in that house had made Jim uncomfortable, but he was good with his hands, and soon he'd remodeled the place until it was completely different. Completely theirs.

The street was almost free of cars, since nearly everyone was at work now. He eased the Fiesta into the shade of a giant maple and turned the engine off. Suddenly he felt that tightening of the scrotum again and the tingle at the back of his neck, but he shrugged it off and reached for the door handle. As he pushed the car door open, he heard rapid footsteps. When he turned to look, a large, heavy hand covered his mouth and pushed him back into the car. He didn't recognize the man pushing him, but there was something familiar about him anyway. If not about him, then about what he was doing.

Instantly, for no reason he could understand, Jim Talon knew he was a dead man. Still, he tried to struggle. He reached up for his assailant's eyes, but Edge moved quickly. Already his knife had punctured Jim Talon's abdomen at the navel. Edge always started at the navel. Then he used all of his 185 pounds to jerk the knife upward. It sliced through intestines and shirt with ease until it hit the sternum. Then it would go no more. Jim Talon's torso opened, spilling blood and organs in a slimy, steaming mess. Suddenly Jim felt very cold and tired. He looked down, saw his wet stomach oozing out of his body, and died.

Edge pulled his knife free, wiped the blade on Jim Talon's pants, grabbed Jim's watch and wallet, and backed out of the car. Immediately the green Honda Accord pulled up next to him, the motor revving. He climbed into the back seat, and the car sped quietly away.

Across the street in her beautifully remodeled house, Alice Talon looked at her watch and hurried to finish dressing in time.

PART ONE

Sunday

1

TINY FEET TROD up his back before the small, warm body collapsed in a heap around his neck. The purring started immediately, and he could feel the gentle vibrations ripple along his neck up into his scalp. He recognized the sensation. A cat. There was just one problem. He didn't own a cat.

A dream, he thought. Ignore it and it will go away. He opened one heavy eyelid and peeked out at his alarm clock. Only his old Little Ben wasn't there. In its place stood a modernistic white plastic digital cube with blue numbers saying it was 9:36 A.M. Where the hell was his Little Ben? Was he dreaming the clock, too? Sleepily, he pressed his face deeper into the thick feather pillow and groaned. He didn't have time to lie in bed in a half-dream. It was past time to get up.

Then it hit him. Why was it time to get up? It was a simple question that a lot of people ask themselves on Saturdays or Sundays or when they're on vacation. He wasn't sure whether this was a weekend or not, and he wasn't sure that he had a job. If he did, what was it?

Christ, he thought, rolling over onto his back. The cat cried out at the movement and dug its claws into his neck in protest before jumping away. "Oooww," he said, reaching around to touch his wound. There was a little blood smeared across his fingertips. "Well, apparently you're real," he told the fat orange cat. He reached over and scratched its ears. It closed its eyes and pressed its head farther into his hand. He seems to know me, he thought. But how did he get into my house? The white flea collar around the cat's neck indicated that it had an owner.

He threw his bare legs over the side of the bed and ground his knuckles into his eyes, trying to rub the sleepiness away. He yawned, stretching his arms over his head. He fluttered his heavy eyelids a few times and glanced around the room. The sight made him gasp.

It wasn't his bedroom!

His bedroom was painted robin's-egg blue, with white molding around the ceiling and floor; this bedroom had textured-canvas wallpaper. *His* bedroom had a hardwood floor that was a bitch to maintain because it had to be polished by hand with paste wax; this bedroom was carpeted with thick white shag. He wasn't sitting on his own oak platform bed; this was a looming mahogany four-poster that hinted of pre-Revolutionary America.

He let out a long, deep sigh and rubbed his eyes again, harder. "A dream," he said aloud, just to hear a voice. "And one helluva a dream at that." He stood up, and the orange cat gave a whine of annoyance at the movement. It was one of those funny dreams you get sometimes when you know you're dreaming, he told himself. All you have to do is order yourself to wake up. He took a deep breath and said, "Wake up—" and then stopped short. He'd wanted to say his own name, but he couldn't remember it. He pressed his hands to his temples as if to release a great pressure. "A goddamn dream," he muttered weakly, sitting back down on the edge of the bed. Maybe if he climbed back into bed and closed his eyes and went back to sleep, he'd wake up where he belonged, in his oak platform bed in his robin's-egg blue bedroom in the middle of downtown . . . Damn! He couldn't remember the name of the city he lived in.

He stood up again and walked to the window. Outside was a backyard, badly in need of mowing, that sloped up into a sizable hill. A battered wooden fence that needed mending and painting enclosed the yard from the foot of the sloping hill to the sides of the house. On the inside of the fence hung a sign: Beware of Dangerous Cat. In the middle of the overgrown yard stood an aluminum pole with a yellow tetherball attached to it. The ball needed air. In the far right corner of the yard he could see a small vegetable garden overrun by ripe tomatoes. It also contained a crop of healthy squash. Whoever lived here wasn't compulsive about keeping the place up. Nothing in the yard told him where he was. He still couldn't put a name to the city. Nor did he know how he got there or why. Or what had happened to his memory.

He pressed his cheek to the window. The glass felt cool and soothing despite the morning sun pouring through. He needed to think. What were the possibilities? How could this have happened? His mind began ordering the details, categorizing things.

First possibility: He was dreaming and would soon wake up. But he had lost hope of that. Everything was too real; the mundane details of his surroundings were too specific. The orange cat let out a loud whine. He turned around, and it stared at him for a moment, vigorously scratched its neck, then started licking its tail.

Second possibility: He'd had some sort of accident that had left him dazed and slightly disoriented. A Good Samaritan had found him hurt and brought him home. The problem with that explanation was that he didn't have any injuries, except the cat scratch—certainly nothing to suggest an accident. And there was one more curious piece of evidence: The bed had been slept in by two people.

Third possibility: He'd attended a wild party and gotten drunk or drugged or both and had wound up in a woman's bedroom. Hmmm. Yes, that sounded the most likely of the three. Maybe he was having the ultimate hangover. He turned his head and placed the other cheek against the cool glass of the window.

The window!

Quickly he fumbled with the handle, trying to open it.

It wouldn't budge. He heaved his whole body weight into it, sending a ripple of cracks along his spine. But still it wouldn't open.

Fourth possibility: He was being held prisoner! He saw the latch that kept the window locked. He yanked it out of the runner, and the window slid open easily. There was a screen that needed washing, but it lifted out with no struggle. He could make his escape right now, stark naked, and run down an unfamiliar street in a city he didn't know, unable to tell anyone his name. No. Best to investigate a little further first.

He leaned out the window for a better view. To his right was another house, very much like this one, but with a neatly mowed lawn and a couple of well-used bikes parked in the backyard. The house to his left was of a similar design, but with a kidney-shaped pool in its yard. A slightly plump woman in her early forties was cleaning the water with a long-poled net. She wore white shorts that had fit her snugly ten pounds ago, but were now pulled taut across her thighs, and a strapless bikini top that wasn't up to the support job it had to do. Every few steps she tugged it back into place. When she rounded the pool she looked up from the water, saw him staring, adjusted her top, and waved happily.

"Cliff, don't tell me you're finally going to wash those windows of yours? You're always welcome to practice on ours." She laughed and tugged.

He ducked back through the window and replaced the screen. Some of the dirt from the screen blew into his face, and he sneezed. Sweat rolled down his sides and back making his skin sticky. He leaned against the window, his heart pumping frantically. The woman knew him! She'd called him Cliff. Wasn't that his name? It didn't sound familiar.

"Hey, Jack," he heard the neighbor woman say, "I just saw Cliff fixing to wash their windows."

Jack snorted. "About time, I'd say."

"I guess he just got tired of trying to outwait Ginger."

Jack snorted again. "She's not exactly the happy homemaker, but she has her good points."

"Yeah, and I've seen you staring at both of them often enough."

They both laughed.

They seemed to know all about him. But who the hell was Ginger?

He scanned the bedroom again, this time without panic. A calmness had come over him without his even realizing it, as easily as if he'd slipped into a thick, heavy coat. A coat of cool, calculating logic. He no longer perceived his surroundings as threatening; they were merely part of a problem he had to analyze. And every unfamiliar object was a clue. A clue that would help him solve this puzzle.

He needed more information, though. He walked over to the telephone on the table beside the bed and picked up the receiver. But whom could he call? And what would he say? Pardon me, is there anyone there who can tell me who I am, what I do for a living, what day this is, what year? Oh, yes, what state and city am I in? He put the receiver back in its cradle. The area code on the phone was 714, but he didn't know where that was.

The bed was queen-sized and both sides had been slept in. He could tell that by studying the arrangement of pillows, blankets, and wrinkles. Maybe he'd been having an affair and didn't want his wife to know. Perhaps his guilt over his infidelity had caused him to have temporary amnesia. The problem with that explanation was that he couldn't remember ever having had a wife. And would he have been so careless as to let his girlfriend's neighbors get to know his name?

First things first. He needed clothes. He couldn't conduct an investigation naked. He grabbed the clothes hanging from the brass coatrack in the corner, hoping they were his even though they didn't look familiar. Everything seemed to fit. The green Jockey briefs (size 34), the gray corduroy Levis (33 waist, 34 inseam), the yellow Ralph Lauren shirt with the blue polo player on the chest (medium). He slipped into the blue Nikes without bothering to pull on the gray socks. Everything felt comfortable, but not familiar.

The fat orange cat on the bed watched the whole process with attentive eyes. He stretched, yawned, and leaped off the bed, then scooted out the partly open door.

He followed the cat to the door and pressed his ear to the opening. He could hear faint music and voices in the distance, but couldn't distinguish the speakers' words or determine their sex.

He decided to search the rest of the bedroom before venturing out to confront the speakers. He tiptoed to the huge mahogany dresser and shocked himself by looking into the mirror.

The man looking back was someone he had never seen before.

At least not anyone he remembered having seen— although he wasn't sure what he'd expected to see. Aside from looking rumpled and unshaven, he looked older than he had thought he would. The wrinkles across his forehead came as a surprise. He looked to be thirty-five or so, but he wasn't sure. He couldn't remember how old he was or when his birthday was. He tried to remember his astrological sign—what did he look for in the newspapers when he checked his horoscope for fun? —but drew a blank.

His hair was different from what he'd expected, too. It was longer than he'd thought it would be, and it waved over his ears and down his neck. It was shaggy, and there were gray strands mixed with the sandy brown.

But the real surprise was that he looked more handsome than he'd expected. He'd never pose for *Gentlemen's Quarterly*—did he read that?—but there was a lean ruggedness to his features that wasn't unpleasant. His nose was long and prominent, straight and commanding; his chin was firm and cleft like Kirk Douglas's. How could he remember Kirk Douglas's name but not his own? His eyes were green flecked with brown, shaded under thick eyebrows. His body was fit enough, despite a stomach that was starting to pucker slightly. He could feel the hardness of well-toned muscles when he moved his arms and legs. He thought he looked like a gunfighter in a B western who's trying to go straight but can't live down his past. A Glenn Ford, maybe, or a Van Heflin.

Quietly he slid open the top left dresser drawer. It was stuffed with a jumble of women's underpants and bras. The bras were size 34B, he noted, and the underpants were mostly cotton of different solid colors. Several had small tears or loose elastic. Rolled up in the back of the drawer under everything else, he found a pair of black lace underpants with no crotch. The rest of the drawers on that side contained more women's clothing: sweaters, blouses, running shorts. The drawers on that side of the dresser had something else in common: They were all untidy. Sweaters had been folded without tucking in the sleeves, blouses were unbuttoned, and running shorts were not folded at all. The other side of the dresser contained men's clothing: different-colored Jockey shorts like the ones he was wearing, and two pairs of nylon bikini briefs rolled up at the back of the drawer; eight different-colored polo shirts; several pairs of running shorts. Everything neatly folded.

The tiny bathroom offered more details, but little help. He found a black Norelco electric shaver next to the sink and a pink disposable Bic razor in the shower, blade up next to the soap. There were two toothbrushes, one wet and one dry, and a tube of Aim toothpaste with the cap off and paste sticking to the counter. An empty cardboard cylinder hung on the toilet-dispenser. The sink needed cleaning.

He returned to the bedroom and searched the walk-in closet, but found only clothes on hangers and more clothes spilling over the rattan laundry basket. The people who lived here didn't break their backs keeping the place neat. He searched the bedside tables but found only a few *Newsweek* magazines addressed to Clifford Remington, a packet of birth control pills, a jar of pennies, and an empty strawberry yogurt container. The dirty spoon was stuck to the tabletop. He was glad it wasn't on his side of the bed. What kind of a slob had he been to bed with? He continued his search, but it wasn't until he lifted the corner of the mattress that he found the gun.

It was a Colt Cobra Model D-3 .38 Special with a four-inch barrel and checkered walnut grip. The metal was blued. He automatically swung open the cylinder to see if it was loaded. It was. Something at the back of his mind nagged him. What had made him look under the mattress? He hadn't thought about it before he did it; it had been purely habitual. A routine that he didn't understand the reason for. He held the gun with such ease and comfort. With such familiarity. He felt at home with its weight in his hand. Somehow complete.

He held the gun in his right hand, eased the door open, and stepped quietly out of the room. He crept down the hall toward the muffled voices. His heart thudded dully in his chest, but he didn't feel afraid, only anxious. Anxious to find out what in hell was happening to him. Anxious to find his missing life.

The music was clearer now. He recognized the song: It was "The Barber's Song" from the *Man of La Mancha.* He took another step forward. The voices were clearer now, too. Two females. One a child, the other a woman. Both of them were giggling.

"Sit still, Liza, or you'll look like Grace Jones," the woman said in a mock-scold.

"Yuk," the young girl, Liza, said.

He inched along the corridor, sliding his back along the wall, holding his gun at waist level ready to swing toward a target. The voices were coming from an open doorway five feet ahead. He moved forward, his thumb automatically releasing the safety.

"Ow! Be careful, Mom."

"Well, stop wiggling in the chair."

"I'm not wiggling."

"Are too."

"Am not."

They both giggled again.

"Oh, I like this part," the woman said and began to sing with the record. " 'Golden Helmet of da-*de*-dum, we'll make golden his-to-ry.' "

"Ugh," Liza said. "That was terrible."

"Thanks. Hey, pal, how about flipping the record for me?"

Then a third voice spoke. "Do we have to listen to that stuff so early, Mom? Can't we put something good on?"

"Yeah, Mom," Liza agreed. "Like Adam and the Ants."

"Flip it, young man, or you're next in the chair."

"I'd rather be in the electric chair," he said. There were sounds of the record being turned and switches being flicked. Richard Kiley started to sing "To Each His Dulcinea."

He heard footsteps returning to the kitchen, and then the boy said, "Just don't sing along this time, okay, Mom? The record is bad enough."

"Kids," the woman sighed.

"*Ow!* Mom, you did it again. Can't you tell the difference between hair and ears?"

"Then sit still. And don't talk so loud. We're trying to keep the noise down, remember?"

"Sorry."

The boy's high-pitched voice interrupted. "Would you two give me a break, please? I'm trying to concentrate."

"Big deal," Liza said. "So concentrate."

"It's impossible around here with all this yapping."

"Then don't stay around here. Go over to Freddy's. The two of you can concentrate together. Like you were doing last week when Mrs. Hanson was sunbathing by her pool. Topless."

"Liar!"

"I saw you."

The woman laughed. "I'm shocked! My thirteen-year-old son a Peeping Tom."

"Aw, Mom," he said, embarrassed.

But the woman laughed again, a loud, booming laugh, and soon all three of them were laughing together.

It seemed innocent enough, he thought, as he moved closer to the doorway, but he didn't want to take any chances. What if it was some kind of trap? He didn't know what to think. All he knew for certain was that he was in a strange house filled with strange people, and he didn't know why. Nor did he know who he was or where he belonged.

He crept up to the doorway and peeked into the room. The young girl was sitting at the kitchen table with a plastic apron around her neck. She was about fifteen, with copper-colored hair and a pale, freckled face that was just starting to lose its childish shapelessness. Scattered over the table in front of her were a dozen magazines—*Redbook, Seventeen, Tiger Beat*—several of them open to photographs of different haircuts.

Hovering over Liza with scissors in one hand and a long comb in the other was the woman with the terrible singing voice and the infectious laugh. Her tongue was lodged firmly in the corner of her mouth, its pink tip poking out. She was about the same age as he was, mid-thirties, with laugh lines etched deep into the corners of her mouth and age lines webbing the corners of her eyes. She had a pleasant face. Her brown hair was thick and curly, with a casualness that bordered on unkempt. It looked as if all she ever had to do to it was to shampoo it and give her head a shake. Again, the effect was attractive. She squinted in concentration as she carefully snipped Liza's hair. She was wearing a yellow T-shirt with a slogan printed across the back: You Belong in a Zoo . . . the San Diego Zoo. She wore matching yellow running shorts, and the sinewy muscles in her tan thighs and calves suggested that the athletic shorts and Nike shoes—which were exactly like his, he noticed—were more than just a whim of fashion.

The woman shifted her tongue to the other side of her mouth. "Und now for zee difficult part of zee operation."

"Just make sure zee patient doesn't die from shock afterwards."

"Ha," the boy said. "I want to die from shock every time I see your face, Liza."

"You little pimp."

"Liza, don't call your brother a pimp."

"Aw, I didn't mean it *that* way. I meant it as short for pimple."

"Oh. That's different."

He saw the boy across the kitchen, sitting on the counter next to the sink, reading a frayed paperback book, *The Stainless Steel Rat*. He was wearing a blue Rams shirt with the number 38 on the front. His hair wasn't red like his sister's; it was sandy. Like his. Occasionally the boy sipped at a big glass of lemonade, trying to capture the ice cubes in his mouth. Whenever he snared one he'd go back to reading.

"How much longer, Mom?" Liza asked.

"Almost."

He walked into the room, the thirty-eight dangling at his side, but with his finger taut against the trigger.

The little boy noticed him first, looking up from his book with a happy grin. "Look who's up. Dirty Harry."

"Mornin', Cliff," Liza said without turning around.

The woman looked over at him, saw the gun, and frowned. "Jesus, Cliff, I don't think you should be carrying that thing around the house."

"Can I shoot it, Cliff?" the boy asked as he jumped down from the counter. "Just once?"

"See what I mean?" the woman said.

"Aw, let them go play their macho games, Mom," Liza said.

He looked at each one of them in turn. His terror was coming back. He was starting to tremble. "Who are you?" he asked.

The woman dropped the scissors on the table and sighed. "Please, not today, Cliff. Really. We promised the kids we'd take them to the beach, and I've got a million things—"

"Who are you?" he said, louder, pointing the gun at her chest.

The woman stumbled back a step.

Liza turned in her chair and looked at him for the first time. "Oh, Christ," she said disgustedly when she saw the gun. "Here we go again."

2

"I HEAR YOU'VE got a memory problem, Cliff. I'm Dr. Kendall, and I'm here to help you." The thin man in the expensive blue suit strolled into the office as he spoke. He had a manila folder tucked under his left arm, and he held an unlit cigarette in his right hand.

Cliff looked up at Dr. Kendall and felt his muscles tighten like steel cables rippling under his taut skin. Despite his casual posture, his whole body was coiled and ready to spring into action, though he had no idea what action would be necessary in a doctor's office. Still he felt the need to be prepared, on guard. This must be what a cornered animal feels, he thought, when it has to rely on its instincts to survive. Somewhere deep inside, he almost liked the feeling.

Dr. Kendall tugged on his earlobe as he sat down behind the glass and chrome desk. He tossed the manila folder onto the desk, opened it to the first page, stuck the unlit cigarette in his mouth. "Trying to quit," he explained as he began to read.

"I was supposed to see a Dr. Jessup."

Dr. Kendall nodded. "Yes, well, today is Sunday, and Dr. Jessup isn't on duty. He stuck the unlit cigarette back in his mouth and went back to reading the contents of the manila folder. "Let's see now. Clifford Remington—"

"That's not my name."

Dr. Kendall looked up from the page and frowned. "Okay, what is your name?"

He stared coldly at Dr. Kendall but said nothing.

"Well, then, what would you like me to call you?"

What indeed? he thought, mentally running through as many names as he could think of: William, David, James, Jonathan, Thomas, Gordon. Maybe something less common: Jason, Randolph, Leif, Brendan, Alexander. Nothing sounded familiar, comfortable. Finally he shrugged. "Cliff will do."

Dr. Kendall smiled. "Good, that's settled. Give me a minute to catch up with Dr. Jessup's notes, and we'll see what we can do. Okay?" He didn't wait for an answer. Instead he dropped his eyes back to the folder and began skimming through the pages, occasionally moving the cigarette from one side of his mouth to the other using only his lips.

Clifford Remington. If that's what people wanted to call him, he could accept it. It was as good a name as any. For now. Until he found his real one. Somehow he knew that Clifford Remington wasn't his real name.

He sat in the orange overstuffed chair opposite the doctor and studied him as carefully as he himself was being studied on paper. He didn't shift in his chair, cross his legs, or even blink. He probed. Dr. Kendall was a slender sprig of a man in his late thirties, with slicked-back brown hair and the thinnest mustache he'd ever seen. He was apparently trying to look sophisticated and dashing, like a young David Niven playing a doomed RAF pilot. Kendall missed the mark by several miles, managing only to remind one of a fussy Clifton Webb. Even on a Sunday, having received that woman Ginger's emergency call only thirty minutes ago, he was dressed in an expensive suit and silk tie, smelling strongly of English Leather. The unlit cigarette rode his lips restlessly as he concentrated on the folder, occasionally nodding or shaking his head in disagreement.

Dr. Kendall read the last page, closed the folder, and pushed it away like an empty dinner plate he'd just wiped clean. He removed the soggy cigarette from his mouth and dropped it into an ashtray. "Let's start with the facts, shall we? Your name is Clifford Halsey Remington." He paused as if expecting an argument. When none came, he continued. "Halsey was your mother's maiden name."

"How do you know that?"

"You told Ginger. At the beginning of your courtship, I believe." He seemed to scrape the word "courtship" off his tongue with his teeth as if it tasted bitter. "You live at sixteen fifty-seven Yale Loop Drive, Irvine, California. Did you know that?"

Cliff shook his head. "She—Ginger told me this morning when she showed me my driver's license and credit cards. As far as I remember, I've never been to California."

"Where did you live, then?"

He thought about it, picturing a large map of the United States and trying to focus on one state. "I don't know. But I get an image of . . . of a pine tree with a thick trunk and a lot of snow on the branches."

"Maybe New England."

Cliff shrugged and shook his head. "Maybe. I don't know."

"Well, let's go back to what we definitely know about you. You live in Irvine with your fiancée, Ginger, age thirty-four, divorced. Also living with you are her two children from a previous marriage: Liza, age fifteen, and Beau, thirteen. His friends call him Bogie. You with me so far?"

"Yes, I heard all this before. That woman, Ginger, my fiancée, explained it all to me this morning before we came here. She told me I've had several bouts of amnesia in the past three months. After getting a clean bill of health from the hospital, I started regular sessions with Dr. Jessup some time ago. Ginger showed me canceled checks made out to Dr. Jessup as proof. That's the only reason I agreed to come here today."

"You don't like shrinks?"

Cliff leveled a steady stare at Dr. Kendall but said nothing. Soon the doctor cleared his throat and looked away.

"Do you believe what Ginger has told you about your life?"

"She showed me photographs of her and me and the

kids all together at Disneyland, Sea World, and the San Diego Zoo. She also showed me magazine subscription labels with the name Cliff Remington and that Irvine address on them. She even has a written estimate from a caterer for the wedding reception we supposedly planned."

"And?"

"And I still don't believe it all. The story seems reasonable and convincing enough on the face of it, and there's certainly plenty of physical evidence, but it doesn't *feel* right. Photographs can be faked. Subscription labels and caterers' stationery can be stolen or even made up."

"Toward what end?"

"I don't fucking know. I just know that none of this makes any sense one way or the other. I just know I'm thinking and doing things I didn't know I was capable of."

"Yes, yes. Ginger told me about the incident with the gun this morning." He stretched his thin, bloodless lips again. "Most dramatic."

"Is that your professional opinion?"

Dr. Kendall frowned. "I can understand your intense emotions right now, Cliff, but—"

"Can you really? Do you know what it's like not to remember who you are, where you come from? Not to know anything about your past? Family? Parents? Do you know what it feels like to be told by a strange woman that you've been living with her for almost two years and that you're going to marry her in three months? Do you know what I do for a living?"

"Do *you* know?"

"I've been told that I own a landscaping business, that I've done quite well at it. But here's the royal punch line: I don't have the slightest idea of how one goes about landscaping. I couldn't name half a dozen plants right now if my life depended on it."

Dr. Kendall reached for the cigarette and began to tear the paper off it. Tiny bits of tobacco spilled out over his fingers as he tore. "According to Dr. Jessup's notes, you've had five of these episodes over the past

three months. They've lasted anywhere from five minutes to two hours. How long has this one been so far?"

"I woke up like this at nine-thirty this morning."

Dr. Kendall glanced at his watch. "About four hours,
then?"

Cliff nodded.

"Well, Cliff, I'm sure you've heard all the medical
explanations of amnesia before."

"If I have, I don't remember."

"No, of course not. Then let me explain. I'll try to
keep it as simple as possible."

"Maybe you could throw in a couple of landscaping
metaphors so I can follow you."

Dr. Kendall frowned but continued. "There are many
different types and causes of amnesia. It can be organic;
in other words it can be the result of something physi-
cally wrong with you."

"Like a concussion or a disease."

"Right. Among the organic types are transient global
amnesia, traumatic automatism, memory defect following electroconvulsive therapy, Korsacoff syndrome, per-
sistent memory defects following encephalitis or brain
surgery, and various brain diseases. When I first heard
about your case, I suspected transient global amnesia."

"Which is what?"

"It was first described about twenty years ago as an
abrupt memory loss lasting a few seconds to a few hours
without loss of consciousness or other evidence of im-
pairment. The individual is unable to store any new experience during the attack. There's also some loss of
memory of the years before the attack. And these attacks may be recurrent, like yours."

"Is that what I have, then?"

Dr. Kendall laid the shredded cigarette aside and
began pushing the spilled tobacco into a small hill. "Apparently not. Transient global amnesia is thought to be
caused by a reduction in blood supply to specific regions
of the brain, and may even presage a stroke. However,
Dr. Jessup had every possible medical test run on you
and she sent you to two neurologists and another
psychiatrist, all of whom tested you further. The results

indicate no organic cause of your memory loss, though I should hasten to add that tests in this area are not always conclusive."

"Thanks. Now what are the other possibilities?"

"That leaves only psychogenic amnesia."

"I don't like the sound of that."

"In many ways it's a hell of a lot less ominous than organic amnesia. At least the psychogenic varieties are usually reversible; the organic types rarely are. So, if we eliminate for the time being paramnesia and conabulation—"

"Christ."

"—we can concentrate on hypnotic amnesia, hysterical amnesia, and fugue states."

"Jesus, are you sure I didn't just get a bump on the head somewhere? Maybe I fell out of a tree while landscaping somebody's garden."

"It's possible, but as I said, we've pretty much ruled out organic causes, including head injuries. Dr. Jessup thinks you have a combination of hypnotic and hysterical amnesia."

Cliff sighed. "Explain."

"Simple. Hypnotic amnesia occurs when someone hypnotizes you and tells you that when you awake you will not remember who you are or what has happened while you were asleep. Irresponsible practitioners do that kind of thing all the time in nightclub acts."

"Have I been to any nightclubs lately?"

"Ginger said the two of you haven't been apart for more than a few hours at a time in the past two years, since she started working for you and the two of you moved in together." Again, Dr. Kendall gave a thin, tight smile that looked somehow malevolent.

Cliff sensed that the man didn't like him, but he couldn't understand why. Or maybe he was just too damn suspicious of everyone. The whole world, from the FBI to *Newsweek* magazine, seemed to be in on the conspiracy, all out to drive him crazy so they could inherit his landscaping empire. The idea almost made him smile.

The psychiatrist continued his explanation. "If the

two of you have been spending so much time together, that would leave little time for you to run off and get hypnotized.''

"Could I have gone to some kind of stop-smoking or weight-loss clinic where they use hypnosis? Maybe something went wrong there.''

"Aside from the fact that you neither smoke nor need to lose weight, Ginger says you would never have gone to such a clinic, since you are known to have poked a lot of fun at such places. Besides, Dr. Jessup called every place in the county that you might have gone to, and no one has any record of you.''

"Where does that leave us?''

"Back with hysterical amnesia, which is very rare and usually only exists where there was a pre-existing amnesia of organic origin.''

"That seems to contradict your earlier conclusion, Doctor.''

"Dr. Jessup's conclusion,'' he said, brushing tobacco flakes from his fingers. "I haven't been involved in this case long enough to formulate any conclusions.'' Cliff caught a slightly petulant tone in his voice. "Let me just state here that people who are unable to remember as much as you are have often been found to be faking. However, I can see no reason for you to fake this, so I must inform you that most cases of hysterical amnesia can be treated with hypnosis.''

"Then why didn't Dr. Jessup use hypnosis?''

"She is planning to. But it takes a while to diagnose the type of amnesia, determine the extent of the problem, and predict all possible complications. And many times the amnesia will go away without any treatment at all. It always has for you before; it probably will again.''

"When?''

Dr. Kendall shrugged. "Five minutes from now, perhaps. An hour. A day. A week. A few months. Hard to say. But if your memory doesn't start to come back to you within a week or so, I'd strongly recommend hypnosis.''

Cliff Remington. It still sounded funny, foreign. Still,

he felt a little better, a little less cornered. Kendall had provided several possible explanations. Logic and science were at work on his problem. No conspiracy was afoot. The memory lapse was just a trick of his mind. Probably temporary. By tonight he'd probably be Cliff Remington again, snuggled up next to the beautiful Ginger. But that frightened him, too. Would that mean that the person he was right now would be lost forever? Was that what he wanted? He didn't know what he wanted. Except to not feel so damned alone, crouched and coiled and ready to spring at anything that came near him.

"Tell me something, Dr. Kendall."

"If I can, certainly."

"Ginger said you recommended that I see Dr. Jessup."

"Yes."

"Did you know me *before* all this started happening?"

"Before the memory losses?"

"Yes."

Dr. Kendall shifted uncomfortably in his chair. "I'd met you a couple of times."

"Uh-huh. And you're associated with Dr. Jessup, right?"

"We cover each other's emergency calls on weekends and vacations."

"Okay. Why did you recommend Dr. Jessup? Why didn't you handle my case yourself?"

"Personal involvement," he said, his lips stretching into a thin, humorless smile that revealed a glint of moist white teeth. "But of course you don't remember."

"Remember what?"

"I'm your fiancée's ex-husband. Ginger was my wife, and Liza and Beau are our children."

3

EDGE CONNORS HUNG up the pay phone and quickly wound his way back to the table, smoothly dodging the french fries that two young boys were throwing across the aisles at each other.

"What're the orders?" Tyrone Willis asked, dunking a Chicken McNugget in a tiny container of sweet-and-sour sauce.

"Same as in Dallas. Terminate."

"With extreme prejudice?"

Edge nodded, peeling back the top bun of his Big Mac and plucking off the limp pickle slices.

"With extreme prejudice," Tyrone repeated. "What's that really mean?"

"Kill the fucker," Edge explained.

"I know *that*. I mean the 'extreme prejudice' part. I've never understood that phrase. Makes me feel funny, like I was racist or anti-Semitic. You know, prejudiced."

Edge took a bite of his Big Mac and grinned.

Tyrone caught the look and shook his head defensively. "I just don't like the word, that's all."

" 'He had but one eye, and the popular prejudice runs in favor of two.' "

"Shit."

"You know where that comes from?"

"No, but sure as a belch follows a beer I figure you'll tell me."

"Charles Dickens. *Nicholas Nickleby*. I've read almost all of his books in the last few months. Great stuff."

"Who gives a fuck? Besides, what does that quote have to do with what I was talking about?"

"Wipe the sauce from your chin, Tyrone." Edge smiled and grabbed a few of Tyrone's french fries.

"Hey, asshole, that's mine."

"I'm just trying to save you from yourself. Have you taken a good look at that gut of yours, buddy? People have been asking me lately if you're pregnant. And whether I'm the father."

Tyrone snorted. "You wish, faggot."

"Faggot? What kind of *prejudiced* word is that? I'm just trying to help you cut down on this fried food."

"Eating here was your idea."

Edge shrugged. "I was just testing your willpower."

"Like fuck you were." He pulled his fries closer, hunching protectively over them. "You get the stats on this guy?"

"Yeah," Edge nodded. "Lives at sixteen fifty-seven Yale Loop Drive. That's about four blocks from here. Name's Cliff Remington."

"Where do we do it?"

"In the house."

"Any I.B.'s?"

Edge hated the abbreviation, a throwback to Tyrone's service in Naval Intelligence. "Three innocent bystanders. One woman, two kids."

"Do they go down, too?"

"Not if we can avoid it. You know, it's a D.D."

Tyrone looked up, tried to decide whether or not he was being kidded, figured he was, but asked anyway. "What the fuck's a D.D.?"

"You don't know?" Edge asked with exaggerated shock. "Discretionary decision. We'll have to decide at the time how much of a risk they'd be to us alive."

Tyrone swallowed a french fry he wished he'd chewed a few more times. He sipped his water and tried to wash the lump of potato down. "When do we do it?"

Edge grinned, snatched a chunk of Tyrone's chicken, and shoved it into his mouth. "As soon as we terminate your lunch. With extreme prejudice."

Tyrone pulled his food out of Edge's reach. "Very funny. I'll remember this next time we're on stakeout and you ask me to go for the coffee and doughnuts."

"Here, you want a bite of my Big Mac?" Edge offered him the half-eaten sandwich. "I'll even give you my pickles and a swig of my milkshake."

Tyrone shook his head in disgust. "You know I don't eat that shit."

The two men were silent for a minute, each staring at the table and eating his own food. Edge knew that silence made Tyrone nervous so he waited for him to break it. Thirty seconds later he did.

"So what do you think we should use on this Cliff Remington?" he asked, swallowing another french fry. "Piano wire?"

Edge clucked his tongue and smiled. "Maybe. What else you got?"

4

"GODDAMN IT, YOU'RE not Gregory Peck and I'm not Diane Baker!" she yelled.

They were driving down Newport Boulevard in the thick of the afternoon beach traffic, trying to squeeze onto the Newport Freeway. She stopped at a red light, and a silver Rabbit convertible pulled up next to them, its quadraphonic speakers blaring the Eagles' "Take It Easy." Two bouncy girls and two bare-chested boys giggled loudly as they shook their wet salty hair in one another's faces. Nothing unusual. You saw the same thing every day of the week on Newport Boulevard. But today their liveliness exaggerated the tense silence that had settled between Cliff and Ginger since they'd left Dr. Kendall's office.

She was driving a rusty maroon bug, jamming the stick shift back and forth with more force than was necessary. Purposely grinding a gear here and there because she knew it annoyed him, whether he could remember it or not. He sat hunched in the passenger's seat, staring at his hands, out the windshield, out the window. Everywhere but at her. A few minutes earlier, she'd tried to comfort him by laying a soothing hand on his arm, but he'd immediately tensed up and pulled away so sharply that she withdrew her hand as if he had slapped it. Finally, unable to bear any more, she'd leaned on the horn, bullied the car into the right lane, pulled into the parking lot of a Stater Brothers super-market, and screamed at him.

"What?" he said.

"I said that you're not goddamn Gregory Peck and I'm not goddamn Diane Baker!"

"What are you talking about?"

"I'm talking about you. And the way you're treating me. You act like I'm some kind of Mata Hari conspiring against you. Like in that movie *Mirage* with Gregory Peck and Diane Baker."

"How do you expect me to act?"

She glared at him for a moment, then softened. "I'm not the enemy, Cliff. I love you."

"That's not fair. You act as if it's my fault that I can't remember who I am or who you are."

"This is the sixth episode, and I'm beginning to wonder."

He twisted around in his seat. "What's that supposed to mean?"

She sighed. "Nothing."

"Come on. What did you mean?"

She tucked a stray lock of hair behind her ear, then fidgeted with a gold hoop earring. "Well, I just think it might be significant that these attacks started a few months after we decided to get married, that's all."

"Oh, for chrissake."

"It's possible."

"I can't believe you. I really can't. You told me that we're engaged and that you love me, and now you accuse me of having amnesia so I can back out of a marriage. Christ, if we were ever engaged, it's obvious I didn't love you for your great sensitivity."

"You son of a bitch," she snapped, swinging around and clubbing him in the arm.

Instantly he returned the punch to her arm.

"Ow, that hurt." She rubbed her arm.

"So did yours." He rubbed his arm.

"Good." They glared at each other for a few seconds. Finally she shrugged. "At least you can't be too far gone. That's what you would have done before.''

He looked appalled. "Did I used to hit you?''

"Not really. You've never punched me or slapped me or tried to hurt me. None of that woman-beating crap. In fact, you broke Stanley Granger's little finger last Christmas when he got drunk and slapped his wife at our party.''

"Who is Stanley Granger?''

"He works for you, but you told him if he ever hits his wife again you'll fire his ass. With real fire.''

"But I have hit you before?''

"Only if I hit you first. And even then you always return the favor with about the same amount of force I gave you. Needless to say, I haven't hit you in a while.''

"What did I used to do that made you want to hit me?''

She grinned at the memory. "Sometimes you're sulky and stubborn. Like now.''

"Damn it, woman, why can't you be a little more compassionate? Can't you see what I'm going through? I can't even remember my own name.''

"Big deal. I wish I couldn't remember mine. Ginger. What kind of name is that? How'd you like to be named after a spice, for chrissake? Everyone expects me to be just like my name—gingery, spicy. I tried to live up to those expectations and became feisty and tough and gingery.''

"It could have been worse.''

"How?''

"They could have named you Pepper. Or Cinnamon.''

"Or Thyme.''

"Or Oregano.''

She laughed her deep laugh, and the tiny VW jostled a little. "At least it hasn't affected your sense of humor too much.''

"Except for being sulky and stubborn.''

"You're always that way when you're sick. When you

get the flu or something, even the kids don't want to be around you. And they like you."

She slipped the car into gear and jerked back out onto Newport Boulevard to the accompaniment of blaring horns and shouts from the drivers she cut off.

"Christ!" he gasped. "What is this, some new kind of shock therapy?"

"Button up, Remington," she said. "And don't criticize me. It affects my driving."

Cliff reached back and wrapped the shoulder harness across his chest, clicking it into place. "Where are we going?"

"Home."

"Your house?"

"*Our* house."

"Your ex-husband told me it was yours. He said I moved in with you."

"Darren's got a big mouth."

"Well, if you didn't want him to talk, you shouldn't have sent me to him."

She slammed the accelerator to the floor, zipping through a light that turned red just as they entered the intersection. He felt his hands tighten on the cushioned dashboard.

"That's what's bugging you, isn't it?" she said. "You're still jealous of Darren."

"My God, woman, I can't believe your incredible ego. I'm sitting here not able to remember anything about myself, certainly nothing about *you*, and you think the only thing on my mind is jealousy. How can I be jealous of a man I don't even remember?"

"It's instinctive with you. You were always jealous of Darren."

Cliff just shook his head. "I can't imagine why."

She turned to look at him and grinned wickedly. "Can't you?"

"I can't believe her," he mumbled to himself. Then he said aloud, "You have to admit it was stupid to send me to your ex-husband right now."

"We didn't have a lot of choices. Today is Sunday, remember? And you were wandering around with that damn gun in your hand. You'd never done anything like that before." She turned to look at him again.

"Look out!" he shouted.

The lane of cars had come to a stop, and it was too late for her to apply the brakes, so she swung the car into the left lane, cutting off a Mercedes with two inches to spare. Its horn echoed after them.

"Besides," she continued as if nothing had happened, "I figured you couldn't remember any of the good juicy stuff to tell him." She wiggled her eyebrows and winked.

"Jesus Christ," he mumbled.

They were quiet during the rest of the drive home. She sped along the Newport Freeway to the San Diego Freeway, then took the Culver off-ramp to Irvine. She kept a bland smile pasted on her face, fighting the urge to break down and cry hysterically. She had to get a grip on herself, she thought. She had remember that her name was Ginger and that she had a tradition to uphold like all the other women who were named after spices. She had to be feisty, spicy, strong. Cliff would snap out of it. He always had before. It's just that this time it was taking so long. And he seemed so frightened. He'd never been this far gone before. The gun was a bad sign. She should have hidden it after his first episode, but she always thought each episode would be the last one. And since the recent robberies in their neighborhood she had felt safer with the gun around, or at least she'd let him believe she felt safer.

Now they were going back to the house. To do what? Sit and stare at each other. Watch "60 Minutes." Play cribbage. Would he remember that she always tried to cheat. And that he always caught her? Would he remember how to play? The thought depressed her. She pulled onto Yale Loop Drive and swung into the driveway.

She found her cheeriest voice. "Say, you hungry?"

He shrugged.

"You haven't forgotten how to eat, have you?"

"I could eat something."

"Good, let's go to a restaurant. Maybe if we're in a public place we won't yell at each other so much."

"What about the kids?"

"I sent them to stay with my sister-in-law."

"My sister?"

"Darren's. She and I managed to stay pretty good friends despite the divorce. So how about it?"

He studied her face a few seconds then nodded. "Fine, but only if I drive. I want to be able to hold the food down."

They climbed out of the car and each ran around to the other side. Cliff strapped on the shoulder harness. "Put yours on, too," he told her.

"That's what you always say."

"And what do *you* always say?"

She looked embarrassed. "That it hurts my nipples."

"And how do I reply?"

"You tell me to put it on anyway."

"Put it on anyway."

She smiled. "Right."

"Now, what kind of food do I like?"

"Chinese."

He nodded approvingly. "Okay, point the way."

They pulled out of the driveway and started down the quiet tree-lined street. Neither noticed the blue Pinto with the rental-agency plates parked across the street from their house. Or the two burly men sitting in it. Watching.

5

"THAT HIM?" Tyrone pointed.

"Fits the description."

"And the woman?"

"It's her house."

"What about the car?" Tyrone squinted after the disappearing VW, his huge frame hunched over the tiny steering wheel.

"His. Maroon VW bug. Same license number."

"Sure doesn't take very good care of it."

"Yeah," Edge nodded. "It's rustier than your crotch."

Tyrone burped. The sour smell of greasy food stung his nose. He fanned the air in front of him with an auto club map of southern California. "What was with the Chinese fire drill? Think they spotted us?"

Edge shook his head. "I doubt it. They were just changing drivers, that's all. He didn't drive as if they were in any great hurry."

"Maybe they just forgot something at the grocery store."

"Probably something like that."

Tyrone burped again, louder this time and with more pungency.

"Jesus, Tyrone," Edge frowned. "Cover your mouth or turn your head next time, will you? Shit, man."

Tyrone rolled down his window a crack and took a

deep breath. "What do you want to do now? Wait or come back later?"

"We wait until they get back. Actually, this is even better since it's already getting dark."

Tyrone nodded, trying to keep his voice casual for his next question. "So, uh, who goes in?"

Edge cocked his head to one side and looked at Tyrone with a confused and disappointed expression. "What do you mean, man? You know damn well who goes in. You do. I did Talon in Dallas."

"Right."

Edge smiled, but it was a hard, thin smile, like a deep scratch on the fender of a new car. "Unless you're starting to jelly and want me to go. You starting to jelly, Tyrone?"

"Fuck you. I'll do it."

"Yeah," Edge said, still smiling and staring at Tyrone. "Yeah."

6

THE TALL ASIAN with gray hair and black eyes stood beside their table and smiled. "How was the lemon chicken, Mrs. Kendall?"

Ginger smiled back. "Excellent as always, Mr. Lee."

"And your sub gum chow fun, Mr. Remington?"

Cliff waved his chopsticks and spoke rapidly in Mandarin Chinese.

Mr. Lee looked startled for a moment; then his smile broadened. He bowed slightly and walked on.

Ginger paled, her eyes wide, her voice urgent. "What did you just say to him?"

"I played with an old saying from Confucius, changing it a little to suit the occasion: 'If a man in the morning eats the right way, he may die in the evening without regret.' Why, what's the big deal?"

"We've been coming here for two years, and that's the first time you've spoken Chinese, or any goddamn language other than bland old southern California English. Usually I have to translate the menu for you and tell you what chow mein is."

"Maybe I learned it in school."

"You took two years of Spanish in college, and the only words you remember are *taco* and *amigo*."

"How do you know?"

"You told me."

Cliff lifted the porcelain cup to his mouth and inhaled

the jasmine-scented steam. He sipped the tea and stared at the red tablecloth.

"What do you think it means, Cliff?"

"What?"

"Come on, don't space out on me here," she said, her voice rising. She took a deep breath. "I'm trying not to get hysterical, but I'd like some explanation of why you just started speaking Chinese."

Cliff shrugged and refilled their teacups. "I don't know. I just did it."

"Can you do it again? Do you just know one saying, like something you might memorize from a crossword puzzle or a quiz show, or can you actually speak the language?"

"I think I can speak the language."

She hugged her shoulders as if she'd felt a sudden cold draft. "This is spooky."

"Yeah." He reached over and patted her hand. "Let's go home. I think we need to relax. I'm even starting to scare myself."

7

TYRONE FELT EDGE'S hard elbow bumping his shoulder. He blinked open his eyes.

"It's time," Edge said.

Tyrone rubbed his eyes and yawned. "What time is it?"

"Howdy Doody time," Edge chuckled, flicking open his Boy Scout knife and waving it in Tyrone's face.

Tyrone ignored it. "They here yet?"

"Nope, but it's dark enough for you to slip inside the house and wait for them."

"What about the kids?"

"No lights on inside. I don't think they're home."

"Good." He opened the car door and climbed out, unfolding his long legs and rubbing the circulation back into them.

"You packed? Just in case."

Tyrone patted his jacket. "The twenty-two."

"Good. The wire?"

Tyrone reached into his jacket pocket and removed a neat coil of wire.

Edge clucked his tongue. "Piano wire?"

"Guitar. An E string. Cuts right through the throat."

"Finally found an instrument you can play, maestro."

Tyrone faked a laugh, hoping he didn't seem too nervous. It wouldn't do for Edge to think he'd gone jelly. He strolled slowly across the street like an executive

coming home after putting in overtime at the office, or
like an old friend coming for dinner. He paused on the
sidewalk and glanced over his shoulder at the car. Edge
was still smiling at him, his teeth gleaming white in the
darkness. Tyrone pulled on his calfskin driving gloves
and waved.

Standard operating procedure called for Edge to
move the car farther up the street and hide in the
shadows. Watching and waiting. Just as they'd done a
dozen times before. Just as Tyrone had done yesterday
in Dallas.

It took less than two minutes for Tyrone to slip
around to the back of the house and pick the lock to the
back door. Once inside he took a penlight from his
pocket and clicked it on. The narrow beam of light offered just enough brightness for him to distinguish
shapes and forms, but not enough for anybody outside
to notice.

He was standing in a tiny utility room, barely large
enough for the gold washer and dryer that stood against
the wall. Two blue plastic baskets overflowed with dirty
clothing, and Tyrone nudged them out of the way with
his foot. A box of Tide lay overturned on the floor next
to a pile of athletic socks. The tangy smell of the
powdered detergent made the inside of his nose itch, so
he hurried ahead.

The kitchen was large and tastefully decorated with
green and white bamboo-patterned wallpaper that
matched the green cupboards and Formica counter. The
metal sink was stacked with dirty dishes, and the kitchen
table was scattered with magazines. Clumps of reddish
hair lay on the table and floor.

Something moved in the dark corner. Tyrone's hand
snapped for his gun as he swung the pen flashlight
toward the sound. A big cat with thick orange fur lifted
his head from the red plastic water dish and blinked into
the light. He licked his mouth lazily, then hopped up onto the nearby windowsill and disappeared through the
special cat door. The heavy rubber flap slapped closed
behind him.

Smart cat, Tyrone thought, his throat suddenly dry.

He covered the rest of the house quickly, memorizing the floor plan while looking for the best place to hide. Since there were two of them to deal with, it would be best to separate them and handle them one at a time. He needed a place where they wouldn't be together for a few seconds. He chose the bathroom off the master bedroom. If Tyrone's experience with his ex-wife was any indication, one of them would come into the bedroom alone at first. The other, probably the man, would wander into the kitchen for a drink, or go into the living room and turn on the TV. The woman would probably go right to the bedroom or the bathroom. That's what Tyrone's ex-wife had always done. But then she'd had a weak bladder. Among other things.

He closed the toilet lid and sat down. Behind him were half a dozen magazines piled on the tank cover. Without looking, he reached back and grabbed the top one. It was *The New Yorker*. With his penlight gripped in his mouth, he began flipping through the pages from the back to the front, stopping only to look at the cartoons. Some made him chuckle, but a lot of them he didn't understand. That bothered him a little because his ex-wife had married some clown who'd once had a poem published in *The New Yorker*. He hadn't understood that either.

He heard a car approaching, its engine loud and straining like Cliff Remington's VW bug. He tossed the magazine back with the others and pocketed his light. His heart was jackhammering against his rib cage. He pressed one gloved hand against his chest and wondered if this was what a heart attack felt like. The car continued down the street without stopping. Wrong car. He sagged against the toilet and tried to bring his breathing under control, but his heart seemed to be beating even faster now, despite the fact that it had been a false alarm.

Tyrone wasn't surprised. He'd felt this way the last few times he and Edge had worked together. The cold sweat would come next, and the diarrhea. The shakes wouldn't start until later tonight, long after he'd finished here. That was the pattern. And Edge seemed to have noticed.

That was the worse part. He and Edge had been buddies since the navy when they'd done Shore Patrol together. Tyrone was forty-two now, four years older than Edge. Hell, even back then he'd looked forty-two, with those heavy frown wrinkles mapping his face. Now that he'd put on all that extra weight and grown a spare chin, he looked fifty-two. But Edge still looked the same thirty years old he was eight years ago. He never seemed to age. Even his body was in better shape than it had been then. Harder, stronger. And his face was as smooth and tight as ever. But he was different somehow. A lot different. For one thing, his sense of humor was odd, like those cartoons in *The New Yorker*. He was always making jokes he knew Tyrone couldn't understand; he seemed to be doing so purposely just to ridicule him. That was something he'd never done in the past. Edge and Tyrone had always laughed at everyone else, never each other. And then there was that quoting business. He was always throwing in these damned quotes from Charles Dickens or Shakespeare, like he suddenly thought he was better than everyone else. Hell, they'd both come from the same kinds of white trash families, even though Edge was from North Dakota and Tyrone was from Kentucky. And they'd both dropped out of high school to join the navy; no amount of Charles fucking Dickens was going to change that.

Tyrone thought that maybe the changes in Edge had a lot to do with his own recent fear on the job. Edge was making him nervous, always staring and grinning like he was waiting for something special to happen. He wasn't sure that he could count on Edge anymore. There was no chance that Edge had gone jelly, but maybe he'd gone something worse.

Tyrone remembered when they'd first been recruited for this job. After four years in the navy, Tyrone had joined Naval Intelligence. Within two years he'd married and divorced an Armenian bitch who smoked cigars and wouldn't touch his penis with her mouth. Edge had quit the navy the same year Tyrone had gone with N.I., choosing instead to join the CIA. He'd married Jenny Wilkins, an art teacher from Hollins College, Virginia, whom he'd had under surveillance for leading an anti-Vietnam War rally on campus. The two men had kept in close touch, Tyrone being named godfather for Edge's son. As near as Tyrone could tell, all being a godfather meant was having to send the kid a present every Christmas and birthday. Still, since his wife had left him for that fag poet she'd been taking a night class from, it was nice to have somebody's birthday to remember. It gave his life some continuity.

Edge and Tyrone had both been approached the same week by the same person, a bald, squat man who looked more like a deli butcher than a government agent. The man had asked them to resign from their positions and go to work as free-lance agents for a government organization that the recruiter would not name. All he'd said was that the work would be steady, though occasionally dangerous, and the pay would be significantly more than they were currently making. In cash. And as a bonus, the recruiter promised to let them work together as partners.

That night they'd met to discuss the offer over a drink at the Holiday Inn. Eight hours later they'd stumbled into Edge's house falling-down drunk with mud on their clothes and bruised knuckles. One of Tyrone's teeth was missing, though neither could remember what had happened. The next day they accepted the offer.

But lately Edge had been acting just plain scary. What could have gotten into him? Tyrone decided to talk it out with Edge tonight when this was over and they were on the plane headed for the next job. Settle it once and for all.

He heard another car puttering down the street. His heart picked up its heavy beat again as his stomach muscles tensed.

The car pulled into the driveway. The motor stopped, and he heard two car doors slam. He reached into his pocket and pulled out the coiled guitar string, wrapping the ends twice around each gloved hand.

He heard the front door open followed by low voices. He stood up and pressed himself behind the bathroom door, his hands outstretched. In the dark, the thin metal wire was invisible.

8

"LET'S POSTPONE THE rest of this argument," she said wearily, closing the front door behind her. "I have to go to the bathroom."

"Me, too."

"How bad?"

"Bad."

"Me, too. I'll use ours; you use the children's."

He shrugged and followed her down the hall.

"Second door on the right," she pointed, veering off into the bedroom.

"Hey, wait a minute."

She stopped, pivoted. "Make it fast. Nature calls."

He smiled at her. "I just wanted to say thanks."

"No sweat, I'd tell anybody where the bathroom is."

"I don't mean that, and you know it."

Her voice was low and tender. "I know. It's just that I'm getting the feeling that maybe I don't know you as well as I thought I did. That's scary."

"Just because I spoke Chinese?"

"Just? Speaking Chinese is no *just*. It's heavy duty. How many Anglos learn Chinese?"

"Maybe it's some kind of manic state. I've heard that some people in a manic state can play musical instruments they've never touched before and even speak languages they've never studied."

She nodded. "Yeah, Darren's told me of some cases like that."

67

"Well?"

"Maybe. I don't know. I'm a little confused right now."

He tapped himself on the chest. "Me, too."

"Yeah, I know." She reached out and brushed a lock of sandy hair from his forehead. "But I still have to go to the bathroom. Pronto."

"Right," he said and hurried away.

She began unbuttoning her jeans as she headed toward the bathroom, kicking her sandals off as she walked. She took one step into the bathroom and was reaching for the light switch when she heard loud cursing from the hall.

"What's wrong?" she called, pausing at the door.

Cliff limped into view, holding a small dumbbell in one hand. "I tripped over this in the bathroom. Who's the goddamn weightlifter around here, me or Beau?"

"Neither. It's mine."

"Yours?"

"I use them to keep in shape."

"You're kidding?"

She put her hands on her hips and frowned. "A less secure person might take that as an insult."

"I didn't mean it that way. I just . . ."

"Yes?"

"Well, what was it doing in the kids' bathroom?"

"Liza's been using them to build up her bust. And I don't want to hear one wisecrack about it."

He held up his hands innocently. "No way. I'll just limp back to the bathroom." He started to leave.

"Cliff?"

He stopped. "Yeah?"

"I think we need to have a long, serious talk."

He nodded. "I agree. But it'll have to wait a few minutes, okay?"

She smiled. "Okay."

As she moved back toward the bathroom, Ginger noticed that she'd somehow rebuttoned her pants while talking to Cliff. A sudden burst of modesty with the

man she'd been living with for two years? She chuckled.
But was he the same man? Aside from the strangeness
of his speaking Chinese, there was none of the old
familiarity, the comfortable companionship they'd had
between them. The friendship that makes marriages
work. But there was something else. A sexual tension
and curiosity that she remembered from the early days
of their relationship. The first time they'd made love . . .

She stepped into the bathroom, one hand tugging at
her pants, the other flipping the light switch. Suddenly
there was something hard clamped around her wrist,
spinning her around. She started to scream, but now
something hard pressed against her mouth, shoving her
against the wall, knocking her breath away. She could
taste the bitter, sweat-soaked leather of the glove
against her lips. She tried to make out the face, memorize the features, but he seemed to tower above her.
She thought of trying to knee him in the balls, the way
she'd taught Liza. But before she could get any leverage, one of the gloved hands released her wrist and
grabbed the back of her neck, pinching hard. It felt as if
he'd pressed a secret switch there and sent a powerful
electrical current pulsing through her veins all the
way to her toes. Her legs went numb under her and she
seemed to be melting into one warm liquid heap. She
sagged forward, spiraling to the floor, thinking vaguely
that she smelled something sour and greasy.

Cliff strolled back up the hall, his hands still damp from
washing. The only towel in the kids' bathroom was
damp and wadded up into a ball in the corner; he'd used
his pants.

He was feeling pretty good, considering. And he
owed much of the good feeling to Ginger. She was sticking by him despite the difficult circumstances. He still
wasn't convinced that he was this Cliff Remington they
were all talking about, but whoever Cliff was, he was
one lucky man. Ginger had blanched when he spoke

Chinese, but who could blame her? She was right, not many Anglos spoke it. His knowledge of Chinese might be a clue to who he really was.

He walked past the bedroom door, glanced in, saw the bathroom light on and the door closed, and continued on toward the kitchen.

It was all so goddamn confusing. And scary. But the worst part was the loneliness, the isolation. With most people, when something bad happened they could retreat within themselves, to their own memories, for strength and comfort. He couldn't. He had to rely completely on instinct. Yet he felt all those memories were just barely out of reach; he could almost graze them with his fingertips. It was like trying to remember the title of the song you've been humming all day.

But Ginger was bringing him out of that isolation. She battered at his walls and shouldered her way into his life. And he was damn glad for the company. He could see why Cliff Remington had fallen in love with her, though he didn't know why she had fallen in love with him. For the first time since waking up in a strange bed this morning, he thought it wouldn't be so bad to be Cliff Remington after all. He tried to ignore the nagging drumming at the back of his skull that said there could be no going back. Not ever.

He flicked on the kitchen light and started opening and closing cupboards in search of a clean glass. He saw several empty spaces where dishes and glasses belonged.

"Hey," he shouted. "Where are the clean glasses?"

No answer.

He grinned. She was ignoring the implied criticism of her housekeeping in his question. He'd almost decided to wash one that was flecked with dried orange juice pulp when he spotted the dishwasher. He pulled the door open and smiled at his first piece of luck of the day: clean glasses. Avoiding the ones decorated with *Star Wars* characters, he grabbed a plain glass that still had some detergent caked inside it. He rinsed it out, filled it with cold water, and drank.

"I thought we were going to have a talk," he hollered, leaning against the counter. "Tonight."

Still no answer.

He shook his head. A talk. What would they say? Should he insist on moving out until he recovered? Would she encourage him to leave? Was she tired of nursing him? Where would he go? And what would he do?

What was taking her so long? He took a few steps toward the bedroom door. Maybe he should check on her. But if he did and she was fine, she might think he was . . . He stopped in the middle of the kitchen. Wait a few more minutes; she'll be out. He raised the glass to his lips and tilted his head back. While he was drinking he felt a sudden tingle of fear. An uncontrollable, irrational fear, like being afraid of vampires or zombies. The hell with what she'd think, he was going to check on her.

But as he lowered his glass he heard a quick shuffle behind him and felt an immediate stinging around his neck. His hands flew to his throat, where a metal wire was slicing through his flesh, pressing into his windpipe. His neck muscles bulged like bridge cables, but muscle was no match for the biting wire. He tried to tuck his chin in, but the man behind him was bigger and stronger, snapping Cliff's head back with a quick tug of the wire. He felt the warm blood running down his neck. Somehow he knew he had only a few seconds to live.

With no knowledge of what to do in a situation like this, he relied on instinct. As he felt his body turning cold, his brain icing over, he could almost name the tune he'd been humming, reach the person he couldn't remember. Then it was gone, and his body surged into motion. He no longer fought the searing wire. Instead, he gave in to its urging, snapping his head backward into the face of his assailant. He heard the sickening pop of a nose being broken. Immediately, the man loosened his grip, and Cliff spun around, his left hand pushing his right fist, driving his right elbow in a slashing arc like a broadsword. The elbow smashed into Tyrone's temple, his head bouncing against his shoulder. Tyrone's knees began to weaken, sagging slightly.

The wire had cut so deeply into Cliff's skin that it stayed around his neck, held in place by cut flesh. Using his elbow like a piston, Cliff battered the big man's head until Tyrone was on his knees, his face a mass of bleeding pulp. His nose was pushed to one side, the skin flapping slightly were it had torn at the nostril. Since Cliff had only worked on one side of his head, Tyrone's face was swollen with black knobs on one side, while the other side looked relatively normal. The result was grotesque.

Tyrone's head rolled, his chin hitting his chest as if he had nodded off. Cliff clasped his hands together, raised them high over his head, and clubbed the back of Tyrone's neck, sending him toppling over with a loud thud.

Cliff unwound the wire from his neck and quickly searched his attacker, not bothering to determine whether the man was dead or merely unconscious. He found the .22 pistol but nothing else. No wallet, no keys. Nothing.

Ginger! he thought, and jumped to his feet to search for her.

But she was standing there in the doorway, rubbing her neck, learning heavily against the wall.

"You all right?" he asked, reaching out to help her. His voice was pinched and hoarse.

She backed away from him, a frightened look in her eyes. "Where did you learn to do that?"

"What?"

"What you just did, Cliff. The beating you gave him. That takes training. Where did you learn it?"

He shook his head. "I don't know."

Behind him Tyrone started to stir.

"How long?" Cliff asked.

Ginger replaced the receiver and sighed. "They said right away. What does that mean in police language?"

"A few minutes."

She walked across the kitchen and stood a little behind Cliff. He was pointing the .22 at Tyrone, who was slowly struggling to his feet.

"Slowly, man," Cliff said, cocking the hammer back. "Very slowly."

"Be careful," Ginger said.

Tyrone finally managed to pull himself to his feet, but he was hunched over, one hand resting on his thigh and one hand holding the side of his face that Cliff had mashed with his elbow. Rivulets of dark blood trickled from his ear and mouth, joining at the chin to form one stream down his neck and over the collar of his shirt and jacket.

"Let's go, sport," Cliff said, waving the gun. "We'll wait in the living room where we can watch for the cops."

"Not in the living room," Ginger said. "I don't want him bleeding all over the carpet."

"Then go outside and keep and eye open for them."

"I don't want to leave you. We'll hear them when they get here."

"Mind if I sit down in the meantime?" Tyrone asked. He started shuffling toward the kitchen table.

"Hold it!" Cliff snapped. "I'll tell you when to move."

"Sure, pal. Sure. Just do me a favor and lower the gun a little. It might go off." But he could see by the way Cliff handled the pistol that he knew what he was doing. There was no way the gun would go off unless Cliff meant it to. For the first time since taking this assignment, he wondered who Cliff Remington was and why they wanted him and the others dead.

"What the hell were you after here?"

Tyrone shrugged. "Whatever I could find. The house was dark, so I figured no one was home. Thought there might be some cash around, maybe some jewelry."

"Why'd you try to kill me?"

"You surprised me when you came home. I panicked."

Cliff studied the thick, heavy face in front of him. The man looked as if he needed a shave, or a bath, or sleep. Maybe all three. But he didn't look as if he ever panicked.

There was a noise at the front door, and both Cliff and Ginger jumped.

He backed up to the doorway, where he could look straight down the corridor at the front door. The knob was turning. He swung his gun toward the door.

The door bolted open and Liza pushed Beau inside.

"Hey, watch it!" Beau scowled at Liza as he stumbled forward.

"Have a nice trip, pimp?" she laughed.

They both spotted Cliff and his gun at the same time. "Oh, shit," Liza moaned, "is he still at it? Sergeant Friday, I presume?"

Cliff turned back to face his prisoner. Tyrone had not moved.

Ginger ran down the hall. "I forgot you were coming back tonight. Where's Aunt Debbie?"

"She's gone," Liza said. "She just dropped us off. She has a date tonight."

"With Boyd Simmons, the fireman." Beau smirked.

Ginger grabbed the kids' arms and ushered them roughly into the living room.

"Hey, what gives?" Liza complained, rubbing her arm.

"What did we do now?" Beau asked.

"Nothing, kids. Just do me a favor and sit here. I'll explain it all later. We've had an attempted robbery."

"Really?" Liza said, delighted. "Neat."

"Let me go see." Beau started for the kitchen.

"*No!*" Ginger screamed after him.

Then came the first explosion.

The bullet dug into the wall next to Cliff, sending powdered plaster flying like a burst of snow. Immediately he jumped back behind the doorway and dropped to one knee. He swung his .22 toward the sound just as another explosion echoed through the kitchen. It sounded like a grenade, but the bullet that splintered the doorjamb confirmed it was only a gun. But a powerful gun. Cliff heard the children screaming in the living room and felt an unfamiliar wave of protectiveness engulf him. He had to do something, if for no other reason than to keep those three people safe.

"Come on!" the voice from the utility room called to the prisoner. Tyrone started to turn.

"One step and you're dead," Cliff told him, aiming the gun at his head.

Tyrone froze.

Another explosion, and the corner of the doorway blew up, sending splinters of wood into Cliff's face. The bullet sizzled past his ear and down the hall. He peeked around the corner and fired two shots toward the utility room, but they were hasty and inaccurate. Both bullets thudded into the wall a foot from the door.

In the distance, he heard sirens screaming.

"It's the police!" Ginger shouted with relief from the living room.

"*Move it!*" the voice yelled at Tyrone.

This time Tyrone lurched toward the utility room, trying to escape. Cliff swung the gun around the corner again and shot him twice in the right thigh. He pitched forward against the kitchen counter, knocking a Snoopy calendar from the wall.

"Shit," he groaned. "My leg."

"Sorry, pal," the voice said lightly. "I gave you a chance." There were two more explosions, and Tyrone's head blew apart, scattering skull chips and globs of gray brain matter over the green cupboards and the no-wax floor.

Cliff heard the outside door of the utility room creak open and slam shut, followed by rapid footsteps. Then nothing. Just the sirens growing louder and louder and louder.

"What are you trying to tell me? That first *you* shot this

mutton, then his *partner* shot him?" Lieutenant Bagg waved a package of Juicy Fruit gum as he talked. "Is that what you're trying to tell me?"

Cliff sat at the kitchen table watching Lieutenant Bagg pace back and forth across the kitchen, absently stepping over the dead man's legs as he walked. "Yes, Lieutenant. That's what happened."

Bagg stopped in front of Cliff, gave him a disbelieving look, then turned to shout at some of his men who were milling through the house. "Hey, let's move it, okay? Get this mutton out of the kitchen. I can't walk in a straight line." He continued his pacing, thoughtfully unwrapping a stick of gum, folding it in quarters, and sticking it in his mouth. He crumbled the wrapper and tossed it into the kitchen sink.

Ginger came into the kitchen and sat at the table next to Cliff. She gave his shoulder a little squeeze as she sat.

"How're the kids?" Cliff asked.

She shrugged. "Fine. Beau's a little shaken, but he's doing his best not to show it. He wanted to call his pal Freddy and tell him all about it."

"What about Liza?"

"She's doing better than I am. She thinks it was terribly immature of someone to try to steal from us. On the other hand, she thinks you were wonderful in saving all our lives."

"Clever kid."

Ginger smiled, but it was a tired smile.

A couple of young ambulance attendants came in with a stretcher.

"Where's the medical examiner?" Lieutenant Bagg asked.

One attendant hooked a thumb over his shoulder. "Out on the lawn smoking a cigarette with Sergeant Crawford."

"He done in here?"

"Said he was."

"Good. Haul this mutton away."

Ten seconds later the attendants were lugging Tyrone out the door.

"Heavy bastard," one of them complained.

The other one grinned. "He ain't heavy; he's my brother."

"How many times you gonna use that joke?"

The other one chuckled. Then they were gone.

Lieutenant Bagg paced over to the table, occasionally grinding a chip of skull under his shoe like gravel as he walked. He leaned against the edge of the table, chewing his gum with a loud smacking noise. "You look a little pale, Mrs. Kendall. Would you like to see a doctor?"

"No, thanks, I'll be all right."

"Fine." He continued to look at them, his gum popping with each chew, his short, broad body looming over them like a brick garage. "Gum?" he said, reaching into his pocket and offering them a stick. They both refused. He shrugged and dropped the pack on the table. "In case you change your mind."

"Thanks," Cliff said. There was a hard edge to his voice that Ginger didn't recognize.

"*De nada*," the lieutenant said. "That's Spanish. I've been taking Spanish at night over at Saddleback College. The department pays for it, and it helps me get promoted." He winked. "Of course, I have a little head start after six years on the force in New York. Naturally, I picked up some Puerto Rican Spanish. But you'd be surprised how different it is from Mexican Spanish." His broad smile revealed short square teeth and his wad of chewing gum.

"If there's nothing else, Lieutenant," Cliff said, "we've had a tough night. We'd like to rest."

Lieutenant Bagg's smile vanished. "So would I, Mr. Remington. So just sit there and let me do my job."

"Fine. Then do it. Quit standing around playing the tough D.A. We've already told you what happened three times."

"Cliff," Ginger cautioned, her hand on his arm.

"All right, Remington," Lieutenant Bagg nodded angrily and snatched the pack of gum from the table. "We've gotten all the physical information we can get for now. We'll have to let the lab boys work their magic, but right now we're pretty slim on leads. The only thing I've to work with is your story. Let me make sure I've got this straight." He leafed through his notepad. "You woke up this morning with amnesia and pulled a gun on your fiancée. Right so far?"

"Yes."

"Where's that gun now?"

Ginger said, "I gave it to my ex-husband to hold for the time being."

"Your ex-husband is the psychiatrist he saw this afternoon? Dr. Darren Kendall?"

"Right."

Lieutenant Bagg sighed. "Okay. After leaving Dr. Kendall, you came back here . . ."

"But we didn't get out of the car," Ginger added, "except to change seats."

"Then you went to a Chinese restaurant, came home, and discovered the burglar. First he gave you—" he nodded at Ginger—"some kind of Vulcan death pinch that knocked you out. Then he jumped you—" he nodded at Cliff—"with some kind of musical wire or something. Somehow you overcame him, got his gun, and held him here for us. But his alleged partner came in to rescue him, failed, and killed him instead. That about it?"

"Yeah," Cliff said, "but without the sarcasm."

Lieutenant Bagg grinned. "That's my Bronx accent. Everything just *sounds* sarcastic." He straightened up, flipped the notepad closed. "Well, it's a hell of a story. Too bad you didn't get a look at the partner."

"It was dark in that room."

"Uh-huh." He started toward the door. Ginger and Cliff stood up to accompany him. "A couple of things just don't make sense, though."

"Like why if he was robbing us there weren't any stolen items on the body?" Cliff suggested.

"Yeah, right."

"And why all the heavy fireworks for a simple burglary of a house they weren't even sure had anything worth stealing."

Lieutenant Bagg stopped chewing his gum and looked at Cliff. "Yeah, that, too. Not to mention the slugs we dug out of your walls."

"Three-fifty-seven magnums."

"Goddamn it," Bagg said, "if you know so much about the gun, why didn't you tell us earlier?"

Cliff shook his head. "I didn't know. I suspected."

"How?"

"The sound, the power. What it did to the walls, what it did to his partner's head."

"Where'd you learn that stuff?"

Cliff looked at the floor, his voice still hoarse. "I don't know."

Lieutenant Bagg turned to Ginger, who was staring at Cliff, her mouth open, her skin even paler. "Has he shown an interest in guns before?" the cop asked.

"Never." Her voice was almost a whisper. "He told me he'd never even shot a gun before. He hated guns. We only bought that pistol because of the robberies over in Woodbridge."

"You hit him twice in the leg. That what you were aiming at?"

Cliff nodded.

"Pretty fair shooting for someone who's never fired a gun before." He resumed walking toward the front door. Ginger opened the door for him, and he went outside, stopping a moment to look back at Cliff. "This case is starting to give me the creeps. Amnesia. Vulcan death pinches. Magnums." He shook his head. "I'm going to run a complete background check on you, Mr. Remington, and try to find out what in hell's going on here. See if maybe there's any mafiosi in your woodpile, because sure as shit those two men weren't your typical burglars. And I don't like what that means. I'm going to leave a couple of men in the neighborhood, just to be sure. Good night."

"I'm sorry," he said.

"For what?"

"For scaring you."

They stood in the bedroom avoiding each other's eyes. Ginger was facing the dresser, slowing removing her rings, earrings, and watch. Cliff was standing in the middle of the room, his hands buried deep in his pockets.

"Don't be silly, Cliff. You saved our lives."

"Maybe. But I put them in jeopardy in the first place by being here."

She watched him in the dresser mirror. "Come off it. They were just burglars, not hit men from the Mafia."

"You heard what Lieutenant Bagg said."

"The hell with him."

"No, he's right. Those men weren't petty thieves. You know that."

"I don't know what I know, Cliff. When Darren and I were married, he pretty much ran everything. His practice, the house, the kids. Me. He always had to have perfect order. No matter what turmoil was going on between us—and there was plenty—he managed to make the trains run on time." She turned from the dresser and sat down on the edge of the bed with a bounce. "After the divorce this place was chaos. My life was as messy as the laundry. I couldn't get a solid grip on anything. Thank God for the kids; they handled it all better than I did. It took a while, but I finally started feeling good about myself, you know, stronger. I got that job at your place, and after six months you finally asked me out. You felt guilty because you didn't think it was good policy to date an employee." She smiled. "You know the one thing I wish you could remember?"

"What?"

"How terrific you were with the kids. It was so hard for you to win them over to where they stopped making faces and pretending to throw up every time I mentioned your name. You took a lot of abuse. Gave plenty out, too. Christ, you were wonderful."

"I wish I could remember."

"Me, too. I wanted you to move in here right away, did you know that?"

He shook his head.

"But you wouldn't. You wanted to make sure I was fully independent first. That I *wanted* you, not needed you. I bitched at you for weeks until I realized you were right. Finally, you moved in, and eighteen months later you asked me to marry you. Everything was about as perfect as it can get. I felt my life had stabilized, maybe for the first time since my own parents' divorce. Then your spells of amnesia started. And now this."

"And suddenly all that stability is gone."

"Yes and no. It's certainly not like it was. Not as comfortable. But I'm still committed to you. I still love you, even though you're a stranger. I didn't know I had that kind of strength in me. I'm almost glad this happened, that I was tested and learned what I'm capable of. That's a special kind of stability, maybe even stronger than the other kind."

Cliff sat on the bed next to her. "When are we going to have that long serious talk?"

"I think we just did," she said, dropping flat onto her back.

Cliff leaned over her, their faces inches apart, their eyes locked. She reached up, the cool tips of her fingers gently brushing the red and blue bruise around his neck. Bits of dried blood flaked off. She slid her hand along his cheek, touched his ear. His scalp tingled at her touch. Slowly he lowered his body to meet hers, his chest pressing against her breasts, his hands cupping her head. At first their lips just brushed; then they clamped against each other with wet probing tongues. It was a long, dizzying kiss that seemed to drain the life from their bodies. When they stopped, Cliff sat up and inhaled.

"Maybe I should sleep on the couch tonight. Until . . . " His voice trailed off.

"Until when? Until your memory comes back? What if it never does? Do we split up? Start dating again? Good night kisses at the front door?"

"I don't know."

"Well, I do. I love you, whoever you are, whatever you were."

"What if Lieutenant Bagg finds something unpleasant in my past. Suppose I was a bank robber. Or worse."

"You weren't."

"Don't be so damned naive. We're not high school kids with a pubescent crush."

"I'm not being naive. I *know* you. Okay, maybe I don't know some details about you. You speak Chinese, and you know about guns. But I know the kind of man you are, what makes you happy and sad. Those things don't change."

He stood up. "Where are the blankets?"

"I need you here, Cliff. With me. Especially now." She frowned. "Don't you need me?"

"I want you."

"It's a start." She reached over and turned off the lamp. Their neighbor's outside lights filled the room with an eerie gray glow. Ginger sat on the edge of the bed and began to undress. She started to unfasten her jeans, stopped, started to pull her T-shirt off, stopped. "I feel a little nervous, as if this were our first time."

Cliff sat on the opposite side of the bed, his shoes and socks off. "Me, too."

"Oh, well," she shrugged, tugging her shirt off. She wore no bra. She stood up, her back to him, unfastened her pants, and wriggled them down over her hips. She wore no panties.

"Don't you wear underwear?" he asked.

"Sometimes. If I feel like it."

He chuckled, quickly stepping out of his pants and shorts with the same movement. Next he pulled off his shirt.

They stood facing each other across the bed, a smoky gray haze outlining their bodies.

"You're beautiful," he said softly.

"Last one in does the morning dishes," she said, pulling the covers back and diving into the bed.

He laughed and jumped in after her. They kissed again. This time Ginger rolled on top of him, pressing her hands against his shoulders, grinding her hips against his. She licked his lips, his teeth, sucked on his tongue, all the while rotating her hips rhythmically against him. He could feel their pubic hairs scratching against each other. He reached around and ran his fingers from the base of her neck down her spine, along the crevice of her buttocks, finally gripping the backs of her thighs. He felt the muscles in her legs shift as she moved faster against him. He tightened his fingers over her hard muscles, forcing her legs apart and slipping his hand between them. She moaned, her toes digging into the mattress as she strained harder against him. His grip tightened even more under her buttocks and he felt her warmth under his fingers.

"Oh, God, Cliff," she gasped and rolled off him. "I don't want to wait. I just want you in me."

He climbed between her spread legs. They continued to look at each other as he leaned forward, guiding his rigid flesh into her. She gasped, her eyes narrowing briefly, but still looking into his. He kissed her tenderly on the lips. Then they both closed their eyes and started to move.

Her legs were locked behind him, her heels spurring his back. His head was buried in her neck. Their bodies were slicked with sweat, the smell mixing with the heavier, more fertile odor that only excited them more. She dug her fingernails into his buttocks, encouraging him.

He felt different to her tonight. His lovemaking was more insistent, demanding. He was considerate, but not as gentle as usual. He moved against her like a powerful animal, all muscles and need. She felt the familiar tingling along her spine, the hot flames licking at her skin. She turned to bury her cries in the pillow so the children wouldn't hear. Suddenly his back arched and his fists tightened around her hair. She opened her eyes and saw his jaw clench in pleasure and concentration, the way it always did when he reached his climax. At least that was still the same. The only thing different was the tiny flap of fresh scab at his throat that had broken open and was now bleeding slightly. She licked the blood away gently.

Afterward they held each other silently for a long time. Finally she pulled away and said, "I feel as if I'm cheating on you with another man."

He laughed. "I feel as if I'm cheating, too. As if I were sleeping with my best friend's girl."

They were quiet for almost an hour.

"You asleep?" she asked.

"No. Thinking."

"About what? Never mind, dumb question."

He laughed and kissed her. "You're terrific."

"Damn right." She bit his ear. "You want to talk about it?"

"Tomorrow. I may have a plan worked out by then."

"Okay." She rolled back on top of him, her fingers walking across his tight muscles and hairy chest. Down his stomach and into his crotch. She wrapped her hand around his penis and squeezed gently. "I'm ready for dessert."

They made love again. But this time he was less intense, more preoccupied. In the quiet time between lovemaking he had devised the beginnings of a plan to discover what had happened to him. It wasn't a complete plan yet, and he knew that it would be dangerous, but he had to take some kind of action. He couldn't sit and wait for them to try to kill him again. He wouldn't risk the lives of Ginger and the kids that way. He would do *something*.

As he moved heavily against Ginger's straining body, he knew the first step was to send her in the morning to her ex-husband. And bring back the gun.

SEATTLE

9

THE TALL MAN with the battered violin case looked out
of place. Of all the adults standing in the ticket line at
the Fox, he was the only one not accompanied by at
least one squirming child. Why would a grown man
come alone to a Sunday matinee of Walt Disney's *The
Love Bug*?

But the tall man would have looked out of place almost anywhere. Despite his neat beige suit, white shirt,
and brown tie, he looked awful. His face was bony and
gaunt, with dark gray circles under his eyes. Even his
skin was slightly gray, except for the green and yellow
bruise on his forehead. His thick black hair looked as if
he had raked it into place with greasy fingers instead of
a comb. His lean face was clean shaven, but there were
several nicks on his neck and jaw. To the other adults in
line he must have resembled Vincent Price or Donald
Sutherland in their more menacing roles.

"Which theater, sir?"

The tall man looked up. "Pardon?"

The ticket seller sighed. "Cinema One, Two, or
Three?"

"I don't care. One, I guess."

"How many, sir?"

"One." He slid a five dollar bill through the opening
in the glass partition. She pressed a button, and a red
ticket popped up. She slid his ticket and his three dollars
change back through the opening.

"Thank you, sir," she said without conviction. "Next."

The tall man walked around the old-fashioned box office toward the waiting usher, a young boy in a red jacket with acne scars quilting his face. The tall man shifted his violin case to his left hand and with his right hand offered the red ticket to the boy.

"Thank you." The boy smiled and tore the ticket in half. "Enjoy the film."

"Thank you," the tall man said. He walked slowly into the lobby as children pulled their parents to the candy counters and clamored for popcorn, ice cream, and soda. The tall man's lips curled into a sneer. He clutched his violin case closer to his chest. He had their refreshments there. The ultimate snack. The real thing.

Now he had to figure out how to carry out his assignment. The Fox was an old theater that had been divided into three smaller ones. Over the entrance to each of the mini-theaters was a small marquee bearing a shortened title of the movie being shown inside. The doors were painted different colors. Several signs on the walls warned against switching theaters. None of that mattered to the man with the violin case. He wouldn't be watching any of the movies.

"Sir?" a voice behind him said.

The tall man swung around, his right hand suddenly in his jacket pocket gripping a small .32 pistol. "Yes?"

It was the acne-scarred usher who'd taken his ticket. He was scratching his face, and the tall man could see where some of the boy's medicated makeup had flaked off. "I noticed you're carrying a violin case, sir."

The tall man laughed. "Don't let the suit fool you, son. This ain't no vi-o-lin; it's just a plain old fiddle. I play with a country-western band at Billy's Longbranch Saloon down in Riverton Heights. You know the place?"

"I know Riverton Heights, but not Billy's, uh . . . ."

"Longbranch Saloon."

"Right."

"Well, that's where I play. I'm between buses right now, so I thought I'd kill some time. Never seen so many kids at one time. You sure must have your hands full."

The boy grinned. "Yes, sir. This is where the parents dump them when they want to go shopping for a couple hours. Now, sir, about your violin . . . "

"Yes, son?" The man's smile broadened as he shifted the gun in his pocket until it was pointing at the boy's stomach.

"With all these kids running around, you might want to leave it with me. For safety. I can put it in the manager's office, and you can pick it up on the way out."

The tall man relaxed his grip on the gun, bringing his hand out of his pocket to tug on his chin. "I appreciate the offer, son. I surely do. But me and this here fiddle been together so long we can't bear to be apart. I guess I'll just hang on to it. Thanks anyway."

"Sure," the kid shrugged, then scratched his face and wandered off.

The man quickly climbed the stairs that led to the projection booth. This was going to be easier than that goddamn hotel in Pittsburgh.

Wendy Cooper sat in the dark next to her father and licked the salt and butter from her fingers. On the floor between them stood a large tub of popcorn and a jumbo-sized bottle of Dr. Pepper. Wendy took her time and enjoyed the treat; she knew her father would buy her more if she asked. Today was the start of their last week together, and she knew he'd give her anything she wanted. But she didn't want anything. Just to be with him, like it used to be before the divorce last year.

On the screen, Herbie the Love Bug was cruising down the street without any driver, and most of the kids in the theater were laughing. Wendy laughed, too, but she didn't find it as funny this time as it had been when Mom took her to see it a few months ago. Of course, she had turned twelve since then, and her tastes had naturally changed. Matured. Still, it had been Daddy's surprise to bring her to the matinee, and she knew it would hurt him if she told him she'd already seen it with Mom. They only had these two weeks to spend together, his vacation time; then she'd have to fly back to Albany, and he'd have to go back to work at the radio station where he was a sound engineer.

The first week he'd taken her camping and swimming. They'd gone to the zoo and to nearly every other place she'd wanted to go—except Disneyland, which he said he couldn't afford to fly them down to. When she'd asked him why he couldn't afford it, he'd frowned and said, "Ask your mother."

A hard kernel of popcorn was stuck in one of her back teeth, and she tried to dislodge it with her tongue. She could have taken some of the Dr. Pepper and tried to swirl it free, but she didn't want to shift around in her seat. Her father's arm was draped around her shoulder, and if she moved, he'd think she was uncomfortable and take his arm away. She didn't want that. She liked it there surrounding her like a tide wall.

Wendy looked at her father and smiled. His eyes were closed, and his mouth was half open. She had known he would be bored with this movie, but he'd insisted that he would enjoy anything that she liked.

During her visit, she'd tried hard to be perfect, like a TV daughter. She was always careful to keep her room neat and hang up all her clothes. She even did all the dishes and tried once to sew a button on Daddy's shirt, though she'd sewn it on the inside by mistake. Still, she had tried to be good. Maybe he'd tell Mom how good she was and they'd live together again because they wouldn't have anything to argue about anymore. Maybe.

Wendy wrinkled her nose. There was a terribly bad smell somewhere. It reminded her of the bathroom at the Albany airport. She looked around, wondering where it was coming from. She giggled. It was coming

from Daddy. He was tooting. When they had all lived
together, sometimes they'd sit around the TV at night,
and suddenly he'd grin at Mom and say to Wendy,
"Come here and pull my finger, and I'll toot your
favorite song for you." And she would go over and pull
his finger, and he'd toot.

"For God's sake, David," Mom would scold and
shake her head, but she'd laugh, too.

Wendy giggled again. "Dad," she whispered, "I can
make you toot." His eyes were still closed as she took
hold of the index finger of his hand which was dangling
over her shoulder. "Toot, toot," she laughed and
pulled on his finger.

There was a small slushing sound. Then the finger
came off in her hand.

She looked at it for a moment, then laughed, thinking
it was a joke he was playing on her. Then she looked at
the mangled hand that still rested on her shoulder, saw
the blood dripping over her new blouse onto her bare
arm, and screamed.

The tall man with the battered violin case stood up at
the sound of Wendy's scream and shuffled quickly
down the aisle, pushing his way through the emergency
exit. A bolt of sunlight shot through the door into the
dark theater like lightning. Then the door slammed
closed, and the theater seemed darker than ever.

A few minutes later the Henderson brothers, on their
way home from St. Mary's Sunday Bible class, found a
battered violin case under a parked Impala. The case
was empty.

PART TWO

Monday

WASHINGTON, D.C.

10

CELIA BEDFORD WAS on her two-hundred-and-thirty-eighth jump when the special security phone buzzed. It took her a few more bounces before she could hop off the trampoline without vaulting into the sofa or chandelier. Even when she stood safely on the floor, the living room still seemed to be moving slightly. She shook her head to clear it and took a couple sips of her diet soda before walking unsteadily across the room to turn down the TV. Jane Pauley was interviewing a rock singer, asking questions about youth, music, and sex.

On her way to the phone Celia grabbed a folded pink towel and threw it around her neck like a scarf.

"Yes?" she puffed into the phone.

"Gilbraith here, Ms. Bedford."

"Go ahead, Carl."

"Eric Morley's down here in the lobby. Wants to see you. Says it's urgent."

"Put him on."

There was a pause as the receiver changed hands.

"Celia?"

"What the hell are you doing here, Eric?" There was no anger in her voice, only surprise that he'd come to her apartment, something he'd never done before.

"Have you heard about the latest outbreak of Brotherhood Disease?"

"When?"

"Yesterday afternoon."

"Where?"
"Seattle."
"How bad?"
"Bad."
"Come on up."

Eric Morley gripped the railing of the express elevator with both hands and concentrated on getting rid of his shit-eating grin. It certainly wouldn't do to stroll into Celia Bedford's apartment looking satisfied. Especially with the news. It would only make her suspicious, and he had to avoid that at all costs.

He couldn't help smiling, though. Ever since the news about the horror in that Seattle movie theater first came in, followed fifteen minutes later by Edge Connor's report of Tyrone's misfortune in California, Eric Morley had been happy and busy—happy because he knew that there must be a way to turn this disaster to his personal advantage, and busy figuring out how.

Finally he had come up with a plan.

Too bad for Celia, he thought, his grin widening, an involuntary chuckle escaping. She was a good executive: imaginative, intelligent, and ruthless. All the qualities necessary to run I-COOP. None of the others in the group even came close to her. None, that is, except himself. She had always teased him about his ambition, warning him that he wasn't ruthless enough. He was about to prove her wrong.

In the end the others would back him, for despite the lip service his colleagues paid to Celia, he'd often overheard them all grumbling behind her back about working for a woman. Constant digs about "that time of month" and such. Ironically, he seemed to be the only one who didn't mind working for Celia, maybe because he was the only one intelligent enough to appreciate her cunning.

Eric nervously jabbed the penthouse button a couple more times, even though the elevator was already whooshing upwards. But he was anxious, excited. This was his chance. Finally. He was dead in the water at the FBI, and he knew it. How they'd found out about him being gay didn't matter. They knew. And because of it, he would stay at the same level for the rest of his career. His only way up was as director of I-COOP. But to land that job he would have to ged rid of Celia Bedford. And there was only one way to do that.

Moonshadow.

Moonshadow had been Celia's brainchild. They had all agreed with her judgment, despite the risks they would run if anyone found out about it. Now that the secret was about to be exposed, I-COOP would not survive, unless Eric could lay all the blame on Celia herself. But how could he manage to do that? No one in the group would dare to accuse her without physical proof. And there was no way to get hard evidence. Nothing incriminating at I-COOP was ever committed to paper; everything was done orally. So the only way was to get her confession on tape. But her office and home were absolutely bug-proof, and she would not discuss business anywhere else.

His one chance was to get her out of the office or apartment, and talking. He ran his finger up the lapel of his red-check coat with the fleece lining. He'd sent away for it last year in response to an ad in *TV Guide*. He had meant it to be a Christmas present for someone special he'd been seeing then—someone he now hoped never to see again. The coat had set him back $159.95, plus shipping costs. Fortunately, the weather today was perfect for it. He'd spent an hour and a half working on the coat with tweezers, magnifying glass, needle and thread, and electrical tape. Now he could barely feel the tiny transmitter sewn into the lapel, or the battery pack hidden in the lining. Another chuckle escaped.

The elevator slid to a smooth halt, and the doors hissed open. Celia Bedford stood in front of him, holding either end of the pink towel around her neck, sweat beaded across her forehead and chest.

Eric Morley's face was grim with bad news.

"Sit," she said, leading him into the living room.

Eric marched over to the sofa and sat down. Celia followed, perching on the arm of the giant wing chair across from the sofa.

"Facts," she said.

"A movie theater in Seattle. Three dead. They're still washing chunks of the the victims out of the seats."

"Positive cause?"

"Moonshadow."

She slid into the chair, throwing her legs over the arm. "Suspects?"

"None observed."

"If it happened yesterday afternoon, why did it take until now for me to hear about it?"

Eric shrugged. "The Seattle coroner and city hall kept it under wraps. It's the tail end of their tourist season, and they don't want it getting out that they have Brotherhood Disease running through their city."

"I take it you've gathered up all the remaining caches."

"Of course."

"And from what you've been able to add and subtract, how much does our friend have left?"

"Depends on how he uses it—a little at a time, as he has done so far, or all at once."

"Roughly."

He shrugged. "Enough to wipe out the entire population of Arizona or New Mexico."

"New Mexico we could do without."

Eric said nothing.

Celia tugged her knit leg warmers up over her knees and straightened the front of her green Danskin leotard. "Christ, it's looking bad."

Eric nodded solemnly. "It gets worse."

"Don't be shy, Eric," she smiled. "Let me have the other barrel."

"Edge Connors phoned in his report from the John Wayne Airport at six twenty-six this morning. He'd been hiding out most of the night, just in case the local police were searching for him.'' He paused to pick a piece of lint off his pants. ''They blew it last night with Remington.''

''How bad?''

''Tyrone Willis is dead.''

''Is Remington?''

''No.''

''You want something to drink?'' she said, though she made no move to get up.

Eric took the hint. He stood up. ''What'll you have?''

''Some of that unfiltered apple juice. The kitchen's right through there.'' She pointed, and he went into the kitchen. He returned a minute later with a glass of cloudy brownish juice for her. ''You're a good boy,'' she said. ''Go on. What went wrong?''

''Connors said that Willis screwed up somehow, and Remington got the drop on him. By the time Connors got into the house, Remington was holding a gun on Willis. Connors fired at Remington, but missed. He heard police sirens, so he left.''

''Who killed Willis? The cops?''

''Connors. 'Security sanction' he called it.''

She smiled and took a sip of juice.

''Aside from our other concerns right now,'' he suggested, ''I think we should keep an eye on Connors. He's getting a little too gung-ho.''

''He's just ambitious,'' Celia said.

''He didn't have to kill Willis.''

She shrugged. ''He couldn't get him out. He had to do something.''

''*We* could have gotten him out. Connors should have let the cops arrest Willis. Then I would have sent in a couple guys from the Bureau to take him into federal custody, and he'd have been back on the streets within twenty-four hours.''

''Ordinarily, yes. But because of the, uh, sensitivity of this particular project, I'd rather we didn't leave a lot of trails that lead back to us.''

"In other words, you're glad that he killed Willis."

"Glad isn't the right word, Eric. Let's just say I don't disapprove of his action."

"Remington's still alive."

"Yes, well, apparently we've underestimated Cliff's abilities. Considering his record, we shouldn't have. Of the four, he was the best."

"At least we know he didn't pull the Pittsburgh and Seattle jobs."

Celia drained the rest of her juice and set the empty glass on the parquet floor next to her chair. "That leaves out Jim Talon and now Cliff Remington. So it's either Albert Boston or Felix McDonald. What do you think?"

He laughed. "I drew Jim Talon in the office pool, so I've already lost my five dollars."

She stood up and sighed. "I'd better get dressed. Looks like a tough day at the office today."

"Right. By the way, I've got Whiz waiting outside in the car."

She raised one eyebrow. "Whiz? Why?"

"Well, he put a lot of Moonshadow together. He knows these four guys as well as anybody. Better, really, considering his unique role. I knew you'd want to ask him some questions, and I figured it would be faster to ask them on the way to the office instead of waiting until we get there."

"Why didn't you just bring him up with you?"

He spread his hands. "I didn't want him to hear the first part of our conversation. We work on a need-to-know basis, remember?"

Celia studied Eric's face for a moment, then nodded. "You've been busy, Eric. I'll be showered and dressed in fifteen minutes."

It took her eight minutes. When they stepped into the elevator, Celia punched the lobby button. The elevator dropped at such a speed they both felt as if their feet were barely touching the floor.

She glanced at Eric. "You still dating—is that the right word?—that reporter from UPI? Brad Lindsay?"

He smiled. "Off and on."

"Good looking boy. Very athletic. Nice ass."

"He used to play football in college. Quarterback."

"Hmmm. So did the President."

"You never know," Eric said, his hand casually brushing the fleece lapel of his jacket, silently activating the transmitter.

Teddy "Whiz" French sat in the back of the Cadillac limousine, feeling a little insecure. That's how he always felt when he was about to see Celia Bradford. Maybe because she was the only one who knew how he'd earned his nickname.

Most of the people he worked with here in Washington knew "Whiz" was a nickname from his high school days. But because of his reputation, they assumed it was the result of his scientific genius. That was a safe assumption. After all, Teddy was the CIA's only twenty-two-year-old Ph.D. in psychology who specialized in behavior modification.

Four years ago, after he'd earned his doctorate, Celia Bedford had brought eighteen-year-old Teddy French to Washington and given him an unlimited budget and complete autonomy to develop a program similar to the one he'd described in his doctoral dissertation. His parents had been thrilled at the government's interest in their son. Naturally they were proud of him. But that pride was also tempered with relief. His father owned a shoe store in Trenton, New Jersey, and had spent the last four years terrified of his own son, who had the unnatural habit of always being right. In those four years, Teddy's father had stopped trying to teach the kid any of the things he'd always wanted a son for—the whole reason he'd let his wife talk him into having a child in the first place—baseball, carpentry, and the shoe business. Teddy had been interested only in math, chemistry, and science. Just two weeks ago, Teddy had received a letter from his mother telling him they were thinking about adopting a ten-year-old Puerto Rican boy who was able to kick a football farther than any of the older kids at the orphanage. Teddy's father was thrilled.

Considering all that, it was natural that everyone should think he was called Whiz because he was a genius. Only Celia knew the truth. One night Teddy and a neighbor boy were late leaving the high school. Once outside the school building, Teddy opened his fly, pulled out his penis, and pissed on the side wall of the school. His friend was surprised and delighted, looking on Teddy with new respect. Teddy explained that a slight bladder problem caused him to have to urinate often, sometimes when there were no bathrooms close by. Of course, as Celia Bedford discovered, that wasn't the truth. Teddy French just liked to piss on buildings, and had been caught twice in high school and once in college outside the library. But because of his youthful appearance and academic standing, the guards always let him go. Once Celia had even shown him an infrared photograph of him pissing against the wall of the Senate Office Building at night. Of course, Teddy knew the psychological reasons for this uncontrollable impulse, but Celia didn't care. He could piss on the President as far as she was concerned. As long as he got results. And as long as he did, the meaning of his nickname, given to him that fall afternoon outside the high school by his neighbor, would remain a secret. Teddy "Whiz" French always got results.

He also got Moonshadow.

After he completed Moonshadow, he was given a permanent position within the CIA as a consultant. As such, he could do pretty much anything that interested him. He liked that arrangement. So when Eric Morley had summoned him to meet Celia Bedford again after four years, he'd begun to feel very insecure. Moonshadow had taken a lot out of him. He didn't want to get involved in anything like that again.

"Well, well," Celia said, climbing into the back seat of the white limousine. "How's my boy?" She slid next to him and patted his knee. He jerked involuntarily.

Eric closed the door behind her and walked around to speak to the chauffeur. "I'll drive, Floyd. Meet us back at the garage."

Floyd nodded, got out of the car, tossed his chauffer's hat through the open window onto the front seat, and walked away.

Eric hopped in behind the wheel, started the engine, and pulled the huge car into the traffic. He rolled up his window to reduce the interference to his hidden transmitter. This conversation would hang Celia Bedford.

Celia was smiling happily as she took Teddy's clammy hand in hers. "How's everything, Whiz?"

He winced at the name. "Fine."

"I hear congratulations are in order."

"What do you mean?"

"You're about to become the brother of a healthy Puerto Rican boy."

He wasn't surprised that she knew, only curious as to how. Maybe she had his mail read. Maybe his parents' phone was tapped. Probably both. "It's not final yet."

"It will be. This is going to be the fastest adoption ever at the Trenton St. Anne's Adoption Home. A present from me to you."

"Thanks," he said evenly.

"Christ, look at this traffic," Eric grumbled from the front seat. "Say, Whiz, do you think you could come up with something that would improve the traffic flow around here?"

Teddy grinned. "My bosses asked me to do just the opposite. The traffic jams make it easier for them to follow people."

Celia crossed her legs and smoothed the wool skirt over her knees. "Just a few questions, Whiz."

"Moonshadow?"

She smiled.

"You know I don't know anything about that, except for the small part I played in preparing those four men."

"That's the part we're interested in."

He adjusted the Windsor knot on his silk tie, pulling it a little tighter. "Okay."

"First, is it possible for the conditioning to wear off?"

"Of course. I warned you of that possibility at the time."

Eric spoke over his shoulder. "But with the help of those special drugs—"

Teddy shook his head. "Experimental drugs. They had no track record in long-term applications."

"Okay," Celia said. "What about side effects? Any new ones discovered since then?"

"It depends on the person involved. His own strengths and weaknesses, or fears. There could be no side effects, or there could be many, some of them quite devastating."

"Considering the personalities of those four men, in your opinion, who would be the first to break out? And who would be most likely to snap under the pressure?"

"Those are very imprecise terms . . ."

"Indulge me," she said firmly.

Teddy loosened his tie, then tightened it again, making sure his collar points were straight. "There's a direct correlation between how well the treatment takes and the subject's IQ. The higher the IQ, the better the treatment will take; the lower the IQ, the less stable the result will be. The more intelligent person is also likely to be more imaginative, more suggestible, better able to live out a fantasy than the individual with a lower IQ. The less intelligent person is generally rigid and unable to sustain fantasy, which is one of the reasons they often don't achieve as much in real life as intelligent people do. It also explains why they are not as unhappy as brighter people. Once they do achieve what they want, they aren't as disappointed with it as the more intelligent people might be. It's fascinating, really."

"Of the four men you worked with, which one is most likely to break out of the treatment soonest?"

Teddy chewed on the inside of his cheek a few

seconds. "I'd say Felix McDonald. He's a very tough individual, but of the four, he had the lowest IQ."

"Low enough to make a difference?"

"Yes. Considering he was also the oldest of the four by seven or eight years."

"Who's the smartest, the cleverest?" Eric asked.

"Those are two different questions. The one with the highest IQ is Albert Boston. A brilliant mind, really. That's why we were able to place him where he is now. But 'clever' connotes quick thinking and resourcefulness. That would easily be Cliff Remington."

Celia nodded. "That figures."

"Yes, he had the second highest IQ, right under Boston's, but he was the hardest to control."

Eric stopped at a light and turned to look at Whiz. "I thought you said the higher the IQ the better the treatment would succeed."

"Generally, yes. But one must take the subject's ego into consideration. Cliff Remington had a very strong ego. He was a very happy man, and he didn't want to lose his identity."

"One more question, Teddy," Celia said, patting his knee again. "Which one of the four is most capable of committing random acts of violence?"

"What kind of violence?"

"Murder. Senseless mass murder."

Teddy tightened his tie again. "All of them are capable of violence. They all have a history of it. But they're all trained men, highly disciplined. Even now. I'd have to say none is capable of mass murder. Except in the same sense we all are; under great enough pressure, anyone would break. But, given those four men's unique circumstances, they would require a lot of pressure, and pressure by itself would not be enough to set them off. It would take something else. An added twist."

"Pull over," Celia snapped. Eric pulled the limousine to the curb in front of the Library of Congress. "Thank you very much, Teddy. I think you can easily find a cab from here."

Teddy "Whiz" French quickly climbed out of the car. They pulled away before he'd even made it to the curb. He loosened his tie, tightened it again, and felt a sudden compulsion in his bladder. He turned to face the Library of Congress and smiled.

"Well?" Eric asked as he drove away.

Celia Bedford leaned back into the seat and sighed. "Well, we know that neither Jim Talon nor Cliff Remington was responsible. I received a report last night that Albert Boston was under surveillance at the times in question, so he's in the clear. That leaves only Felix McDonald. He is supposed to be in the Rocky Mountains photographing wildlife for the Sierra Club."

"What about his wife and son?"

She shrugged. "They don't answer the phone, and nobody's seen them. They probably went with Felix."

"Since he's the only one whose time can't be accounted for, then it has to be him."

"Looks that way."

"Then you knew that before you talked to Whiz."

"I suspected it. With these guys you can't even trust physical evidence. Remember, they know all the angles. But now that I've talked to Whiz, my suspicions are even stronger."

"Then we should concentrate on finding Felix. We can forget Albert and Cliff."

"And risk the same thing happening to them? Hardly. Look, we tried an experiment with them; it didn't work. They had their chance. You forget, we defied a direct presidential order by developing Moonshadow. If anyone finds out, it's our asses."

Eric raised his voice. "You mean you had Jim killed, and now you want Cliff and Albert killed, too, even though you're pretty sure they're innocent?"

Celia nodded. "Nobody involved with Moonshadow is innocent."

Eric stroked his fleece lapel and smiled.

11

CLIFF DID NOT open his eyes when he felt the barrel of the gun lightly tapping on the back of his head.

Then the tapping stopped, and he decided it was probably just a bad dream. After everything that had happened, it was no wonder he was a bit paranoid. He was lying in bed naked, his arms wrapped around Ginger, his legs tucked up behind hers, his hips pressed against her warm buttocks. His face was buried in her hair, and he could smell the strawberry scent of her shampoo. He wrinkled his nose and smiled; her hair made him hungry for strawberry shortcake.

When he felt the tap at the back of his head again, he knew it was no dream.

He turned slowly, one hand automatically gripping the corner of his pillow as a weapon. The muscles in his arms tensed, and his feet sought purchase on the slippery sheet.

Then he saw his tormentors.

"Jesus," he sighed, shaking his head.

Beau and Liza were standing next to the bed staring at him. Liza held a green plastic bowl in which she was stirring something, while Beau poked Cliff in the shoulder with a spatula.

"I'm awake! I'm awake!" Cliff said.

"Do you remember us?" Liza asked.

"Sure."

"No, I mean *really* remember us. Like you used to."

Cliff paused, thought about lying, but didn't. "No."

"I told you," Beau sighed with disappointment.

Ginger stirred behind him, stretched, yawned, and sat up. "What's going on here?" She yawned again, fluffing her mussed hair. The covers had fallen to her waist, revealing her naked breasts, and Cliff wondered if maybe she should cover them while the children were in the room. Ginger saw him staring, guessed what he was thinking, and gave a loud laugh that turned into a cough. "Don't worry, Cliff; they've seen them before."

Liza continued stirring. "He's still sick, Mom."

"He doesn't remember us," Beau added.

"Listen, Beau—" Cliff started.

"Bogie! Everyone calls me Bogie. *You* gave me that nickname." He threw down the spatula and ran out of the room.

"He'll be okay," Liza said. "It was his idea to make breakfast for you." She tilted the bowl and showed them the thick yellow paste inside. "We eat in ten minutes." She marched out of the room still stirring.

Ginger began scratching Cliff's back. "Well?"

Cliff shrugged. "I still don't remember anything that happened before yesterday morning."

"Shit."

"How do you feel?"

She forced a smile. "Okay, I guess. As long as you remember last night."

"Which part?"

"Bastard," she laughed and hit him with her pillow.

"Okay, gang, here's the plan." Cliff looked around the breakfast table at Ginger and the children. They leaned forward. "After breakfast, you're each responsible for writing down as many details as you can remember. Everything, no matter how small. Anything I've ever said about my parents, for example."

"You were an orphan," Beau offered.

"Very good, Bogie. That's just the kind of thing I want you to remember."

"You were raised by your grandparents," Liza said happily, then frowned, "but they died, too."

"Good. Write it all down. When it's all over, the person who can remember the most gets a present."

"That's not fair," Liza said. "You've told Mom a lot more than you told us. In bed and all."

"She doesn't count," Cliff announced.

"Hey, thanks," Ginger laughed.

"What's the present?" Beau asked.

Cliff looked at Ginger for help. She was smiling, sipping her coffee. "Well, what do you want?" he asked.

"A Harley-Davidson motorcycle," Beau said.

"A Fiat convertible," Liza said.

"We'll compromise. A new ten-speed bicycle."

"Deal," they said in unison.

Ginger nodded her approval while Cliff pretended to wipe the sweat from his forehead.

"So what's for breakfast?" he asked.

"Our own special treat," Liza said, going over to the stove. "Corn muffin pancakes."

"Fried in an inch of bacon grease," Beau added excitedly. "Makes 'em crisper."

"Sounds, uh, good."

"It should," Liza said. "You taught us how to make them."

"That's right," Ginger said.

Cliff drank his orange juice in one gulp and refilled the glass. "What about the landscaping business?"

"I'll call Glenn Tompkins after breakfast. He should be able to handle it for a few days."

"And after that?"

She tightened the belt on her green flannel bathrobe. "Depends."

"Bogie?"

"Yeah, Cliff?"

"What's this say? I can't read your writing."

Beau cocked his head to one side and stared at the paper. "It says 'clams.' You used to like fried clams. You'd dip them in honey and mustard dressing."

"He dipped *everything* in that dressing," Liza said.

"Yeah, but especially fried clams."

"And artichokes."

"Yeah," he reluctantly agreed. "Artichokes."

"That's one point for both of us then."

And so it went for three and a half hours. After Ginger, Liza and Beau had finished writing their individual reports, Cliff and Ginger eliminated the repetition and all the information together into a three-page profile.

"This is your life, Cliff Remington," Ginger sighed, tossing the profile on the coffee table and stretching out on the sofa, her bare feet on his lap.

"So who wins the bike?" Beau asked.

"You both do," Cliff said.

"Really? Can we go get them now?"

Cliff picked up the report and began leafing through it again. "Later, kids."

"How much later?" Liza asked. "An hour?"

"Maybe tonight."

"Awww."

"Knock it off, guys," Ginger said. "This is your last week before school starts. Wouldn't you like to spend some of it outside?"

"Okay, Mom." Liza winked, eager to show she was mature enough to pick up adult signals.

"We could have a lot more fun outside if we had our new bikes," Beau grumbled as Liza escorted him out of the room.

Ginger massaged her temples with her fingertips.

"You okay?" Cliff asked.

"Headache. I'll take a couple Tylenol."

He wrapped his hand around one of her feet and rubbed. "Tough morning?"

"A little. Doing all this was strange. I felt as if the Cliff Remington we all knew was dead and never coming back."

"We'd better start considering that possibility."

"Oh, God, Cliff, do you really think so?"

"It's possible."

She slid her feet to the floor and sat up. "Now what?"

"Now I call Lieutenant Bagg and see what he's found out. Our main concern right now is finding out why those two guys tried to kill me." He walked over to the phone, glanced at the business card Lieutenant Bagg had given him the previous night, and punched out the numbers.

"Sergeant Copello here."

"Lieutenant Bagg, please."

"Sorry, but he's not in his office, would you . . . Here he comes. Just a second. Hey, Larry, phone for you. You can take it here."

"Lieutenant Bagg speaking."

"This is Cliff Remington."

"Oh, yeah. Hold on a second." There was some noise as the receiver changed hands. "Copello, I'm going to take this in my office. Hang it up for me, will you?"

"Sure thing." Sergeant Copello chuckled. "Sorry my desk isn't neat enough for you."

After a minute, Bagg came back on the line. "Got it," he said and the other receiver clicked. "Remington, you still there?"

"Yeah. What have you found out?"

There was a pause, and Cliff wondered why the tough city cop of last night suddenly sounded so nervous.

"Look, Remington, I'm still, uh, waiting for the reports to come in. Nothing new yet."

"Nothing?"

"Yeah, well, it takes, um, time. You know."

"I know. You've had all night. From what I could tell about you, I'd say you've had the computer and telephone lines humming all last night and this morning. Am I right?"

No answer.

"Why the stall, Bagg?"

Lieutenant Bagg's voice barked through the phone. "If you've got an accusation to make, Remington, call my captain. In the meantime, keep your nose clean." He slammed the phone down.

Cliff replaced the receiver.

Ginger was leafing through the three-page profile. "I take it all the shouting meant he didn't know anything new."

"He knows. He's just not talking."

"Why not?"

Cliff looked her in the eyes. "He's scared."

"Of what?"

"I don't know."

"I don't like it, Cliff. It sounds dangerous."

"What can be dangerous about it? I'm just going to visit old friends. According to our little profile, I'm thirty-five years old. My parents were killed in an automobile accident when I was three. I was raised by my grandparents, who died eight months apart of various diseases. Immediately after high school I attended UCLA, majoring in anthropology. Finding the job market a little slim for anthropologists, I used the modest inheritance from my grandparents to travel around Europe and the United States for a couple years. Then I worked at odd jobs here and there, and eventually bought an ailing landscaping business in Santa Barbara. After turning it into a profitable enterprise, I sold it four years ago to move here and start my own landscaping business. One question. Where did I learn landscaping?"

"Your grandfather was a gardener in the Beverly Hills and Bel-Air sections of Los Angeles."

"Okay. Then except my infancy in—" he flipped the page—"Pennsylvania, I'm a Southern California boy. Have you ever met any of my boyhood chums?"

"No."

"Relatives?"

"No."

"Traveling companions?"

"No."

"College classmates?"

"No, but you do get letters from UCLA asking for donations. And I've already shown you your goddamn college diploma."

Cliff turned to Ginger and laid a hand on her shoulder. "What are you getting sore about?"

"I don't know," she snapped. "It's just that you seem to be making more of this than is necessary. You're so skeptical about everything."

"Ginger, someone did try to kill me last night. You and the kids could have been next."

"Maybe. But maybe it *was* just a burglary. Maybe they really were just a couple of amateurs who bungled the job."

"They weren't burglars. And they weren't amateurs."

"How do you know?"

He shrugged. "I just know."

"Terrific," she said, throwing up her hands. "You just know. Great answer."

Cliff leaned back into the sofa. "What do you want me to do? Just wait for them to try it again?"

"No, Cliff. I want you to wait until the police have had a chance to check this whole thing out. Then I want you to start seeing Dr. Jessup again. Maybe she'll start with hypnosis."

"Not yet." He stood up and walked to the center of the room.

Ginger rose and faced him, glaring. "When?"

"When I've answered some questions."

"Lieutenant Bagg said—"

"Lieutenant Bagg is holding out on me. I can't wait around for him to loosen up."

"Maybe you think because I don't want to get your stupid gun back that I'm holding out on you, too?"

Cliff said nothing.

Tears appeared in Ginger's eyes, and she nodded slowly. Her voice was weak with hurt and disappointment, barely a whisper. "Okay, Cliff, I'll get it."

He wanted to go to her, to hold her close and beg forgiveness for hurting her this way. But something inside wouldn't let him, and right now he hated that something. Still, he just stood there, his hands deep in his pockets.

●   ●   ●

Cliff was sitting on the sofa reading the *Los Angeles Times* when he heard Ginger's Land Rover pull into the driveway. He quickly put the paper aside and stood up.

Ginger walked wearily through the front door as if she were exhausted. She saw Cliff staring at her expectantly, almost happily, and she shook her head and pushed past him, avoiding his eyes.

"Well?" he said, following her.

She reached into a purse, pulled out his gun, and tossed it on the sofa. It landed on the newspaper, bounced once, and lay there on page one like a freshly unwrapped fish.

Cliff picked it up, swung open the cylinder, checked the cartridges, and flicked it closed with one snap of his wrist.

"You do that well," Ginger said quietly.

Cliff dropped the gun back on the sofa and went to Ginger, closing her within his arms and hugging her. At first she just stood there, her body limp. Then suddenly she was hugging him fiercely, her hands locked behind his back, her face pressed to his neck. Though she made no sound, he could feel her warm tears against his neck.

"I'm not a nagging woman, Cliff. For God's sake, if you don't remember anything else about me, please remember that. But I'm scared. Since yesterday morning, since you lost your memory of us, I've had the feeling that you're dangling over the edge of a ravine and I'm holding on to you by your sleeve. You're slipping, but as long as I keep holding you, I know you won't fall all the way. Do you understand?"

"I think so."

She moved away from him. "As long as you're with me, I keep thinking your memory will come back and everything will be the way it was before. Now you want to go away."

"Only to L.A."

"It doesn't matter where. You've got a gun, and you don't want me to go with you. That scares me. I feel as if the sleeve I've been holding on to is tearing and you're about to fall away. Forever."

"I love you, Ginger. I don't have to have my memory

to know that I loved you before yesterday." The words came smoothly, though unexpectedly from him, and he wasn't sure he meant them. They seemed to be the words she wanted to hear, so he said them. Instinctively. He hoped he meant them, because he didn't want to think that kind of lie came so easily to him.

She looked into his eyes and smiled. "I know, babe, I know."

Suddenly he had to get away. He needed time and distance to sort things out. But now wasn't the time, and this wasn't the place. He had other plans. He stuffed the gun into the waistband of his pants at the hollow of his back. Then he slipped into a tweed sports jacket he'd dug out of the closet.

Ginger watched him with a grim frown. "You look just a little too happy."

"For God's sake, Ginger," he said. But it was true. He could almost feel the blood surging through his veins, entering his heart, and being pumped out again. He felt as if he'd discovered a lost part of himself. A strong part. But was it the best part?

He kissed her quickly on the lips and started for the door. "I'll be back by this evening. Early."

"You'd better leave L.A. by three o'clock if you want to miss the commuter traffic."

"Check."

"You remember the directions I gave you?"

"Yes."

"Want me to write them down?"

"No."

He stood with his hand on the front door, staring back at her. The Cobra Model D-3 .38 Special was pressed snugly against the small of his back. He liked the feeling. He wondered if he should tell her he loved her again or wait to figure out if it was true. "I love you," he said, and went out the door.

"Be careful," he heard her say as he closed the door behind him.

He started the VW and headed toward the San Diego Freeway. It wasn't until he'd entered the on-ramp that he realized he was being followed.

12

"Shoot the sherbert to me, Herbert."

"Pardon?" Cliff said.

She laughed a light, airy laugh that tickled his ears. "Oh, don't mind me today, mister. I just found out that I got an A on my physics test. My first test this semester, and I got an A. Isn't that terrific?"

"It's marvelous. Keep it up."

"You can bet your bongos, mister. This is my last year, and I intend to graduate smack into a job that starts at twenty-five grand. No more three roommates in a two-bedroom apartment overlooking a cracked driveway and a scummy pool. And no more work-study jobs like this. It's condominiums and Hawaiian vacations after this year."

"Not on twenty-five thousand a year."

She frowned at him and placed her hands on the counter between them. "It's a start, man. I just need to put a down payment on one little piece of property, then keep trading up. That's how my brother-in-law started, and he's cleaning up."

"Good luck." Cliff smiled.

"Thanks." She smiled back. "Now, what can I do for you?"

"I'd like a copy of my transcript."

The young girl across the counter looked surprised. "You went here?"

"Sure. Why so surprised?"

She wrapped a lock of shoulder-length blond hair around one finger. "This is my fourth year at UCLA, and as far as good-looking men go, well, it sucks. The real handsome ones are gay, and the rest are into all kinds of kinky stuff. The only ones worth the effort are the professors, and they're all married." She unwound the lock of hair from her finger and smiled. "I guess I came here a few years too late. You married?"

"Yes."

"Happily?"

"Deliriously."

She shrugged. "I'll get your transcript now. Name?"

"Clifford Remington."

"Nice," she smiled and turned away.

Cliff watched her walk away, purposely putting a little extra action into her hips. She was pretty, with just a touch of baby fat that was in danger of becoming permanent if not immediately disposed of. But that was not his concern now. The transcript was. And the man in the cheap gray seersucker suit waiting outside the records office. The one who'd followed him from Irvine.

It hadn't been much of a tail job, and somehow Cliff had known that he could shake the blue Mazda any time he wanted to. He could imagine all the proper moves, the dodges and fakes, that would send the other car miles off in the wrong direction. But he'd decided against it. As long as he knew where the car was, he knew where to look for trouble. If he lost this guy and the bastard managed to find him again, it might be harder to spot him next time.

So Cliff had driven the lazy ninety minutes along the San Diego Freeway to Wilshire Boulevard, and woven his way through the Westwood shopping district. All along the streets were theaters showing first-run movies. It was funny. He recognized the titles on the marquees, but couldn't remember where he'd first heard of them. He'd felt the same way while reading the *Times* that morning. He was familiar with all the events going on in the world; he just didn't remember how he knew or where he fit in with any of it. All the details of the world around him were still in his memory. All that was gone was *him*. Cliff Remington.

Maybe with his transcript in hand he could track down some of his former classmates and teachers. They might be able to help him. Had he studied Chinese here? He needed to fill in some gaps. Jog his memory. Something. Anything.

He watched the young blond girl as she went to the back of the room where dozens of four-drawer file cabinets lined the wall. She tried several different ones, rummaged through the drawers, twirled her hair around her finger again, and checked yet another file cabinet. Finally, still empty-handed, she went to an older woman with bifocals and frosted hair. The woman listened to the girl with an expression of disapproval. She took her bifocals off, tapped the stem against her teeth, then looked at Cliff. Disapprovingly.

She marched over to the same file cabinets that the blonde had checked, scanned the same drawers, and also came up empty. The two stood facing each other for a few seconds, the blonde winding and unwinding her hair, the older woman tapping the stem of her bifocals against her teeth. Then the woman seemed to get an idea. She went over to a file cabinet at the back of the room and unlocked it with a key she had pinned to her waist. Cliff noticed it was the only cabinet that was locked. The blonde did not follow the older woman, but merely waited in the middle of the room looking bored. She glanced over at Cliff and shrugged elaborately.

The older woman was hunched over the cabinet, walking her fingers over the tops of the files. Finally she found what she was looking for and slid a manila folder from the drawer. She quickly read through it, closed it, and disappeared into a cubicle at the back of the room.

The blonde walked back to Cliff, leaning her elbows on the counter.

"Problem?" Cliff asked.

"We're having a little trouble finding your transcript. My supervisor is checking it out now."

"Does this happen often?"

"Not often. But it happens."

The door to the cubicle opened, and the supervisor stuck her head out. "Angie," she called, "may I see you a moment?"

Angie rolled her eyes for Cliff before turning and walking to the cubicle. Once she was inside, the woman pulled the door closed with a slam. Several other employees glanced up from their work and exchanged looks.

Five minutes later the door opened again, and Angie came out alone. Gone was her confident swagger, her easy smile, her happy mood. She looked pale and frightened. Her eyes were a little red, as if she was fighting tears. She approached Cliff timidly.

"I'm sorry, sir, but your transcript was in the batch we sent out for microfilming."

"You okay?"

She nodded. "Yeah, sure. I just got yelled at, that's all. Too friendly with customers. Too slow to do my work. It's not the first time."

"How can I get a copy of my transcript?"

"You can't for a week. That's when this batch will be back."

"Is there any particular order in which transcripts get sent out for micofilming?"

She looked nervously over her shoulder. "Sorry, sir, I really don't know. All I can suggest is that you come back in a week. I have to get back to work now. I need this job if I'm going to graduate. Sorry." She forced a weak smile. The sudden shift of facial muscles caused a tear to roll down her cheek.

When Cliff emerged from the building the man in the gray seersucker suit was nowhere in sight. Yet he knew the man was watching him. He no longer questioned how he knew these things; he just accepted it as one accepts breathing.

He looked up into the sky and squinted. It had been heavily overcast and cool when he'd left Irvine, but the cloud ceiling had burned off, and now the sun was glar-

ing down. The temperature was at least eighty-five, and
seemed even hotter after the crisp air-conditioning of
the records office. He wished he could take off his
jacket, but it wouldn't do to walk around campus with
his gun exposed. He settled for loosening his tie.

A tall boy wearing an orange backpack walked past
him, absorbed in a small computer game. His fingers
jabbed the buttons causing flashing lights and loud electronic beeps. Cliff stopped him and asked directions to
the anthropology department. The boy mumbled them
without looking up or breaking his concentration on his
game.

Cliff found the old brick building after only two
wrong turns. As he walked in, he spotted Gray Seersucker leaning against a nearby tree, pretending to read
a UCLA catalog as if he were considering enrolling.
Cliff noticed that he, too, had kept his jacket on.

This building was not as cool as the records office,
but it was certainly more comfortable than the damp
heat outside. Cliff straightened his maroon tie and
straightened the shoulders of his jacket. After what had
just happened in the records office, he realized getting
information was not going to be as easy as he'd hoped.
Maybe Angie's story was true; maybe his records really
were being microfilmed. It made sense. They couldn't
keep the paper around forever. Still, you'd think that
they would have been microfilmed before now. Why
hadn't Angie looked in the microfilm catalog? Why had
the supervisor chosen that moment to yell at Angie?
None of it was concrete enough to take to Lieutenant
Bagg, even if he trusted Bagg. But it was enough for him
to recognize that he wasn't going to get anywhere playing it straight.

He smoothed back his sandy hair and strolled down
the corridor, reading the plastic nameplates next to the
office doors. When he found the one that said "Department Chairperson," he walked in.

The woman behind the small metal desk continued
typing on her IBM Selectric without looking up. She
was remarkably thin, with curly black hair, and slightly
prominent teeth. She looked about Cliff's age. On her

desk was a silver-framed photograph of twin girls who appeared to be about ten years old, both with curly black hair and slightly prominent teeth.

Behind the woman was a closed door. The plastic nameplate read: Dr. Leonard Sands.

"Excuse me," Cliff said with a friendly smile. "I'd like to see Dr. Sands, please."

The woman looked up as if unaware that anyone had been in the room. Her fingers were still poised over her typewriter as she talked. "Do you have an appointment?" She smiled like a person who only asked questions to which she already knew the answer.

"Yes, I do," Cliff said.

She looked surprised, then doubtful, finally annoyed. She switched off the IBM and swiveled around to the appointment calendar on her desk. "I don't see any appointment here."

"The name's Steve Lansing. My secretary made the appointment for me."

"There's no Steve Lansing here."

"God, that girl is going to ruin me yet. That's the trouble when six reporters have to share the same secretary. Nothing gets—"

"Reporter?"

"Right. *Los Angeles Times*. She was supposed to set this appointment up for me while I was at the mayor's office. Look, I hate to barge in without an appointment, but this is important. It will only take a few minutes."

She continued to stare at the appointment calendar while she thought it over. "I'll see if Dr. Sands is busy." She pushed her chair back, got up, smoothed her skirt, and disappeared through the door.

She returned a minute later, holding the door open for Cliff. "Dr. Sands will see you now."

"Thanks," Cliff smiled and walked into the office.

Dr. Sands lifted his massive body up from his chair and smiled. "Come in, Mr. Lansing. Come in."

The room was larger than Cliff had thought it would be. Beside Dr. Sands's large wooden desk, it contained a sofa, a water cooler, a conference table surrounded by eight wooden chairs, and a card table with a coffee maker on it. Every inch of wall space was covered by filing cabinets and bookcases.

Cliff guessed that Dr. Leonard Sands weighed close to three hundred pounds and was in his late forties. He stretched out one hand to greet Cliff, keeping the other flat on the desktop as if to support his tremendous bulk. As far as Cliff could determine, not a pound of it was muscle. He was completely bald, except for a fringe of long, thin hair on the sides and back of his head, but he had masses of beard and mustache that almost obscured his gold tie and blue vest. His matching blue jacket hung on a wooden hanger behind the door.

Cliff shook his hand and accepted a seat across from the desk. Dr. Sands seemed relieved to be able to sit again, and did so with a noticeable thud. On his desk stood a half-eaten pear, a Diet Dr. Pepper, and an open magazine that looked to Cliff like the *Atlantic Monthly*.

"And what the devil would the *Times* want with the anthropology department?" he asked. "Someone discover a new tribe somewhere?"

"Nothing like that, Professor."

Dr. Sands looked disappointed. "Then how may I help you?"

"It's a simple matter. We're thinking of hiring a graduate of your department, and we want to check up on him first."

Dr. Sands frowned, tipping his chair back a little. "Verifying an applicant's background in person is a little unusual, isn't it?"

Cliff shook his head. "Not for us. Since the Pulitzer Prize scandal, we've tried to make triple sure about the background of everyone we hire. We've even run checks on some reporters who have worked for us for years. So far we've caught three in serious lies. Two claimed to have worked for newspapers they'd never worked on, and one said she had a diploma for a graduate school she'd only spent one semester at."

"I see. Then all you need is a transcript of this student's record." Now that Dr. Sands realized he wasn't going to be quoted in the newspaper, he was no longer interested in the matter. "I think the records office could best help you."

"Sure, we'll check with them, too. But in my business it doesn't hurt to have a second confirming source. Just to cover our butts." He winked.

Dr. Sands sighed impatiently. "Just what do you want from me, Mr. Lansing?"

"To merely confirm that you had a student by this name and see if you remember anything about him."

"What's his name?"

"Clifford Remington."

"What year did he graduate?"

"Sixty-nine."

Dr. Sands tipped back farther in his chair until the legs creaked. "That's quite a while ago. I had only been teaching here a couple years then."

"He said he remembered you. You were his adviser."

"Remington, you say?"

"Clifford Remington."

"Hmmm. That does sound familiar. Let me just refresh my memory." He got up and went to one of the two file cabinets next to the coffee maker. A box of Sweet'n Low sat on top of the cabinet next to a box of Hostess doughnuts. He pulled open a drawer, tugged out a file folder, and read its contents. When he turned back to face Cliff, he was smiling, but his face was stiff. He spoke louder than before as if to mask a sudden nervousness. "Of course, now I remember him. Just had to tickle the old gray cells." He chuckled weakly.

"Then you were his adviser."

"I certainly was. He was a top-rate student. Could use a few more like him around here today. Always had his nose in a book."

Cliff tried not to look as surprised as he felt. This man claimed to remember him. Add that to the diploma Ginger had shown him, and the fact that even though they hadn't shown him his transcript, they at least had a record of him. Maybe Ginger was right: he *was* just being overly skeptical. Maybe he was becoming a conspiracy nut. He stared at Dr. Sands and tried to remember him. He couldn't.

"Well, thank you very much for your help, Professor."

"You're welcome." He jammed the file folder back into the packed drawer and closed it with his knee. "I guess it's quite a jump for Cliff from anthropology to journalism, eh?"

Cliff stood up, shook Dr. Sands's hand, and smiled. "We like to hire reporters with diverse backgrounds."

Dr. Sands nodded and returned to his chair.

Cliff reached for the door, hesitated, then opened it. But before he went through, he turned back. "One last question, Professor."

"Yes?"

"Did Cliff have any special problems?"

"Special problems?"

"You know, racial problems."

Dr. Sands looked confused. "Uh, none that I recall."

"I just wondered what his attitude was toward whites. Sometimes a minority's personal outlook can prevent him from being objective in reporting."

"Clifford never demonstrated any animosity toward whites," Dr. Sands huffed with indignation. "In this department he was treated with respect, as an equal. There was never a problem."

"Never one incident relating to his being black?"

"None."

"Fine," Cliff smiled. "That's just what I wanted to know."

13

"Bastards!"

Cliff drained his Coors and slammed the empty can down on the counter. The noise wasn't loud enough to offer him any satisfaction, and that only made him madder. He wanted *Crash!* and all he got was clunk. He glared across the kitchen at Ginger, who was sitting at the table matching clean socks and rolling them into balls, the tip of her tongue peeking out the corner of her mouth. He slammed the can again to get her attention.

"Well? Are you going to tell me now that I'm imagining everything?"

"No," she said quietly. "But I am going to offer a possible explanation, just for argument's sake."

His eyes narrowed. "Go ahead."

"All right. And let me finish before you jump in. Remember, Cliff, I'm on your side." She tossed a pair of rolled up athletic socks on the table. "Okay. Let's suppose that they really did send your transcript out to be microfilmed. Maybe it's their policy to wait a certain number of years before doing that. Or maybe their budget was cut and they have to do it whenever they can. Possible?"

"Yes, but—"

"Let me finish. Maybe that blonde girl got what was coming to her. From your description she sounds as if she needed a good talking to anyway. Instead of yelling at her in front of everyone else, her supervisor properly

123

took her into a private office—not to warn her to keep her mouth shut, as you suggest, to but to tell her to quit flirting with every guy who comes into the place."

"Okay, but what about—"

"Now, as far as Dr. Sands goes, you popped into his office pretending to be a reporter from the *Times*. You know when someone from the media suddenly confronts an ordinary person, that person will be shaken up a little. You burst in on that poor man, asked him about a student from fourteen years ago, and were surprised when he didn't remember him. Then on top of that, you tricked him with that story about the student being black. What if he felt embarrassed because he didn't really remember Clifford Remington, but wanted to give one of his students a good recommendation anyway?"

"But when he checked his file, his whole demeanor changed. He became nervous."

She shook her head. "Maybe he was just embarrassed. He looked in his files, still couldn't remember Cliff Remington, but didn't want to hurt a former student's job opportunity."

"You've ignored one detail. The guy in the gray seersucker suit who followed me there and back. You saw his car pull away from here a few minutes ago. I'm certainly not imagining that, am I?"

"No, Cliff. I saw him, and he definitely was watching the house. But didn't Lieutenant Bagg say he was going to have someone watch us? For our own protection. Maybe that man was a policeman keeping an eye on you. Is that possible?"

Cliff took a deep breath, rubbed his eyes with his fingertips, and exhaled. "Doesn't that stretch the socks, rolling them up like that? Maybe that's why socks never stay up."

Ginger tossed another pair on the pile. "Answer me, Cliff. Is my explanation possible?"

"Yeah, it's possible." He smiled. "Maybe even probable." He sat down next to her, picked up a pair of rolled socks, tossed them into the air, and caught them. "I don't know. Things have been happening so fast.

Maybe I overestimated the reliability of my instincts this time. Have you always been this goddamn logical?''

"Always. You men are so damned emotional." She reached out and squeezed his hand. He leaned across the pile of socks and kissed her.

"Where are the kids?" he asked.

"At the community pool. They're gathering data on the best ten-speed bike to buy."

"Can we afford the best?"

"Not unless you suddenly remember a fortune you've kept hidden from me."

"I wish. In the meantime, I noticed a healthy collection of credit cards in my wallet. Let's splurge this time. The best that Sears, J.C. Penney, or Montgomery Ward has to offer."

She laughed and hugged him, kissing him loudly on the lips. "I'll drive over and pick the kids up. Give you a chance to change into something more comfortable. And less metallic."

"Right," he said, pulling the gun out of the waistband of his pants. "I'll find someplace to hide this until we can get rid of it. Permanently."

"Thanks, Cliff. I'll feel a hundred percent better."

He smiled. "Me, too."

"Goddamn it, Bagg," Cliff shouted into the phone. "I want some straight answers. *Now!*"

"Look, Remington," Lieutenant Bagg said, "I've told you everything we know."

"Which is nothing, right?"

"So far. We're still working on it."

"You've been working on it all day."

"So have you, from what I hear."

"Then the guy in the blue Mazda was yours."

"Harrison's a good man. Wanted me to thank you for the tour of UCLA. His ex-wife goes there. She divorced him, married their insurance agent, and is now going for her master's degree in French. Some life, huh?"

Cliff clenched his fist tighter around the telephone

and looked up at the kitchen clock. Ginger had been gone fifteen minutes and was due back any time now. He wanted to get off the phone before she returned and discovered that he hadn't bought her careful explanation of everything that had happened, that he had simply pretended to agree with her to make her feel better. It had been another performance, an easy act. Too easy. He realized now that he was good at lying, a natural. What he didn't know was how much of his life with Ginger before the memory loss had been a lie.

Or did it really matter? Right now he needed answers. Sure, her calm explanation had been plausible. But it still *felt* wrong. And with everything else gone, he had to rely on that feeling, wherever it came from. His instinct was all he had left of the man he had once been.

"Remington," Lieutenant Bagg said, "if you tell me what you were doing at UCLA today, I might be able to fill you in on one or two items. How about it? Tit for tat?"

"Look, Bagg," Cliff said, his voice straining like taut cable, "you and I both know something suspicious is going on here. Somebody has already tried to cancel my ticket, and there's reason to believe they'll try again. What if they succeed the next time? What if they also kill Ginger or the kids? Are you willing to take the responsibility?"

Lieutenant Bagg hesitated, started to snarl something, then stopped. "Goddamn it, Remington. Goddamn it all to hell." Then he released a long sigh of defeat. When he spoke again, his voice was low. "All right. I've had enough of this secrecy shit anyway." His voice went even softer. "I can't talk now. Meet me later."

"When and where?"

"Can you shake your girl? It'll be my ass if anyone finds out."

"I'm taking them to some shopping mall, uh, South Coast something."

"South Coast Plaza. Good. Drop them in a department store and meet me by the carousel in an hour." He hung up.

• • •

"There they are!" Beau said and ran down the aisle.

"Whoa, pal," Ginger called after him. "They aren't going anywhere."

Liza shook her head, maintaining her sophisticated pose. "He's such an immature pimp."

"Liza, it makes me nervous to hear my son being called a pimp all the time."

"I told you, Mom, it's short for 'pimple.' "

"I'm not sure that's much better. How about just calling him Bogie again? For old times' sake?"
She shrugged. "Okay."

They entered the sporting goods department of Sears, passing the pool tables, Ping-Pong tables, and video games. Beau was already examining the bikes—rubbing the seats, squeezing the hand brakes, hefting them to determine their weight. The excitement of it all even got to Liza, who dropped her Joan Fontaine demeanor long enough to wax enthusiastic over a sleek yellow ten-speed. Beau had mounted one bike and was getting ready to pedal down the aisle toward the hardware department.

"No free rides, Bogie," Cliff said, grabbing the handlebar.

"Just a short spin. You wouldn't buy a car without taking it for a test drive, would you?"

"Beauregard!" Ginger said firmly.

Beau winced and climbed off the bike with a long sigh. "Yes, ma'am."

Cliff checked his watch. Five minutes. Everything was right on schedule. He leaned over and bit Ginger's earlobe.

"Cliff," she laughed, "that sort of thing just isn't done in Sears. Roebuck tried it once and they took his name off the store."

"The lout." He leaned over and bit her other ear. "I have my needs. Look, I noticed a B. Dalton bookstore on our way in. You lead the great bike hunt while I run back and look for a book about amnesia."

"Christ, Cliff, that store's way on the other side of the mall."

"I'll hurry. Be back in ten minutes. Time me." He winked, turned, and sped down the aisle toward the main mall before she could protest.

On his way across the second floor of the mall he made a few precautionary maneuvers, dodging in and out of several stores, backtracking, even sitting on one of the benches for a minute. But he was sure no one was following him. Still, he pressed his left forearm against his hip as he walked, just to feel the six-inch steak knife he had taped to his wrist. He'd snatched the cheap, sharp knife from the kitchen sink while no one was looking. With Ginger and the kids along, he hadn't wanted to carry the gun. The knife would have to do. He couldn't remember ever having used one as a weapon before, but he had the feeling that he'd know how to handle it if he had to.

He heard the calliope long before he saw the carousel. It was playing a speeded-up version of "When You Wish upon a Star," the metallic sounds echoing off the plate-glass windows of the surrounding stores. Cliff peeked over the edge of the railing at the crowd milling around the carousel. A line of eager children waited impatiently for their turn to ride. Their parents stood next to them, clutching their children and their shopping bags.

Lieutenant Bagg leaned against the metal rail that surrounded the carousel, unwrapping a stick of gum. He crumpled the wrapper and dropped it on the floor. After a couple chews he looked at his watch and drummed his fingers on the railing.

Cliff's eyes never left the lieutenant's back as he stepped onto the escalator and rode down to the ground level. He strolled casually toward Lieutenant Bagg, loosening the masking tape on his knife as he walked.

Lieutenant Bagg glanced over his shoulder at Cliff's approach, but then looked back at the carousel. "No brass ring."

"What?"

"There's no brass ring. What's the point of riding a merry-go-round if there's no brass ring to grab for?"

Cliff shrugged. "For the hell of it, I guess."

"Doesn't make any sense."

"I don't think carousels are supposed to make sense. They're supposed to be fun."

Lieutenant Bagg shook his head. "My kids prefer the roller coaster."

"There's no brass ring there either."

"Yeah, but at least you've got something to show for it afterward. You're sick." He smiled.

"I've got to get back to Ginger and the kids."

"Right." Lieutenant Bagg cupped his hand under Cliff's elbow and guided him away. "Let's keep moving. That way I don't feel so much like a target."

"Any reason you should?"

"Being seen with you, for one." He looked at Cliff and frowned. "I don't know all the details of what you were into, pal, but it must have been something heavy. The phone lines between our office and Washington have been smoking all day."

"What about?"

"Beats me. I'm only told what to do, not why."

"But you hear things."

Lieutenant Bagg grinned. "Yeah, I hear things. Things like don't look too closely into the shooting at your place last night. Make it look good, then drop it."

"Why?"

"Don't know." They stopped in front of Hickory Farms and pretended to study the list of cheeses displayed on the window. "I do know that my boss wasn't thrilled with that kind of federal pressure. He tried to loosen up his own contacts in Washington, but it was no go. They came down on him so hard his teeth are still rattling."

"That's not much to go on."

"It's more than you had, pal."

"What else have you got? You didn't risk a face-to-face for that."

Lieutenant Bagg snorted. "You've been around a lot, Remington. This amnesia act may fool some people—"

"It's no act," Cliff snapped.

"No shit?"

"No shit."

"You're in worse shape than I thought."

"Thanks for cheering me up. Now what have you got?"

He rubbed his stubbled jaw and nodded. "Sometimes I really hate this job." He glanced over his shoulder and motioned Cliff forward. "Let's keep walking. Being with you is making me nervous."

They strolled along past the shops.

"All right, Remington. I've got one thing more to tell you, but it comes with a speech. Those are my terms."

"I'm listening."

He hesitated, as if not sure where to start. "Look, I'm not much good at this. I've been a cop forever, man; it's the only job I've ever had, and it means something to me. I've never done anything like this before, going behind the back of the department, and I'll tell you up front that it makes me sick."

"Then why are you doing it?"

"I'm not sure. It seemed clearer to me this afternoon. Anyway, it has nothing to do with you, Remington. I figure you probably deserve whatever's going to happen to you whether you can remember what you did or not. You're no innocent citizen being unjustly picked on. If the Feds want you, they probably have a damn good reason."

Cliff said nothing.

"Yeah, you're a cool one all right. But your old lady and the kids," he shook his head, "they deserve better than to wake up and find you with your throat slit. Hell, maybe you deserve better too. Who knows? I just know how I'd feel if my wife and kids had to go through something like that. And it'll get worse."

Cliff stopped walking and faced Lieutenant. "Okay, Lieutenant, let's cut to the bone. You've got a guilty conscience because you know damn well I'm being set up for murder and you've just been handed a starring role in the production. Believe me, I appreciate your concern and the risk you're taking, and I'd like to be more polite, but I don't know how much time I have. So tell me what you know. All of it.''

Lieutenant Bagg looked around as he reached into his jacket pocket and took out a folded sheet of typing paper. He handed it to Cliff, who opened it and began to read:

MOONSHADOW

James Talon
Dallas, Texas

Clifford Remington
Irvine, California

Albert Boston
Boulder, Colorado

Felix McDonald
San Francisco, California

"Moonshadow," Cliff whispered. His scalp tingled, and he felt a tightening in his throat. A sense of foreboding engulfed him, but he didn't know why. The word looked familiar, and he had that same sensation of having heard a tune whose title he couldn't remember. Something haunting by Dukas or Saint-Saëns. He turned to Lieutenant Bagg. "What's this Moonshadow?"

"I don't know. This is just what I managed to read upside down off Captain Juarez's notepad after he got off the phone with Washington. Don't you know what it is?"

Cliff shook his head absently. "No, I, uh, can't quite remember."

"Maybe I got it wrong. The captain's handwriting looks like snail slime, and besides, reading upside down isn't all that easy."

"Yeah, maybe." Cliff's voice was distant, preoccupied.

Lieutenant Bagg shrugged. "Whatever. Look, Remington, this is far as I go. I'm out of it now. I've even been told to pull Harrison away from your house. You won't have any more special protection. And once I walk away, that's the last I want to see of you. Don't call me again.''

"Okay." He offered his hand. "And thanks, Lieutenant. I mean it.''

Lieutenant Bagg smiled, gave Cliff's hand a firm shake, and quickly walked away without turning back.

Cliff hurried back up the escalator and down the mall to intercept Ginger and the kids. He kept reading through the names on the list as he walked, trying to memorize them. But he couldn't. What did they all have in common? And what did it have to do with Washington? And why did he feel such horrible dread when he saw the word *Moonshadow*? He had to know.

They were waiting for him by the cash register, Beau and Liza each holding on to a new bike, Ginger signing a credit card slip. There was something so comfortably domestic about the scene, something so safe, that he ached to remain a part of it. As he passed the Ping-Pong tables he waved, and they all waved back.

"Look, Cliff, look!" Beau was grinning.

"Isn't it neat?" Liza squealed.

Ginger was smiling. "Ah, the phantom book hunter returns."

Cliff smiled at them all and wondered if he should tell them the truth about what he was going to do next. Or was it just too insane for them to comprehend?

Lieutenant Bagg fished through his pocket and came up with two dimes, a stick of Juicy Fruit gum, a broken rubber band, and a paper clip. For a moment the contents reminded him of the collection he might find in his thirteen-year-old son's pockets, though it lacked such exotica as dead reptiles and insect wings. He dropped the dimes into the pay phone and dialed the number he'd been told to memorize a few hours earlier.

"Yes?" Celia Bedford said across three thousand miles of telephone wire.

"This is Lieutenant Bagg."

"Go ahead, Lieutenant."

"It's done. I gave him the list."

"Excellent. What about phone numbers and addresses?"

"Just the names and cities. You told me not to make it too easy for him."

"Quite true. You did the right thing. We appreciate it."

"Yeah, sure," Lieutenant Bagg said angrily.

Celia's voice was slow and soothing. "Look, Lieutenant, I know you feel as if you've just betrayed an innocent man, but you haven't. You've just helped your government solve a very critical problem. We won't forget your help, and we'll make sure your department knows how much we appreciate your assistance."

"Do me a favor, lady."

"Name it."

"Don't make sure my department knows anything. Don't tell them, the President, the U.N., or nobody. Just let it drop."

"If that's the way you want it."

"It is."

"Consider it dropped."

"Just one question," Lieutenant Bagg added. "What happens to Remington now?"

"Sorry, but that information is on a need-to-know basis. I can tell you this much," she chuckled. "Remington is about to take a long trip."

"Where?"

"Sorry."

"You going to have one of our men follow him?"

"That won't be necessary. We have a very capable man in the field right now heading for the same destination. A man already familiar with Mr. Remington, having more or less introduced himself last night at his home."

"Jesus," Lieutenant Bagg whispered, remembering the shooting.

"Again, thank you for your help, Lieutenant. We

couldn't have done it without you.''

"That's what—" he began, but the line was already dead.

Lieutenant Bagg slowly hung up the receiver, as if it weighed fifty pounds. Suddenly he felt very sleepy. "Bone weary" his wife would say. He thought he might have to lie down right there in the middle of the mall and take a nap. But he forced himself to march across the huge parking lot, picking his way among the cars until he found his wife's red Pinto with the dented fender. As he climbed into the driver's seat, he glanced back at the mall and shook his head sadly. "Goddamn job," he muttered and drove home to his family, breaking every speed limit on the way.

Something was terribly wrong.

Ginger pressed her ear to the bedroom door and tried to make out Cliff's words. Nothing. She unclipped her gold leaf earring and tried again, her ear flat against the door. She heard Cliff say, "Are you sure? I'm terribly sorry to hear that . . ." The rest was just low mumbles. What she would have given for Darren's stethoscope at that moment, she thought. Or a drinking glass like the ones she used to use in the dorm at college whenever her neighbor's boyfriend managed to sneak upstairs for the night. For a moment Ginger considered tiptoeing out to the kitchen for a glass then sneaking back to listen, but he'd be sure to hear her. Lately he seemed to be aware of all kinds of sounds and movements that he never would have noticed before.

She frowned at the closed door, gave it the finger, and stomped off to the living room to put on a record at top volume. If she couldn't hear, she'd make it hard for him to hear, too. Childish, but effective. To hell with his problems for a few minutes. There ought to be a Cheer Up Ginger time somewhere along the way.

All her show albums were scattered next to the stereo in a disorderly heap, just as she'd left them. She began picking through them, looking for something to lighten her gloomy mood. *Man of La Mancha*? She had O.D.'d on that during the past few days. *Guys and Dolls*? Too happy. *Gypsy*? Too energetic. *Getting My Act Together*? Too preachy. *Porgy and Bess*? Too serious. Finally she found her two records of *Camelot*, decided on the Richard Harris movie version over the Richard Burton stage version because Harris looked better in tights, and slipped it on the turntable.

As she lowered the arm, she noticed a thick, furry dustball on the tip of the needle. It must have taken weeks for it to get that big. Just the kind of thing that would drive Cliff crazy. If he saw it he'd probably say, "When you die, your gravestone will read, 'Here Lies Ginger Kendall, Dustball Queen of Orange County,' " or something like that. They'd once had a major not-speaking-to-each-other, door-slamming fight over black footprints in the tub. Ginger liked to go for long bare-foot jogs along the beach, then take a shower, leaving black beach-tar footprints in the tub. After scrubbing the tub two days in a row, Cliff had finally exploded on the third day. They'd negotiated a peace that lasted until the great kitty litter debate two months later. That had ended with Cliff threatening to flush the cat down the toilet. Liza had once joked that Cliff was born with Lysol in his veins, and they had all cracked up over that, especially Cliff. But that was the old Cliff Remington. Happy, lively, loving Cliff Remington.

Not at all the same man locked in their bedroom right now making secret phone calls to God knows where.

She had known something was wrong the moment he'd rejoined them in Sears earlier that evening. She'd sensed a slight change in him. Nothing drastic, just a tightening of movements, a hardening around the mouth. A watchfulness. After shopping he'd taken them all out for dinner at Marie Callander's, and the whole time she'd had a feeling that he was hovering over them protectively. He hadn't liked the table they'd been given, insisting instead on one in the back corner near the emergency fire door. When they pulled into the driveway later on, he had made them all wait in the car while he searched the whole house. In the dark.

When he finally allowed them inside, he'd told the kids he wanted to be alone with their mom, and they had winked, giggled, and trooped dutifully off to Liza's room to watch TV. But as soon as the kids had closed the door, Cliff had locked himself into the bedroom to make a few calls, promising to explain everything when he was done. That had been twenty minutes ago.

She looked over her shoulder toward the bedroom, then gave the volume control a sudden twist. Richard Harris bellowed, "I know what my people are thinking tonight." The sound echoed throughout the house, and the antique lamp on the library table rattled. Ginger smiled. Let him whisper around that!

"Hey, Mom, what's going on out there?" Beau shouted from the hallway. "We can't hear the TV."

"Sorry," Ginger shouted back and turned the volume down. The resentful mood had passed anyway. She was back to being worried.

It wasn't until Richard Harris finished singing "How to Handle a Woman" and the record clicked off that Ginger heard the bedroom door open. She got up to flip the record, wanting to show a lack of concern, but when she saw him she stopped cold.

He was carrying a suitcase.

"Sending your laundry out?"

Cliff shook his head, started to say something, then shook his head again.

"Well, then, you must be running away from home." She tried to sound light, but her voice caught in her throat. "You coming back?"

He dropped the suitcase and walked toward her. "Of course."

"So, I know that you're going somewhere and that you're coming back. What happens in between?"

Cliff stood in front of her and reached out to hold her shoulders, but she twisted away from him. He motioned to the sofa. "Sit down and I'll try to explain."

"Don't tell me to sit down! This isn't some innocuous family comedy, and we're not having a goddamn domestic chat about the children's latest capers. We're talking trust here. Our future's going out the door in that suitcase. So if you've got something to say, spit it out. Otherwise, just get the fuck out." She flopped down onto the sofa.

Cliff pulled the folded sheet of typing paper out of his pocket and handed it to her. Then he told her everything he knew. Almost.

Ginger sat in stunned silence for a minute staring at the paper. "Where did you get this list?"

"I can't tell you. Promised."

"Lieutenant Bagg?"

He shrugged. "Promised."

"Okay, then, we know that the federal government is somehow involved, and that you're connected in some way with these other men on the list, and that you had your nose into something called Moonshadow. So what were the phone calls about?"

Cliff refolded the paper and tapped it against his palm. "I've been trying to learn the whereabouts of the other men on this list. It took a little verbal finesse to get information about them on the phone."

"What'd you find out?"

"Nothing conclusive," he mumbled and stood up. He walked over to the stereo, blew the dust from the needle, and closed the plastic cover.

"Come on, Cliff, it must have been conclusive enough to get you to pack your suitcase."

He spun around, his jaw clenched. "Can't you see I'm trying to keep you out of this?"

"How? By not telling me anything? You've never tried to play my father before, don't start now. It's a role even he didn't do well."

"I just don't want you hurt."

"Ignorance is no protection, Cliff. They already proved that last night."

Cliff dropped back onto the sofa. She had apparently allowed herself to be convinced, finally, that the intruders of the previous night were not, after all, just burglars. Was that bad or good? Right now, she was repeating every argument he'd already made to himself while he'd been packing. He hadn't been able to refute the logic then either, but there was still something inside him that abhorred divulging vital information. A nagging at his ear, a wagging finger in his face warning him not to trust anyone. Was it a new feeling, or had he been that way before?

He had a sudden vision of the world as a huge dark room. Everyone in the room was armed and trying to kill the others, but no one could see anyone else. Certain information was like a candle, giving only its possessor the ability to see. That candle was a weapon as well as a shield, and only a fool would share that light with others, thereby making himself vulnerable to them. After all, what did he really know about Ginger Kendall? Only what she had told him. And what he felt about her. Was that enough?

"Meow," came a loud cry as something flapped in the kitchen. Seconds later the fluffy orange cat sauntered into the room and jumped into Cliff's lap.

"Zero!" Ginger scolded. "Where have you been? We've been worried sick about you. Don't you know there are coyotes out there?"

Cliff and Ginger looked at each other for a moment, then laughed. It was a long, loud, rollicking laugh of two people caught in the absurdity of a moment, like an injured accident victim worrying if he has clean underwear on for the trip to the hospital. Ginger's sudden outburst at the cat in the middle of their tense conversation shattered the wall they'd been painfully constructing between them.

"Zero? What kind of name is that for a cat?"

"You named him. Liza brought him home one day and asked you what were the chances of keeping him. And you said, 'Zero.' "

"I see my opinion carried a lot of weight around here."

Zero lifted his head, opened one eye, licked his paw, then went to sleep.

"Okay," Cliff said to Ginger, "you win."

"I don't want to win anything here, Cliff. I just want you to trust me."

"I do." He wiped his mouth with the back of his hand. "But once I tell you, you may be sorry you asked."

"Try me."

"I phoned Jim Talon first, the one from Dallas, the first name on the list."

"And?"

"And I spoke to his wife. Or I should say widow. Talon was murdered last Thursday."

"Oh, my God. How?"

"Muggers supposedly. But from what his wife told me, I doubt that, the same as I doubt we were being burglarized last night. Oh, yeah, here's the part you'll like. He was killed coming home from his shrink. Guess what for?"

She whispered her answer. "Amnesia?"

"Bingo. Intermittent amnesia. Been going on for the past few months."

"Jesus."

"Oh, there's more. It seems Jim Talon appeared in Dallas a few years ago with enough money to buy a restaurant and enough know-how to keep it in the black. Tough business, but fortunately he had a chunk of money left over from an inheritance he got from his parents, who were killed when he was a kid."

"An orphan, like you."

"Yeah, like me. I also called Felix McDonald in San Francisco, but his answering service told me he's out of town shooting wildlife photographs for the Sierra Club. His wife and son aren't around either. The other fellow, Albert Boston, lives in Boulder, Colorado, but he's not home, or not able to answer his phone."

"What do you mean by that?"

"I mean that maybe some burglars recently wrapped a wire around his throat and sliced his jugular in half."

Ginger nodded, then glanced at his suitcase. "That's where you're going, isn't it? Boulder, Colorado. To see this man."

"To see if he's still alive."

"And if he is?"

"To ask him some questions. About his past. About Moonshadow."

"Moonshadow. Sounds romantic. Do you have any idea what it means?"

"Only that I get an uncomfortable feeling every time I see or hear the name. A cold knot forms in my stomach."

"Cliff, I was worried before, but now I'm scared. I mean it, really scared. For you, for me, for the kids."

"That's another good reason for me to go. As long as I'm not around, you're no threat to them. If they want me, they'll have to follow me around. You and the kids should be safe."

"But we want to be safe *with* you, as a family. Can't you just keep calling this man's number? Talk to him over the phone?"

"What if he's dead? Or what if he doesn't want to talk to me?"

"You won't be able to make him talk to you when you get there, either, if he doesn't want to."

Cliff looked away. "Yes, I will."

Ginger stared at him.

"Let me try to explain to you how I feel. Maybe then you'll understand why I have to go. I remember a comic book I read once. It was about an evil man who liked to torture people. This kind of comic book always ends with some appropriate form of justice, so at the end of this story, the evil guy is placed in a narrow maze in total darkness. The corridors of the maze are just wide enough for him to squeeze through, but they are embedded with razor blades from floor to ceiling. Just when he's decided he can outwit them by moving carefully through the maze, his tormentors release a rabid Doberman behind him. Now he must run blindly away from the dog and be sliced to pulp by the razor blades or stay where he is and be torn to shreds by the rabid dog."

He breathed a long sigh. "Right now I feel like that man. Total darkness, rabid dog behind me, razor blades all around me. Still, I've got to find a way out."

Ginger got up and slipped her Nikes back on. "Have you called the airport yet?"

He looked at his watch. "There's a flight out in forty minutes."

"You want to say good-bye to the kids?"

He shook his head. "I'll be back tomorrow or the next day at the latest."

"I'll drive you to the airport." As she started for the front door, he grabbed her around the waist and kissed her. She kissed him back, hard. "I don't know about that rabid-dog-and-razor-blade story of yours, Cliff, but I do know this: I don't want your search for your past to destroy our future. Is that understood?"

Cliff nodded, pulling her close again. She wrapped her arms around his waist and felt the hard lump of the gun under his jacket. She closed her eyes and squeezed harder.

14

ERIC MORLEY PRESSED the Play button.

"What about side effects?" Celia's voice.

He pressed Stop, then Fast Forward, then Play.

". . . take ego into consideration. Cliff Remington had a very strong ego." Whiz's voice.

Stop. Fast Forward. Play.

"What about McDonald's wife and son?" Eric's own voice. It sounded funny to him, high and nervous, like those Chipmunk records. He hoped Celia hadn't noticed.

Stop. Fast Forward. Play.

". . . had their chance. You keep forgetting that we defied a direct presidential order with Moonshadow. If anyone finds out, it's all our asses."

Stop. He marked the number on the automatic counter and leaned back in his chair with a smile. The perfect quote; that one would hang her ass out to dry. When he played this tape back to certain well-connected people, Celia Bedford would be no more.

"Quoth the faggot, 'Nevermore,' " he chuckled. He would miss her. Sure, she rode him all the time about being gay (she was the *only* one he allowed to do it). But she rode everybody about something; that was just her way of reminding them all how vulnerable they were. Yet she also delegated most of I-COOP's major projects to him, and for that he was grateful. Grateful, and anxious for more responsibility. Well, he'd made no secret about being after her job. He'd given her ample warning. Smug little Celia's problem was that she didn't think he was clever enough to take it away from her. Yeah, well he just hoped to Christ he'd be in her office when the fancy black phone began its frantic beeping, when the voice requested that she drop in at the White House for a little chat. Then she'd know for certain where she stood, and who had put her there.

Eric adjusted the gooseneck fluorescent lamp on his desk and hunched over his favorite jacket. The miniature transmitter's battery had leaked, the acid burning part of the lining. Cheap government equipment! He'd have to sew the damn device into another jacket before his next recording session with Celia. God, he hated sewing, wishing for a second he was less rugged and outdoorsy and more of a flaming queen. He could climb the steepest mountain, shoot the most powerful gun, fix anything electronic, but he couldn't thread a needle without stabbing himself.

He looked at his watch and leaned over to switch on the TV. Just in time for the late news.

". . . still can't seem to agree on the cause. But on one thing they all agree: This disease is one form of brotherhood they hope won't spread." Meaningful pause. "Brian Gilbert reporting from St. Francis Hospital, Seattle, Washington."

"Wow," the anchorman nodded gravely at his partner. "Kinda scary, huh, Betty?"

Eric tipped back in his chair and frowned. Earlier that afternoon he'd been in the office with Celia when she'd suddenly snapped her fingers and grabbed one of the telephones in front of her. Within minutes she was talking to some shitkicker cop in California, giving him orders, hinting at threats, and finally mentioning Moonshadow and reading the list of names only I-COOP knew about. When she hung up, Eric had asked for—almost demanded!—an explanation, but she'd only grinned, obviously pleased with her own deviousness, and said, "In time, Eric. You should know better than to rush a woman." She'd smiled, displaying her capped teeth and crossed her perfect legs. "But then again, how could you know about such things?"

He smiled. All he had to do now was wait and see, and keep his transmitter and tape recorder active. Hiding the tape recorder in the trunk of the car last time had been a nice touch, though dangerous. She might have asked for a quick search of the car, as she sometimes did. But with a range between the transmitter and receiver of only a mile, he had to be careful to keep the recorder within the operative distance. If he could record a few more quotes like the ones he had already, one month from now people would be standing at a Rose Garden reception sipping martinis and wondering whatever happened to that good-looking Celia Bedford. She'd had quite a head on her shoulders.

"Yes, indeed," Eric chuckled, flicking off the lamp. "Only by then it won't be attached."

PART THREE

Tuesday

15

EDGE CONNORS THREW his first dart into the black.

"Too bad."

His second dart hit next to the first one, also in the black.

"Tough luck."

Edge's third dart stuck in the double eleven.

"Nice shot. That gives you two seventy-nine." The skinny kid with the wire-rimmed glasses wrote 279 on the chalkboard under the name Bill.

The skinny kid picked up his thin, tungsten darts with the orange flights and stepped up to the white line on the black rubber mat. He squinted at the board a moment, his dart balanced lightly between his fingers like an expensive cigar; then he threw. The first dart hit the double bull's-eye.

"That's fifty points," he said.

His second dart hit the triple twenty.

"That's sixty points. A hundred and ten all together."

His third dart hit the triple twenty again.

"A grand total of one hundred seventy points." He walked over to the dartboard and plucked out his darts. "That makes my score one thirty-one."

Edge grinned and wrote 131 on the chalkboard under the name Jeff. "You've done this before, haven't you, Jeff?"

Jeff grinned back. "Once or twice."

"I think I've been hustled."

"Just don't break my thumbs, Bill, like Paul Newman in *The Hustler*."

Edge laughed.

"Your turn, Bill."

Edge shook his head and sat down. "Forget it, man. You're too good. I concede." He waved a hand at a chubby barmaid who wore a velvet bow tie. "Two beers. Michelobs."

"Right," she said, snatching their empty glasses and rushing away.

Jeff sat down and began plucking the flights out of his darts and packing them neatly into his wooden case.

"Nice darts."

Jeff nodded. "I won them in a game. Some guys drag race for pink slips; me, I like to play for darts."

Edge nudged the thick wooden ones with the torn feathers he'd used, house darts. "I'll bring my own next time. Not that it'll make much difference."

Jeff shrugged.

"You go to school here?"

The beers arrived. "Two bucks," the waitress said.

Edge gave her $2.50.

"Thanks," she said and left.

Jeff stared at her as she walked away. "Nice ass."

"You go to school here?" Edge asked again.

"Sure, doesn't everybody?"

"What're you studying?"

"Comp Lit. You know—Tolstoy, Balzac, Goethe. All those short, hairy foreigners."

"You ever hear of Professor Albert Boston?"

Jeff sipped his beer, wiped his mouth with his fingers. "What's he teach?"

"Political science."

"Shit, poli sci. I haven't taken that since I was a freshman. And then all I had was some T.A. named Burke. Why?"

"An old professor of mine. Thought I'd look him up while I was in town."

"You went here?"

"No, Columbia. He was teaching there then."

"Oh."

They chatted awhile longer, until Jeff looked at his watch and jumped out of his chair, grabbing his wooden case and paperback copy of *The Magic Mountain*. "Gotta run, Bill. Don't want to be late for Meyer's noon lecture; that Prussian son of a bitch eats the balls of choirboys before each class. Thanks for the game and the beers."

Edge smiled and waved. "Thanks for the lesson."

When Jeff was out the door, Edge stood up, his face dark and angry. "Damn," he muttered, grabbing the thick wooden darts and rapid-firing them into the dartboard. He turned and walked away before seeing where the last one landed. He didn't have to look; he knew it had struck right where the other two had: in the bull's-eye.

Edge sat cross-legged on the bed, an open book in his lap, a loaded gun in one hand. The habit of sitting cross-legged came from his martial arts training in the CIA, though he was the only one in the group who had actually felt comfortable sitting that way. The bed was king-sized with a slight sag in the middle, in a small room on the second floor of the Best Western motel just a few blocks from the campus. The open book in his lap was *American Art of the 20th Century*, a textbook his wife used in the art history class she taught at Hollins College. The loaded gun was an eight-inch Colt Python .357 magnum with a Colt-Leupold 2X scope mounted on the barrel.

Both the gun and the book would play a part in what Edge Connors had to do, not only to fulfill his assignment but also to carry out his own personal Connors Master Plan. He and Jenny called it Comaplan for short, though she had little idea exactly what he did for a living and even less of an idea what his plan called for.

She knew his work was confidential, so she rarely asked about it. Once when she pressed him, Edge told her he arranged security in cities the President was going to visit, and that seemed to satisfy her. He smiled at that notion, but only for a moment. He'd worked too hard too take this lightly now.

The manager of the motel had checked Edge in, telling his whole life story in the time it took to hand over the room key. That was one of Edge's assets: He was an attentive and sympathetic listener, and people liked to talk to him. The manager had once owned a much smaller motel on Sunset Boulevard in Los Angeles, and had spent his entire time there on the lookout for movie stars. He'd had visions of lining his office walls with framed photographs of him with his arm around dozens of movie stars, each autographed with something like, "To Eddie, one helluva guy," like the ones he often saw in barber shops. But in thirteen years living on Sunset Boulevard, Eddie Brokaw was the only person in Los Angeles who'd never seen a single goddamn movie star. Not even a lousy sit-com star. When Edge had checked in last night, Eddie had thought he might be Bruce Dern, but he couldn't imagine why Bruce Dern would be in Boulder at this time of the year.

That was another of Edge's assets. He reminded people of someone else. With his powerful build and craggy features, he looked like a cross between a professional athlete and a tough-guy actor. So on those occasions when police wanted a description of the man seen near the scene of the murder, all they got was conflicting descriptions of well-known football players or actors.

He clucked his tongue and read the same page of his book again, using the barrel of his gun as a pointer. When he finished the page he closed his eyes and recited, "Willem De Kooning shared the leadership of the avant-garde with Jackson Pollock. Uh, became its most influential figure in the early fifties. Okay, name a couple of Pollock's works, smart-ass. *Lavender Mist* and *The She-Wolf*." He opened his eyes, glanced down at the book, and smiled. "Fucking genius, Edge." He closed his eyes again and rattled off the dates of the Pollock works. Then he checked his answers. Right again! "Okay, genius, name three works by De Kooning. Um, there's *Effervescence* and—no, that's Hofmann. Damn!" He peeked at the book again. "Right. *Excavation, Night Square*, and *Pink Angels*." He reeled off the dates and checked the book once more. "Got it."

This, too, was part of Comaplan. He brushed the book off his lap and grinned. Comaplan. Okay, maybe a little cornball sounding, but nonetheless it was important. Comaplan. Less of a plan than a realization, one that had to happen to finally get him off his ass and thinking.

His lips tightened, and his face flushed as he remembered the origin of Comaplan. It had begun on a Monday. He and Tyrone had been tailing an air force colonel down to Mexico City, where some thick-necked Soviets were waiting to buy the colonel's imitation leather attaché case and its top-secret contents. At about the same time Edge and Tyrone were sitting near a fancy Mexican tennis court watching the colonel sip his third strawberry daiquiri, some junkie creep was busting the bedroom window in Edge's apartment and hauling off his and his wife's TV, stereo, wedding silver, blender, microwave oven, and a whole shitload of other stuff. Fortunately, Jenny had been at school teaching advanced charcoal sketching, and three-year-old Aaron had been at the campus day-care center. But they might have been at home. And what if they had been? What then?

Jenny had told Edge about the burglary when he called her, and he had returned from his trip in a rage. How dare some shit-ass punks violate his home? He'd even tried to get I-COOP to hunt the bastard down, but except for putting a little extra pressure on the police, there wasn't much I-COOP could do. What the fuck good did it do to belong to that elite bunch of spooks if they couldn't even keep his own goddamn family safe? he'd wondered. He realized then that he'd have to figure out a way to protect Jenny and Aaron while he was away. That's when he'd made up his mind to buy a house, move into a secluded neighborhood with trees and lawns and cops patrolling every ten mintues to earn their under-the-table Christmas bonus. When he'd told Jenny his decision, she'd stroked his chin and shaken her head. "Sorry, Bluto, but we don't have the bucks." Bluto was her pet name for him, going back to his time in the navy when he wore one of those fringe beards like the cartoon character. "What do you mean?" he'd asked. And she'd showed him. Since their marriage, Jenny had handled all the family finances, paying the bills, balancing the checkbook. Everything. Despite their two incomes, they were just able to meet monthly expenses, go out a lot when he came back from trips, and save a few hundred now and then. They had enough to buy a small condominium somewhere, but not enough to move into the kind of house Edge wanted.

And so Comaplan had been born. It was a fancy name for what other people had been doing all along: getting ahead. And getting ahead was just what he planned to do. He had to reassess where he stood in the I-COOP organization, and he wasn't happy with his conclusion. He was nothing more than a gofer. Well paid, well trained, but still a legman. He was street smart, but uneducated. No college. And there was no way he could get ahead in Washington without at least a college degree, not with all those Harvard-Yale-Princeton types with their briar pipes and tinted glasses. So he'd get one. He and Jenny laid out a program of reading and self-tutoring to prepare him for an equivalency exam that would earn him some college credits. His traveling made attending classes difficult, but with the help of some of her faculty friends, he could do a lot of independent studying.

He'd even changed the way he dressed. Gone were the baggy pants and shapeless polyester jackets. Now he favored pleated slacks and corduroy jackets with patches on the elbows. The academic look that was popular in Washington.

He glanced over at the other bed and started to say something, then realized there was no other bed, because there was no Tyrone. That had also been part of Comaplan. A sad part, but necessary. Without Tyrone lumbering around, Edge had a better chance to call attention to himself, more elbow room to display his new style. Besides, Tyrone had started to jelly the last few times. It was only a matter of days before he'd freeze and blow Edge's game plan. Or worse, get him killed. The way Tyrone had bungled the Remington matter the other night was proof of just how right Edge had been.

Now that he was working alone, he could successfully complete this assignment, show them the stuff he was made of, then start pushing for a promotion out of the field and into the carpeted offices where the real power and money were. Screw the preppies and the Ivy Leaguers with alligators on their chests. Edge Connors could hold his own with any of them. Willem De Kooning, *Woman in Landscape III,* 1968. He slapped the book and grinned.

But first things first. Right now he had to locate this Albert Boston. He'd been ringing the guy's goddamn phone off the hook, but the bastard hadn't been home all day yesterday, last night, or this morning. Probably shacking up somewhere with a broad, but where? That's what Edge had spent the morning trying to find out. Eddie Brokaw, the motel manager, had assured Edge that lots of students came to the motel's English-style pub to shoot darts and drink beer, and Edge had planted himself there last night and at opening time this morning, buying drinks and trying to locate the professor's love nest. But no go, Bluto. Some knew of Boston, one guy had even taken a course from him. The student had bitched his way through two free beers about how tough a grader Boston was, but no one knew where to find him except on campus. Edge wanted to avoid doing anything there. The flow of witnesses at a school was just too unpredictable.

Edge shifted slightly on the bed and looked through the Leupold scope on his Colt Python Hunter. Removing the black anodized aluminum cover from the elevation turret, he slowly turned the knob, enjoying the clicks it made as he adjusted it by several minutes, clucking his tongue to imitate the sound. Then he tightened the windage adjustment. The ammunition loads were the real key, though. A .357 magnum wasn't known for its accuracy, only for its power. The .22 favored in mob executions was best for accuracy. It made only a tiny hole going in, but once inside the body it rattled around, chewing up organs like a starving rat. The magnum just blew off hands and legs, or blasted a six-inch tunnel through the chest. But with the No. 19106 .357 load, with a full metal-jacketed wad cutter weighing 158 grams, he was assured of reasonable accuracy as well as power.

And he wanted to be accurate, not just in eliminating this Boston fellow, or the next mark in San Francisco, but also in settling the score with that Remington guy. No matter whose fault it was, that little episode in California had gone down as a miss, a failure. And since Tyrone wasn't around to take the blame, it went down as Edge's failure. And failure was not part of Comaplan.

He laid the Colt Python gently on the bed and picked up his Boy Scout knife, pulling open the blade. Then he grabbed the whetstone, squeezed a tiny drop of oil on it, and began sharpening the blade in smooth, scraping circles. He smiled and clucked his tongue. Yes, sir, he was looking forward to meeting Clifford Remington again, and maybe introducing his navel to old Howdy Doody. But whether it was Howdy Doody or the Colt Python that did the trick, the next time he saw Mr. Remington, he was going to make him into hamburger.

Edge leaned back against the headboard and lifted the phone onto his lap. After a quick call to Information, he dialed again.

"University of Colorado at Boulder. May I help you, please?"

"Yes, Dr. Albert Boston."

"What department, please?"

"Political science."

"Thank you. It's ringing."

It was ringing, and it continued to ring for a full minute before being answered.

"Dr. Boston's office. May I help you, please?"

"Is Dr. Boston in?"

"Not yet. His first class isn't until two."

"And when are his office hours today?"

"Let me check . . . uh . . . oh, he doesn't have office hours today. He lectures from two to five, eats dinner, then teaches a graduate seminar from six until eight. Would you like to make an appointment for tomorrow? His office hours are noon to one."

"No, thanks, I'll try to catch him later."

"Fine."

"Good-bye," Edge said pleasantly and hung up. He swung his legs over the side of the bed and cracked his knuckles one at a time, then his wrists, and finally his neck. With practiced deftness, he removed the scope from the Colt Python. He would have no need for it this time. If he had to use his gun today, it wouldn't be from a distance; it would be up close. He slipped on his custom-made shoulder holster and fitted the gun snugly into place along his rib cage. Then he wiped the excess oil from Howdy Doody, dropped it into his pocket, tied his desert boots, and pulled on his down jacket, allowing his knit tie and maroon sweater to show through. Dressed this way he figured to be mistaken for an older graduate student or perhaps a professor.

He'd wasted enough time waiting for Professor Albert Boston. And what if the bastard didn't return home tonight after class? There was still that McDonald fellow in Frisco to take care of. And Remington. I-COOP wouldn't wait any longer, and Comaplan couldn't wait any longer. Edge would hunt the professor down on his own terrain.

16

CLIFF TURNED UP his jacket collar, hunched his shoulders forward, and blew warm, steaming air on his numb fingers as he hiked across the chilly Boulder campus. The previous night when he boarded the plane, the temperature at John Wayne Airport had been a comfortable sixty-eight degrees. But here, according to the Wells Fargo Bank thermometer he'd passed a half a block from the campus, it was only forty-four. And dropping. The gun tucked against the small of his back felt like a block of ice freezing his spine.

The students he passed gave him puzzled side glances and sympathetic smiles. Sure, they could afford to be amused. They were sensibly dressed in thick sweaters and down coats, while he was wearing the same thin sports jacket he'd roasted in the day before at UCLA.

Despite the cold, the campus was remarkably green. Trembling, Cliff tried not to look at the heavy snow capping on the surrounding mountains. He shoved his hands deep into his pants pockets and picked up his pace to something of a trot.

When he finally saw the building looming ahead, a glow of satisfaction spread through his chest. With nothing more than a name and city he'd been able to track Albert Boston at least this far. It hadn't been easy. And he'd had to do a few things along the way he hadn't known he was capable of. Like commit crimes.

He'd arrived late last night, rented a car at the airport, and checked into a Holiday Inn. For more than two hours, until three-thirty in the morning, Cliff had called Albert Boston's phone number every five minutes.

No answer.

Finally, he'd kicked off his shoes, laid his head back on the pillow to rest his eyes, and, with the telephone still sitting on his chest and the TV droning on, fallen asleep in the middle of a "Mission Impossible" rerun.

When he woke up, he rubbed the sleep from his eyes and dialed Albert Boston's number again. Still no answer. After a quick shower and a few more calls, he'd decided to hunt down his quarry in person.

Albert Boston's home address—357 Roan Street—he'd gotten from Information. The complicated directions he'd gotten from a leggy waitress in the motel coffee shop. She'd had to consult two other waitresses, the cashier, and one of the fry cooks before she finally handed him a napkin with a map to Roan Street on one side and her phone number on the other.

Roan Street proved to be a pleasant residential neighborhood. Boston lived in a well-kept Victorian house with the best lawn on the block and a lush garden that bordered on being fussy. A couple of rolled-up newspapers lay on the porch, indicating that Albert Boston had left home two days ago. Or had been inside the house for two days.

Cliff had kicked the newspapers aside and jabbed the doorbell. He put his ear to the door and jabbed again, but he couldn't hear the bell sounding inside. He knocked on the screen door, then pulled it open and knocked on the inside door. His hands were so cold that each knock sent pinpricks stabbing through his knuckles. He kicked the door a few times, but still no one answered.

He glanced over his shoulder at the sleepy street, ignoring the occasional car, and went to work on the lock. Had he read how to do this somewhere—in *Newsweek*

—or seen it done in a TV cop show—an old "Dragnet"? Wherever he'd picked it up, he'd learned his lesson well. He slid his Montgomery Ward credit card between the door and the frame, and with a nudge and little twist of the wrist, pushed the door open. He quickly slipped inside and closed the door behind him, throwing the dead bolt to prevent anyone from surprising him.

It was funny; from the moment he'd decided to go in, he'd forgotten all about the cold. His body had taken on an almost dizzying energy, as if a sudden electrical charge had rippled through his blood. Every sense was keen. It was like being omnipotent, in complete control of everything around him. It was the feeling kings must have, or pro basketball players, or chess masters. Once inside, the feeling gave way to apprehension.

He searched half the house before realizing that his gun had been drawn and pointing ahead the whole time. For a moment he considered the seriousness of the crimes he was committing, but that passed quickly. There were other laws at work now.

No one was home. The mail on the kitchen table confirmed that Albert Boston lived here, and the papers in the study indicated that Boston was an associate professor of political science at the University of Colorado at Boulder. Several letters revealed that a publisher was interested in the textbook Boston was writing on lobbies and their influence on federal legislation; the book was tentatively titled *The Power Pushers*. The bedroom closet contained only a man's clothing. The bed hadn't been slept in, and there were no dirty dishes in the sink, no half-filled coffee cups in the bathrooms. The house was surprisingly immaculate, and Cliff smiled, remembering Ginger's throw-it-in-the-closet housecleaning technique. But, like the garden, this house was too neat, too fussy, too sterile.

Finding nothing of interest in the house, Cliff headed for the University.

The buildings looked newer than those at UCLA, but inside the history and political science building everything was pretty much the same. Teachers hurried down the halls to the safety of their offices while students wandered aimlessly about.

Cliff sauntered down a corridor wondering what kind of college student he had been, if he'd ever been to college at all. Had he gone to fraternity parties, raised hell in the dorms, crammed all night for exams, dreamed of humping the homecoming queen? Memories like that made college special, didn't they?

He knew he must have had *some* advanced education. He spoke Chinese, and had recently discovered he could get by in Russian, German, and Spanish. He hadn't told Ginger about that. He could rattle off the theories of several philosophers, and he could remember the plots and main characters of many literary classics. But he could have picked up that kind of stuff in a lot of places, or he could have educated himself. But who had time for that? Students and prisoners. Was that it? Had he been a criminal? Well, if he hadn't been before, he was one now.

Tacked to a bulletin board in the hall he found a list of poli sci faculty members with their office numbers and hours. Dr. Albert Boston's office was on the third floor, but he had no office hours that day. Cliff wandered into the office of the department chairman and hovered over the secretary's desk. She was a frail woman in her early sixties with good skin and bad teeth. She smiled at Cliff.

"Help you, son?" she offered.

"Yes, ma'am. I'm looking for Dr. Boston."

"My, he's popular today." Despite the huge wall clock next to her desk, she consulted her wristwatch. "He's got his International Law class in five minutes."

"When does that let out?"

"Five. Though he usually runs a few minutes over. Over the years we've had a few anonymous complaints about that. Most kids figure three hours at a stretch is plenty. Can't say that I blame them much."

Cliff glanced at the wall clock. "It's important that I see him now."

"The class takes a fifteen minute break at three-thirty. When Dr. Boston remembers.''

"It's urgent,'' he pressed.

She shrugged her thin shoulders. "Might be able to catch him before class. They're meeting in the chemistry building lecture hall.'' She told him the room number. "Just two buildings away. Go out the side door there.'' She pointed.

"Thanks. How will I know him? What's he look like?''

"He's black,'' she said simply, and resumed typing.

Cliff raced out the door, ignoring the cold blast of air that scrubbed his face as he ran. It took less than two minutes to reach the chemistry building and fight his way through the crowded halls to room 101, Albert Boston's classroom. He looked inside, but there was no teacher, only students removing their scarves and coats and sweaters. He pushed his way to the glass doors at the front of the building and scanned the milling students outside. Not one of the faces was black.

Then Cliff saw him. Immediately he knew that this was the man who belonged to the house he'd just searched. He was walking along the sidewalk, despite the fact that everyone else was cutting across the grass. He was black. Not brown, not cinnamon, not mahogany. Black as deep space. His face was narrow with strong features and hooded eyes. He smiled broadly and often at the young Asian girl whose arm was hooked through his. He was wearing well-cut jeans with sharp creases that sliced the air in front on him with each long, assured stride. His jacket was suede with a lot of zippers crisscrossing the front. Beneath the jacket Cliff could see a plaid flannel shirt that had cost three times more than the workman's shirt whose style it echoed. He wore glossy cowboy boots with sharply pointed toes, and his briefcase was hand-tooled leather.

Class.

As they approached the building, Dr. Boston leaned over and kissed the girl in something more than a friendly fashion. Cliff now had an idea where the elusive professor had been for the past two days. She ran off toward another building, her school books tucked up against her chest.

"Dr. Boston?" Cliff said, cutting off the teacher's entrance to the classroom. Dr. Boston was a little shorter than he was, but about twenty pounds heavier. None of it fat.

"Yes?"

"I'm sorry to interrupt you here, but I need about five minutes of your time."

He looked annoyed. "I have a class right now. You'll have to make an appointment with the department secretary." He started to move around Cliff.

"I'm Clifford Remington."

"Congratulations. Now, if you'll excuse me—"

"The name doesn't mean anything to you?"

"No, it doesn't."

"How about Felix McDonald or James Talon?"

"Zip."

"And Moonshadow?"

"A song by Cat Stevens. End of quiz. Now back off, please." He strode past, his massive shoulders nudging Cliff aside.

"Look, Dr. Boston, there's no simple way to say this, but time is running out."

"Listen, Mr. Remington, I—"

"So I'm just going to tell you straight out that someone's going to try to kill you. Probably soon."

Dr. Boston swung around, his jaws clenched in anger, apparently ready to take a swing at Cliff. "I'm warning you—"

Cliff ignored him. "You're an orphan, right?"

Dr. Boston hesitated. "So?"

"Had any instances of amnesia recently?"

"No."

"No brief losses of memory?"

Boston's face tightened, his thick brows crowding together. "I had a little too much wine a few nights ago. Tapped out for a couple minutes, but . . ." His voice trailed off.

Cliff removed the folded paper from his jacket and

handed it to Dr. Boston. ''Three of the men on this list
are orphans and have had recent bouts of amnesia. One
of them was murdered three days ago. Two days ago
someone tried to kill me.'' Cliff lifted his chin to reveal
the red welt around his neck. ''I can't reach the fourth
man, Felix McDonald. He may already be dead.''

''What does being an orphan have to do with this?''

''I don't know. Right now four things tie us together:
We're all orphans; we've all had amnesia; we're all on
this list; and someone's trying to kill all of us.''

''What the hell is this list? Where'd you get it? Who
made it up? What's Moonshadow?''

Cliff nodded at the classroom full of students.
''We've got to talk.''

Dr. Boston rubbed his chin and frowned. He studied
Cliff's face with cold, hard eyes. Cliff took back the
paper, folded it, and shoved it into his pocket, all the
time returning the professor's icy stare.

''I think you're being straight with me,'' Dr. Boston
said quietly, shaking his head. ''I've got this annoying
feeling next to my ulcer that you know what you're talking about.''

''Instinct,'' Cliff said. ''It's a wonderful thing.''

''Whatever.'' He handed Cliff a key. ''Meet me in my
office in an hour. I'll discuss their next term paper for a
while and give them the rest of the class time in the
library. That's going to play hell with my reputation as a
hard-ass.''

Cliff restrained the urge to argue, not wanting to wait
even an hour. He knew persuasion wouldn't work. Dr.
Boston seemed too conscientious to dismiss his students, even for something this important. It was a major
concession for the man just to cut the class short.

''In an hour,'' Dr. Boston said and marched into the
classroom, his voice booming at the students. ''Okay,
scholars, settle down.''

Cliff pocketed the key, checked his watch, and
pushed out into the cold. An hour could be a long time.
A lifetime.

• • •

Less than a minute later, Edge Connors shoved his way through the glass door on the opposite side of the chemistry building. The halls were relatively empty now that classes had started, just an occasional student or two hanging around or walking through the building because it was a warm shortcut to another building.

Edge walked down the corridors, his desert boots soundless, his manner friendly. He grinned at a couple of passing girls, one of whom smiled back while the other giggled and elbowed her friend. He noticed a couple of burly football types shuffling off to the men's bathroom with the unmistakable look of guilt mixed with defiance. Probably some dope was about to change hands. For a moment he thought about crashing through the door and pretending to bust them just for the hell of it, just as he and Tyrone used to do while working Shore Patrol in the navy. But there was no time. Still, the thought made him smile.

He walked passed room 101 just as Dr. Boston asked one of his students to close the door. But Edge had seen enough to know this was the guy he was looking for. Today's target. He grinned. That was the term they used at the CIA training school. "Today's target, ladies and gentlemen, is Fidel Castro." Then they'd break into teams, and each would plan the best way to "terminate the target with extreme prejudice." The next day's target would be a Soviet general or the Israeli prime minister—made to look like an Arab hit. All make-believe. Practice for the real thing. He walked past the door again just before it closed completely, wanting to make sure. He preferred the real thing.

Edge checked his watch. Three fucking hours. What the hell could they do in there for three hours? He wished he could kill the time in the classroom, at least that way he'd learn something while waiting, helping Comaplan along.

He leaned against the wall and watched a bearded boy and pigtailed girl standing near the water fountain. The boy was speaking in sign language, rapidly flexing and fluttering his hands and fingers in what was obviously a long story. The girl stared at his hands and lips, nodding encouragingly. When he finished, they both burst out laughing, though her laughter was soundless and his was more like grunting. They they put their arms around each other and disappeared around the corner still chuckling.

That must've been a hell of a joke, Edge thought as he checked his watch again. Only two hours and fifty minutes to go. He hoped it would be a stimulating class for Professor Boston, because it was certainly going to be his last one.

17

"IMPOSSIBLE!" HE THREW his briefcase into his chair and slammed his fist on the top of the desk. "Ridiculous!" He bent over and snatched a scrap of paper from the floor, rolled it into a tiny ball, and tossed it into the wastebasket.

Cliff watched but said nothing. He sat on the metal folding chair and stared as Dr. Albert Boston paced.

This office was much smaller than Dr. Sands's room at UCLA, but it was also much neater. The books were all arranged by subject and author. A small silver espresso machine stood in the far corner with three delicate cups and saucers neatly stacked next to it.

"It just doesn't add up," Dr. Boston said, but his voice was quieter, less outraged now. The problem was no longer merely a personal concern, but an abstract equation, a thing to be solved. Find the key. Cliff remembered his own thought processes the morning he woke up not knowing who he was. He'd approached it the same way.

"Do you remember any details of your past?" Cliff asked.

"Of course. I grew up in a middle-class neighborhood in Atlanta, went to Howard University, then got my Ph.D. at Stanford. I did a couple of years in the G.A.O. in Washington before coming here three years ago. I remember everything quite clearly."

"Have you kept in touch with any of your old bud-

165

dies from Atlanta or from college or maybe from Washington?''

Dr. Boston straightened a row of books. ''Well, no. But I moved around a lot. Besides, I was never very gregarious.''

''What happened to your parents?''

''Mom died in childbirth two years after I was born. The baby died, too. Dad was killed by a drunk driver three years after that. I was raised by my—''

''Grandparents.''

''Right. But then they both—''

''Died of natural causes right before you started college.''

''Dr. Boston stopped pacing and stared at Cliff. ''You, too?''

''Uncanny, huh?''

''Damn near impossible odds.''

''Yup. And it gets better. Jim Talon's parents died in a plane crash, and he was raised by his grandparents who then died of natural causes when he was seventeen.''

''So he went to college?''

''Nope. The Marines for six years.''

Dr. Boston seemed stunned as he sat on the edge of his desk. ''Spooky.''

Cliff laughed.

''So you think I'm going to have more of these amnesia episodes?''

''Probably. Do you remember where you were last night?''

Dr. Boston nodded. ''Stayed over with a, uh, friend.''

''Does anyone know about her?''

''People have seen us together, but you don't advertise that you're dating one of your students.''

''If you want to keep it a secret, I'd suggest you stop kissing in front of the building before class.''

Dr. Boston sighed, spreading his hands helplessly. ''Her youthful passion.''

''It might be a good idea for you to stay with her

again tonight. Then you should seriously think about disappearing for a while.''

"I can't just disappear. I've got classes to teach."

Cliff shrugged. "You can't teach if you're dead."

There was a sharp knock on the door. Dr. Boston ignored it, nodding at Cliff. "You're probably right. I'll get some sort of family emergency leave or something. What are you going to do?"

"Go to San Francisco and check out Felix McDonald. See if he knows anything about this Moonshadow business."

Another knock on the door.

"Go away!" Dr. Boston growled. "Make an appointment with the secretary."

Another knock. "Dr. Boston?" The voice sounded hesitant, intimidated.

"Pesky students," he mumbled and started for the door. "I have an idea, Remington. I think I'll just tag along with you to San Francisco and help you check this Felix McDonald out. I've always done quite well with puzzles. That is if you wouldn't mind the company of a truly brilliant mind."

Cliff smiled. "It'll be nice not having to prove to everyone that I'm not crazy."

Another knock. "Dr. Boston?"

Dr. Boston stood with one hand on the knob. "Who is it?"

"K-Kathy's father," the voice said timidly, as if the man was uncomfortable talking to professors. "I've come to talk about her grade."

"Kathy?" he mumbled to himself. "Kathy who? I've got a dozen Kathys in my classes." He turned the knob and pulled the door partway open with a great sigh of annoyance.

Cliff could see only the back of Albert Boston's head as he held the door. But something about the man's sudden posture sent an alarm jangling through his stomach, up his spine, and along his scalp. He leaped to his feet knocking over the metal chair, and pulled out his gun. *"Albert!"* he screamed.

Too late.

Dr. Albert Boston gave a loud croaking grunt and stumbled backwards into the office, his hands covering over his heart. He looked surprised and confused as he stared at his own chest, watching with detached curiosity the blood seeping out between his fingers, turning his suede jacket red. "Shit," he gasped, and collapsed backwards over the desk, his head cracking against one of the bookshelves.

Without hesitating, Cliff crouched into a half-squat, thrust his gun out with both hands, and fired two shots through the partly open door. Over the sound of wood cracking and splinters flying, he heard a muffled cry and knew he'd hit the assassin.

Somewhere down the hall a woman screamed, and footsteps slapped against the tile floor. Cliff flung open the shattered door and leaned out into the hallway with his gun pointed toward the footsteps.

The running man was holding his wounded left shoulder as he crashed into a suddenly opened exit door leading to the stairway. He paused for a second, just long enough to turn and face Cliff. In that moment their eyes locked, and Cliff knew this was the man who'd invaded his home that night. Cliff took steady aim, but people were pouring into the hall half in a panic and half to see what was going on. Several screamed and immediately dropped to the floor, but there were still too many for a clear shot.

The other man didn't think so. He raised his Colt Python and fired two rounds at Cliff. The first slammed into a nearby wall, blowing a baseball-sized hole through it. The second caught a panicky young woman in the hip as she bolted for the elevator. Then the exit door banged shut and the gunman was gone.

The wounded woman screamed as she pressed her hands to her hip and realized much of it was gone, splattered in a grotesque pattern against the wall.

Cliff ran down the hall around the screaming woman and through the exit door. He swung his gun into firing position, but no one was there. At the bottom of the three flights he heard another door bang open, and he clattered down the stairs in pursuit.

But when Cliff burst out the building into the crisp cold air, he could find no sign of the killer. No wounded gunman lumbering across campus, no trail of fresh blood to follow. Nothing.

He stuffed the gun back into his belt and continued jogging to his car. Sirens wailed from all directions as he climbed into his rented Gremlin and pulled out into the Boulder traffic. There was only one place left to go now.

18

CLIFF JUMPED OFF the cable car at the intersection of
California and Polk. After consulting the street map
he'd bought at the airport, he headed north up Polk
Street. It was almost dark now, and the weather in San
Francisco was nearly as crisp and bone-biting as it had
been in Boulder. Fortunately, he had found time to
make a few prudent purchases, including a puffy black
ski jacket and a blue TWA flight bag. Knowing that the
police would be searching for him as well as for the
killer, he hadn't bothered to stop at the Holiday Inn to
pick up his suitcase. He'd driven straight to the airport,
nudging the speed limit but careful not to get stopped.
But once there he had faced the problem of how to
sneak his gun through the metal detectors. He solved it
easily by purchasing the flight bag and checking it
through with the luggage.

He zipped his jacket tightly around his neck and
thanked the gods for MasterCard and Visa. So far they
were financing this whole operation.

At Sacramento Street he turned right. Someone had
used red spray paint to write on the sidewalk: "I left my
heart in San Francisco, but I shot my wad in San Jose."
Cliff checked his map again. Felix McDonald's apartment was a block away.

He walked slowly up the hill, trying to organize his
thoughts, to understand what had happened. Albert
Boston was dead. Cliff hadn't needed to check the

body; he had known from the placement of the wound that if he wasn't already dead, he soon would be. But why hadn't he gone back to check on the wounded woman? No reason, really. He had just known he had to get out of there, to avoid the police at all costs.

He sighed as he crossed another street. At the back of his mind he had an idea of what a good man was supposed to do: the decent thing. Without ever having thought about it these last few days, he'd assumed that no matter what he discovered about himself, there'd be some reason, some justification for the callousness he sometimes displayed. He had believed that deep in his heart he was a good man. Now he wasn't so sure.

Damn, he had liked Albert Boston, had been pleased when the man offered to come with him to San Francisco. Damn. He shoved the street map into his coat pocket and began scanning the numbers on the buildings. Felix McDonald's was three buildings farther down on the other side of the street.

Cliff had tried phoning him from the airport, but he got the answering service operators, who still maintained that Mr. McDonald was out of town on a photography assignment. They didn't know exactly when he'd be back. Cliff had decided it was time to do some checking on his own.

The apartment building was as old as the others around it, but someone had built a modern wooden facade that covered the entire six-story front. Elaborate wrought-iron lettering announced it as Bayside Arms, though the bay was two miles away.

He avoided the elevator, preferring to climb the stairs to the third floor. It was a pleasant building, with freshly painted walls and carpeting that was apparently in the process of being replaced. The new carpet, a bold rust color, ended halfway up the first flight of stairs.

When Cliff reached the second floor landing, he knew something was wrong. By the time he stepped onto the third floor his stomach was twisting and grinding in protest against a thick heavy odor, somehow both cloying and bitter, like that of spoiled food. He cupped his hand over his nose and continued walking down the hall. When he reached 312, he found several notes taped to the door. "Take out your garbage, McDonald. Tom Burke." Another one bore today's date; it read: "Mr. McDonald. This is notice that unless otherwise contacted, I will be forced to enter your home tomorrow with my pass key, as per your lease. Mr. Timmons, Manager, #118." The last note was friendlier: "Felix & Susan, Ruthie and I stopped by to kvetch about life. Catch you when you've done the spring cleaning and patched things up with your neighbors. Arn & Ruthie."

Cliff tried the door, but it was locked. He looked around the corridor. Across the hall a TV was tuned to a baseball game. Every once in a while the crowd would roar, and a gruff voice would shout, "You clumsy bastards!" Two doors away a stereo throbbed with the earthy voice of Edith Piaf. Someone was frying fish, but the greasy odor was losing the battle with the nauseating smell seeping out of the McDonald apartment.

"Well, it worked once," Cliff mumbled, pulling out his Montgomery Ward credit card, which was a little chewed at the edges from the last time. He worked it into place and began jiggling and coaxing, but this lock wasn't as simple as Albert Boston's. He unzipped his jacket and leaned into it.

Suddenly a door banged open behind him, and the sounds of the baseball crowd cheering poured out into the hall.

"What the hell do you think you're doing, bud?" the gruff voice demanded.

Cliff slipped the credit card down the front of his shirt before spinning around to face the voice. "Who are you?" Cliff snapped back, just as gruffly.

"I live here, man." The owner of the gruff voice stood three inches taller than Cliff and weighed fifty pounds more. With his huge hands on his hips and his thick face twisted into a scowl, he looked eager for a fight. "Now, what're you doing fucking around with that door?"

"I'm an inspector with the Health and Safety Department. We've had complaints about this smell. I'm checking it out."

The man glared skeptically at   Cliff. "Got some I.D.?"

"Sure thing." Cliff reached for his wallet, then stopped suddenly. "Hey, is that smell coming from your place? Yeah, I think it is." He walked across the hall and stuck his head through the open doorway. A horse-faced woman in curlers and a running suit was bending over an ironing board arranging an extra-large shirt while watching the baseball game. Neither seemed to interest her.

"It's not coming from here, man. It's coming from across the hall." The man followed Cliff.

"At first that's what I thought," Cliff said, wrinkling his nose and sniffing again. "But now . . ."

The woman looked up sleepily from her ironing, then yawned, and returned her attention to the game.

The big man seemed genuinely nervous now. "It's across the hall, man. Didn't you see the goddamn notes on the door? The bastard's been gone for days now. Must've left his fucking trash all over the place. Could be rats in there."

Cliff looked unconvinced. "Well, I'll check it out. But I might have to talk with you later, bring a lab crew by your place."

"Like hell!" the big man said and slammed the door in Cliff's face. Through the closed door he could hear the man hollering. "Fucking government bastards." A loud roar went up from the TV crowd. "Goddamn Billy Martin. The bastard."

Cliff returned to the locked door and eased the credit card into the crack, trying to force the spring tongue back into its hole. Down the hall Edith Piaf was replaced by the husky crooning of Marlene Dietrich. Across the hall the crowd roared again, and the big man's voice boomed happily, "About fucking time."

Finally the card slid into place, and the door swung open.

It was like being hit by a tidal wave. The sickening

odor rushed out the door, washing over Cliff like a thick soup. His eyes stung, and his mouth tasted sour. He kept his breathing as shallow as possible as he stepped inside, closed the door behind him, and flipped on the light switch.

He gasped, stumbled back into the wall, and felt his knees begin to buckle.

He stood with his back pressed against the door and stared, his mouth hanging open, his face contorted with horror and disgust. They lay in the middle of the living room, between the sofa and the coffee table, as if they'd been sitting there and had suddenly fallen off. As far as he could tell, one was a woman, and the other had been a child of three of four. They resembled dried branches or burned newspapers more than humans. There was no substance or weight to them. Their blood had leaked out of a hundred different places, staining the blue carpet for three feet in every direction. The skin was torn and parched into stiff flakes like potato chips. There were no eyes in the heads, only crusted holes. The child's arm lay completely detached two feet from the body. The woman's right leg was hanging at the knee by blackened strands of muscle.

Cliff felt the vomit bubbling up in his throat, but forced it back down and took a step forward. A dozen flies rose from the bodies and buzzed about, as if to protest his intrusion. Cliff staggered back again. More vomit surged into his throat, but he swallowed again and walked slowly forward like a man swimming the same lake the day after a drowning.

The living room window was open, which explained why the smell in the hall wasn't stronger. He searched the rest of the apartment and found all the windows open. Unusual for this time of the year. As if someone had deliberately raised them to postpone the discovery of the bodies. A small hole in the rusty kitchen screen had let the flies in, and black ants marched across the kitchen floor to a half-filled garbage bag under the sink.

Cliff conducted the search holding the front of his jacket over his nose as a makeshift gas mask. When he

walked from the kitchen back to the living room, he
passed near the bodies and stepped on something hard.
When he lifted his foot he saw it was a tooth and
jumped back.

At that moment the front door exploded open, hitting
the wall with a thud, and two guns were shoved into his
face. Behind the guns were the horse-faced woman and
the brawny baseball fan from across the hall. Their guns
were identical Colt Super .38s, which they held two-
fisted and steady like pros.

"Hands up against the wall, feet spread apart," the
woman snapped, both eyes on Cliff, her gun waving
him toward the wall. *"Move!"*

"Jesus, the smell!" the big man complained, his face
wrinkled in disgust.

Then he looked past Cliff at the bodies on the floor
and pointed with his gun. "Oh, my God! Oh, my
God!"

The woman took a few steps forward, glanced at the
mess, frowned, and looked at Cliff. "I told you to
move, mister."

Cliff leaned against the wall, his hands and legs
spread.

"Cuff him, Glenn," the woman ordered. "I'll call
in."

"Huh? Yeah, right," Glenn said weakly, his face
pale. He held the cuffs in one hand, the gun loosely at
his side in the other. He took a few wobbly steps toward
Cliff, then suddenly doubled over and vomited on the
carpet.

"For chrissake, Glenn." The woman sighed with
disgust. She bent over, snatched Glenn's handcuffs, and
jerked Cliff's hands behind his back, clicking the cuffs
into place. She patted him down with experienced
hands, plucking the gun out of his belt. There was a
slight movement behind his back, then a sudden sharp
pain in his buttocks where she'd stuck a hypodermic
needle.

"What was that?" Cliff asked.

"Let's go," she said, pushing Cliff toward the door.

"Where we going?"

"Across the hall for now so we can breathe. Then you're going for a little trip, Mr. Remington."

"Where?"

She drew her chapped lips across her huge teeth in a smile. "Why, our great nation's capital, of course." She gave Cliff another shove out the door, pausing to issue some final instructions to her sick partner. "Call in and then lock this place up. We'll wait across the hall for the others. This stuff should start taking effect in a few minutes. Okay, Glenn?"

Glenn nodded slowly and wiped his sweaty face with his sleeve. He hauled himself to his feet with obvious difficulty. "Sure, Bev, I'll just . . . " Then he was back on his knees, dry-heaving in the corner, his shiny new gun lying in a puddle of vomit.

19

EDGE UNBUTTONED HIS wool shirt and yanked it down over his left shoulder. A drop of blood had seeped through, but the gauze bandage looked as if it would hold well enough. He smoothed down the adhesive strips along the edge of the bandage and gently pulled his shirt back up. It wasn't a bad wound, hardly any blood. Certainly not serious enough to report to Washington. After all, he'd told them the important part, that Dr. Albert Boston was dead. Assignment completed.

He leaned over the tiny sink, splashing cold water on his face. Suddenly the plane hit an air pocket and threw Edge back against the flimsy door. His stomach did a slow roll. He sat down on the toilet seat and caught his breath.

Someone knocked on the door. "Are you all right, sir?" It was the stewardess with the southern accent.

"Yes, fine."

"Okay, then." He heard her walk away, her cart of drinks tinkling along the aisle.

He buttoned his shirt, stood up, and checked his appearance in the narrow mirror over the sink. Perfect. They'd never be able to tell he'd been hit. Of course, he'd had to tell them that Remington had been there; they'd have found out anyway. But that the son of a bitch had clipped him with a slug, well, that was his little secret. One that he was going to share with only one per-

son: Clifford Remington. When the time was right. He
used his sleeve to wipe a few drops of water from his
chin with his sleeve.

What the hell was Remington doing in Boulder with
Albert Boston? How had he known about him?

More important, why had Washington suddenly
ordered Edge home before he'd completed his San Francisco assignment? It didn't make any sense.

Something was screwy.

He opened the bathroom door and pushed past a little
boy who'd been waiting.

" 'Bout time," the little boy mumbled slamming the
door behind him.

Edge walked slowly along the aisle bracing himself on
the seats. The plane did another tiny dip, and Edge
cursed louder than he'd meant to. A few disapproving
faces swung toward him. He plopped into his seat and
opened his art book. He was finally into the Recent
Sculpture chapter. He didn't make judgments about the
strange and puzzling works he studied; he merely
memorized the names of the sculptors: a row of stain-
less-steel cubes by Don Judd; a twisted hunk of aluminum called *Around and About*, by Clement Meadmore.

Slowly his gaze drifted away from the book and out
the window toward the thick clouds swirling around the
plane. Why had they abruptly called him back to Washington? As soon as he'd told them about Remington
being in Colorado, they had put him on hold for twenty
minutes. Then Hawkins, the CIA liaison, had come on
and ordered him home. It had something to do with
Remington; that much was certain. But what would it
do to Comaplan?

Hell, if they were calling him in before the assignment
was completed, it didn't look good.

Well, whatever setback Comaplan suffered would be
Clifford Remington's fault. And no matter what else
happened, Edge was going to even the score. He felt just
like the man in that book Jenny had given him to read,
Moby Dick, the one where Ahab was nuts to get the
whale that bit off his leg and ruined his life. And Edge

planned to hunt Remington just the same way. He would harpoon the bastard as he had Talon and Boston. Only this time he'd have a little fun first.

Edge slammed his fist down on his book. It was all that damn Remington's fault. First, with Tyrone the other night, and now with Albert Boston in Colorado. Washington would probably blame him. One complete failure and one sloppy success. The information was probably already stored in some computer and in his file: Field Status: Unreliable.

He thought of Jenny and little Aaron, vulnerable in that cheap apartment as they waited for him to come home. Since the break-in Edge had installed a sophisticated alarm system he'd gotten from I-COOP. That made him feel better when he traveled, but they couldn't stay inside all the time.

The pilot announced that they were approaching Washington, D.C. Edge fastened his seat belt, leaned back into the seat, and closed his eyes. He imagined Clifford Remington floating on his back in a mountain lake, the front of his body slit open from the throat to the crotch, the bright sun glistening off his blood-soaked organs.

The plane vibrated as the landing gear lowered. As always, Edge gripped the armrests until his knuckles were white.

20

IT WAS CLOSE to midnight when the tall, gaunt man walked through the lobby of the hotel with his canvas tennis bag slung over his shoulder. Because it was a luxury hotel where famous people often stayed, several guests stared, trying to place him. His clothes were casual; Levis and a yellow turtleneck sweater under a brown leather jacket. But they couldn't remember him from the opens or Wimbleton or any other major tennis match. In fact, he didn't really look much like an athlete at all. He was tall enough, but much too thin, almost fragile. And the gray pallor of his skin, the dark circles under his eyes, the green and yellow bruise over his eyebrow, all conspired to make him look decidedly sickly. Besides, he was too old, past forty. With that realization, they moved on, disappointed.

The tall man carefully lowered his tennis bag to the carpet before signing for his room.

The hotel clerk, a veteran of thirty years in hotel service, politely ignored the man's unhealthy appearance and smiled as he handed over the key. "Enjoy your stay, Mr. McDonald." Just don't croak on the premises, he added silently. "Any luggage?"

Felix McDonald smiled back, hefting the tennis bag. "Just this."

"It's a good thing you had a reservation, what with all the hoopla tomorrow."

"Expecting a big turnout?"

"Yes, sir. At least five hundred thousand, probably more. Every hotel in town is booked solid."

"Good," he smiled. "Very good."

"Would you like a bellboy, Mr. McDonald?"

"I can manage this by myself. Thanks anyway."

"Yes, sir." When the tall man turned away, the hotel clerk tapped his assistant on the shoulder and nodded at the new guest, rolling his eyes. The assistant smiled and nodded back.

Felix McDonald headed across the lobby for the elevator. This was a much nicer hotel than the one in Pittsburgh. More class. Twice as expensive. The carpet was at least half an inch thicker with not one cigarette burn anywhere. Too bad this wasn't the target. With all the celebrities who stayed there, there would be a hell of an outcry.

He stepped into one of the three elevators.

A young girl in a skimpy red uniform and a pillbox hat smiled up at him. "What floor, sir?"

"Eight."

The door slid closed, and the elevator lurched upward. Felix watched the floor lights over the door and smiled to himself. He wasn't going to waste his time anymore with hotels or movie theaters. It was time for the big dramatic action. He would release it all at once at the place where he could expose the most people in the shortest period of time. Hundreds, probably thousands would die writhing in the dirt, their bodies disintegrating, choked by their own blood.

"Eighth floor," the young girl announced, tugging down the hem of her tiny skirt and straightening her little hat as if it embarrassed her. "By the way, I saw you play at Forest Hills, and I thought you were wonderful."

"Thank you." Felix McDonald smiled and stepped off the elevator. She was blushing as the door slid shut between them. As he searched for his room he wondered who she thought he was.

Once inside his room, he gently laid the canvas tennis bag on the bed, unzipped it, and checked the contents. Everything was in order.

He undressed and climbed between the cool sheets. It had been a long, boring flight with nothing to do but refine his plan. He'd sent the telegram from the airport, so I-COOP would be waiting for his call in the morning. He smiled as he thought of them sitting around worrying.

He set his alarm clock for seven in the morning. That's when the final phase would begin. Tomorrow everybody would be busy.

PART FOUR

Wednesday

21

EVERYTHING WAS HAZY and red.

Cliff rubbed his eyes, fighting his way back to consciousness. He fluttered them open again and looked around. The room he was lying in glowed with a smoky red light, like a cheap waterfront nightclub. At first he blamed it on his throbbing headache, but then he realized that the light was actually relaxing, and he had no trouble adjusting to it. However, the sofa he was stretched out on was not only too soft but also a foot too short. His legs stuck out over the arm at an awkward angle. But when he tried to use his hands to pull himself up, he discovered they were still handcuffed. He ignored them for a moment and tried to remember what had happened to him during the past few hours.

He remembered getting the injection in San Francisco from the horse-faced woman in the running suit. He shifted and felt the dull pain in his buttocks. Whatever she'd injected into him hadn't been enough to knock him out, but it had sure taken the fight out of him. Two suit-and-tie agents in their late twenties had carried him out of Felix McDonald's apartment building. One of the agents had smacked his elbow on the door of a drab brown Buick and Cliff remembered laughing idiotically as they shoved him into the back seat.

He wasn't sure how long the drive had been, because somewhere along the way they'd given him another

shot, this time in the neck. He remembered frantically
warning them about air bubbles in the syringe; even a
tiny one could kill a man. Then the driver had said
something curious: "You would know, pal." And the
one giving the shot had chuckled.

They had driven to a small airfield. It was not a commercial airport; that much he could tell even in his haze.
He'd tried to ask questions, but he couldn't get his
tongue to move. It just flopped around in his mouth,
thick and numb, dry as an ashtray.

The two suit-and-tie agents handed him over to a
couple of guys in U.S. Air Force uniforms, who then
dumped him in a golf cart and drove him to a military
jet. One of the air force men asked the other if Cliff had
been given a shot recently, but the other guy said he'd
forgotten to ask the agents. Cliff had tried to say yes,
but now even his lips wouldn't open. "We'll just have to
take a chance," the first one shrugged and gave Cliff
another shot in the neck. "Can't hurt, Captain," the
second one had said. After that Cliff had passed out.

Now he was stretched out on a short sofa in a room
drenched in red light, locked in a pair of handcuffs. He
must have lain on them funny during the plane trip,
because there was a raw blister on his right wrist. At
least they'd shifted the cuffs from behind his back to the
front. Not that it mattered. He could get out of them
either way.

Again, he wasn't sure where he'd learned the technique. Maybe in that *Houdini* movie with Tony Curtis, or
in a Bruce Lee film. That didn't matter, as long as he
knew it. Using his left hand, he firmly kneaded his right
hand at the thumb joint until the thumb dislocated. The
bones moved under his urging as if sliding into well-
worn slots, and he wondered how often he'd done this
before. Now that the thumb was movable, he easily
coaxed his hand out of the cuff. He popped the thumb
joint back into place, then went to work on his left
hand. The cuffs were off in less than two minutes.

"Ta-*da*," he said with a pleased smile.

Suddenly the soft red lights changed to a bright white,

blinding him. As he shielded his eyes, he could hear a door opening nearby.

"Excellent, Cliff," a woman's voice said. "Not quite up to your old record time of twenty seconds, but then, none of us are what we once were, eh?"

The lights came down a few notches in intensity, and Cliff could see again, though he had to squint until his eyes adjusted completely. Four people were standing in front of him, three men in suits and a fashionably dressed woman. The woman seemed to be doing all the talking.

"Yes, Cliff," she continued. "I knew you could handle yourself, even in your present condition."

Cliff dropped the cuffs on the coffee table but said nothing.

Celia Bedford nodded to the others, who sat down across from Cliff. Celia sat on the sofa next to him, her smile radiant, her manner jubilant. "I can't tell you how good it is to see you again, Cliff."

"Celia Bufford," Cliff said quietly. "No, Bedford."

The men leaned forward, startled.

"You remember me?" she said.

"Just the name. It sort of popped into my head, like this headache."

"Anything else about me?"

He shrugged. "I don't like you."

Her smile faded briefly, then was back even bigger. "I see."

Eric Morley grinned and leaned back in his chair. "At least you made a lasting impression, Celia."

Tom Hawkins from the CIA stared at his fingernails and noticed a little grease from his model trains that he'd been unable to scrub loose even with Lava. He tried to scrape it away with his other fingernail, cleared his throat, and quietly spoke. "Can we get on with it?"

General Steve Gerrard, who'd arranged for the air force jet to bring Cliff to Washington, nodded in agreement. "Indeed."

Celia sighed and crossed her legs. "It's hard to know where to begin."

"Let's start with Moonshadow," Cliff said.

General Gerrard leaned even farther forward until his knees were almost touching Cliff's. His breath smelled of coffee and bacon. "How much do you know?"

"Nothing. Except that you've killed two people, maybe three, because of it and you've been trying to kill me."

"Come, come, Cliff," Celia laughed. "If we'd been trying to kill you, we could have done it at any time in the past few hours. But we didn't."

"Why not?"

Celia rummaged through her alligator purse. "Thank God alligators are coming off the endangered species list so I can start carrying this thing in public. I've got two pairs of shoes sitting in my closet I haven't been able to wear for two years, just because the First Lady's got a bug up her ass about saving the alligators. Now they've got them coming out of their ears down South. Ah, here it is." She tossed the watch to Cliff. "Yours was broken in flight. Handcuffs, you know. You're going to need a watch. Time is very important now."

He checked the time. It was six forty-five. "Is it morning or evening?"

"Morning."

Cliff strapped the watch to his wrist. "I'm hungry."

General Gerrard leaned back in his chair, frowning his usual military scowl. "Christ!"

"Don't mind the general," Celia said. "He just resents you because you've been living in sin with that Ginger Kendall woman and her kids, just like the guy who moved in with Steve's ex-wife and daughters. Suddenly the general's become terribly moral. Right, Steve?"

"Let's get on with it," General Gerrard grumbled.

"Yes, let's, Celia," Eric agreed.

Celia smiled and shook her head. "Boy! When did everyone in this business turn so serious? Well, all right, then. Down to brass tacks, I suppose. You'll just have to eat breakfast after we're finished, Cliff. Sorry."

Cliff shrugged. He flopped back against the sofa with

a bored sigh, trying not to show how excited he was. Inside, his heart was thumping, his mouth salivating. Finally he was going to learn the truth. About himself. About everything.

Celia put one hand on Cliff's knee. "Just how much do you remember about your past?"

"What difference does it make? My past isn't real." The three men exchanged looks.

"You're quite right, of course. The four of you boys are what you might call born again. Test-tube babies with manufactured identities and memories. But before you start shouting about civil rights, you should know that we did all that for your own good."

Tom Hawkins cleared his throat, still digging at the grease behind his fingernails. "We saved your lives."

"Thanks," Cliff said. "Only now you've decided you want those lives back."

Celia's smile was still intact, but her voice took on a harder edge, hinting at the power beneath it. "Let me finish, Cliff. Then you can pass judgment."

Cliff bowed.

"First, all four of you were agents of the United States government. As such, you knew the risks you were taking."

"Even from our colleagues?"

"If necessary. I must say, you don't seem surprised."

"You mean about being a spy? It explains a lot. Also, it's a bit of a relief. For a while I thought I might be a mob hit man or something. Although, after seeing you people, I'm not so sure that this is any better."

"Now, now, Cliff, you agreed to save your judgments."

Eric tapped his watch. "Let's hurry this up, Celia. The call should be coming through soon."

They all looked nervously at their watches. Celia nodded and continued. "I'm afraid we're going to have to skip the moral debate and just get to the facts, Cliff. We're on a rather tight schedule, which I will explain shortly. As I said, you, McDonald, Boston, and Talon were all agents working for me."

"I-COOP," Cliff mumbled.

"You remember?"

"The name. Lots of names are coming to me, but I don't know what they mean."

"You'd been with the CIA for years, working mostly out of Europe, Soviet Union, and Asia."

"That explains my knowledge of languages."

"Hawkins here requisitioned you for I-COOP for a particular assignment a few years ago, and you'd been working with us ever since. Talon and McDonald were military intelligence brought in by the general, and Boston was FBI out of New York. You'd never worked together before being assigned to us for Moonshadow."

"And what the fuck is Moonshadow?"

"Ever hear of something called Yellow Rain?"

Cliff nodded. "Read about it in a magazine, I think. Some kind of chemical warfare the Soviets are supposed to have used in Laos and Afghanistan."

"Right. It's main chemical agent is tricothecene toxin, known as T-2. It's made from a grain fungus and is as deadly as the worst synthetic poison. If you breathe it, swallow it, or just get it on your skin, you're dead in minutes. And those minutes are the most agonizing possible."

Hawkins abandoned his fingernails and cleared his throat. "This T-2 causes the victim's blood vessels, arteries, and capillaries to contract, and the tissues to rupture so that the body explodes. Basically the victim becomes a walking hemorrhage, drowning in his own blood."

"Jesus," Cliff said.

"Oh, it gets worse," Hawkins continued. "Your body feels as if it's on fire while at the same time you're having spasms and convulsions. And since there's no place for the blood to go, you end up vomiting pints of it while more blood pours out of every orifice."

Celia was no longer smiling. "We've known about T-2 for years and began research on our own variation. Finally we developed a toxin that acts on the body much the same as T-2 does, but worse. It also causes an immediate breakdown of muscle fibers and eats away at the bone joints.''

"American ingenuity,'' Cliff said. "Keeping up with the Jonesovitches. I take it you gave this stuff its catchy name, right?''

Celia explained. "One of the research scientists was a young genius who played rock guitar as a hobby. He happened to be on a Cat Stevens kick at the time and named it Moonshadow after one of Stevens's songs.''

"Clever. Nice to know you people enjoy popular music just like us plain folks.''

Celia ignored him. "The scientist's supervisors didn't know where the name came from, but they thought it was suitably sinister, so it stuck.''

"But something went haywire, right?''

"Admittedly there were some problems with the first batches of the substance. For one thing, it didn't affect everyone, just selected groups with certain blood types or specific genetic makeup. In one case, it affected only people with naturally red hair. Those batches were sealed and hidden in various locations around the country while we perfected the formula. Unfortunately, when the new administration came in, the President found out about Moonshadow. In a fit of moral outrage he ordered the project stopped and all caches immediately destroyed. That was almost four years ago.'' She leaned back against the sofa arm and stared into Cliff's eyes. "Have you heard of the outbreaks of Brotherhood Disease that hit this past week?''

"Sure, I . . . '' Cliff stopped, a deep frown of disbelief creasing his face. "My God! You mean you *didn't* destroy the toxin?''

She took a deep breath. "That's right. Administrations come and go pretty damn quick these days, but our enemies stay the same. No, not the same; they get stronger. I couldn't do anything to save the research project, but I could damn well save what we already had, and I could make sure the Soviets knew we had it. At least now they'll think twice before they try releasing Yellow Rain again.''

"So you defied a presidential directive."

Celia laughed. "It isn't the first time. A few years ago one of our distinguished Presidents ordered me to assassinate the prime minister of a friendly nation because he thought it would dramatically boost our own economy right before elections. I refused to do that, too. If you refuse to follow the orders of one President, you're a good guy; if you refuse to obey the other, you're bad, right?"

Cliff shrugged.

"Well, I'm not afraid to take responsibility for my actions."

"No matter who has to pay for it."

She smiled. "The greater good and all that hogwash. Anyway, the Brotherhood Disease isn't a disease at all. It's caused by exposure to an early form of Moon-shadow that usually affects only people with B-negative blood, which is not very common, and AB-negative blood, which is quite rare."

"Usually?"

"As I said, this was an early and not totally successful batch. We know that, once exposed, some ninety-eight percent of the people with these blood types die. But the toxin also affects certain people who don't have those blood types. We aren't sure why. Someone has released the toxin twice, and according to a telegram he sent us last night, he intends to release the remainder of his batch this morning."

"How much does he have?"

General Gerrard answered, "If administered for maximum efficiency, say at a pro football game, enough to expose sixty to seventy thousand people. Taking into consideration the average number of people in any typical crowd whose blood types make them vulnerable, he could kill six or seven thousand people."

Cliff smiled thinly. "And the inevitable investigation would reveal that you guys disobeyed the President. I hear he's got quite a nasty temper."

Gerrard bristled. "Naturally we are primarily concerned with the welfare and security of this great country of ours and—"

"Knock it off, General," Eric interrupted. "We have no time for that shit now."

Cliff looked at each of them in turn. "You've given me a lot of information that is pretty dangerous to you. Why?"

"Simple, Cliff." Celia smiled brightly. "Someone has to stop this man before he kills several thousand innocent people . . . and that someone is you."

The phone wailed like a civil defense siren. Celia stood up and marched to the round table behind the sofa. The three other members of I-COOP followed in a line. Cliff twisted around on the sofa to watch.

"Everything set up?" Celia asked before she picked up the phone.

"Check," Eric said. "They'll start tracing as soon as you pick it up. We'll need at least two minutes, so keep him talking."

The four of them took chairs around the table, with Celia in front of the buzzing telephone and a telephone amplifier. The table was round, but it was obvious to Cliff that wherever Celia sat was considered the head of the table.

Celia pulled her chair closer to the table, nodded to the others, and punched a button on the amplifier. "Yes?" she said firmly.

"That you, Celia?" an answering voice asked.

"Yes."

"Well, then, I guess the rest of the Dalton gang must be hovering nearby. Howdy, boys."

"What's on your mind, Felix?" She sounded casual and friendly, as if she were talking to a favorite nephew.

"What's on my *mind*, Celia?" He chuckled again. "That's a good one. Did you get my telegram?"

"Yes."

"Then you know what's on my mind. Wholesale

death and destruction, as the comic books say.''

Celia checked her watch. "I don't understand, Felix. What do you mean?''

"Oh, I get it. You're stalling for time so the trace can find me. Tsk, tsk, Celia. They trained us better than that. But I've got a few seconds to spare, so I'll spell it out for you. As I said in my telegram, I've got a vintage batch of Moonshadow. A particularly potent year; smooth yet with a dash of insolence. And as you know from the unfortunate incidents in Pittsburgh and Seattle, I'm willing to share it with the public. In fact, I intend to use it tomorrow in a way that will guarantee a kill factor of thousands. Thousands of people will spit their blood and guts into the dirt.''

"What is it you want, Felix? Money?''

The voice became strained and agitated. "Money! I don't want your money. I don't want anything. That's the genius of this whole plan. I didn't call to talk about blackmail. I called to give you the facts of life, Celia. Fact: Twenty-four hours from now I'm going to murder thousands of people with your toy. Fact: I'll make sure the whole country knows about you and Moonshadow. Fact: The public will rise up in outrage, probably storm the fucking White House. But not before you and your eunuchs disappear forever, and I'm not talking about retirement. You know what they'll do to you? One of the President's goons will drop in on you with his hands in his oversized pockets. Then it'll be bye-bye to Celia and her acolytes. Yes, I remember everything now. It came back to me in bits and pieces at first, just a few words here and there, then the names, then the faces, then everything else. Remembering all that was like being swept through a sewer. The worst part was realizing what a big part I'd played in it all.''

Eric flashed all his fingers twice to tell Celia she had to keep the caller talking for another twenty seconds.

Celia nodded. "But, Felix, why are you doing this? What did those people do to you?''

The caller laughed. "Consider them casualties of war,

sweet pea. I'm doing this for the good of the country. Doesn't that justify everything? It used to. I'm going to wake people up to this danger before you destroy the whole country. The whole *world*!"

A loud noise came through the amplifier. At first Cliff thought it was static; then he realized it was a sob.

"It wasn't supposed to be this way," the voice continued. "For the past three years I've been photographing wildlife and mountains. I was good at it, too. Those three years were the best time of my life. I got married and adopted a kid. But when I started remembering, I couldn't live with the guilt. I talked it over with my wife." He choked down another sob. "She agreed we had to do something. So I broke into one of your secret storage chambers and stole some toxin, just enough to take to the authorities. I meant to tell them how you had disregarded a presidential order and put millions of lives in danger."

The sobs were deeper now, almost groans. Cliff felt his own eyes watering, his fists clenching.

"But one of the containers must have been faulty. I took the stuff home, and it . . . oh, God, it killed them! Susan and the baby. They . . ." His voice trailed off into a piercing wail.

Eric Morley crossed the room and picked up another phone. He spoke softly into it, then came back and gave the thumbs-up sign to Celia. She nodded.

Her voice was soothing. "Listen, Felix. You can't blame yourself—"

"I don't blame myself!" he shouted. "I blame you. You and the others who went along with you. *You* killed my wife and child, *you* killed all those other people, and *you* will be killing those people tomorrow. That's enough talk. Twenty-four hours, just like in the movies. After that you can read about it in the newspapers." He hung up.

Celia turned to Eric. "What have you got?"

"A phone booth in Miami. He was clever, though; he rerouted it through New York City. If we hadn't been watching for it because of his army communications background, we'd have been looking for him in the Bronx.''

Hawkins cleared his throat. ''No wonder he wasn't concerned about the trace.''

''Okay, General Gerrard growled, ''so we know the bastard's in Miami. What do we do now?''

Everyone looked at Cliff.

Cliff threw his head back and let out a loud, bitter laugh. Then he stared at them in wonder and disgust. ''You people have some nerve. First you try to kill me; then you ask me to help you.''

Celia walked around the sofa and sat down next to Cliff. The others followed, reclaiming their seats.

''Look at it from our side,'' Celia smiled, reaching over to pat Cliff's knee again. He pulled away from her. Celia's smile broadened. ''We knew that it had to be one of you four because you were all involved with storing Moonshadow. Boston was in charge of logistics; you were in charge of security, and Talon and McDonald took care of transportation. Since we couldn't immediately be sure who was innocent without risking a lot of lives, we did the only thing we could—tried to silence all of you. Permanently. It was a hard decision, but it was the only one to make. You'd have done the same thing.''

''If you'd followed the President's orders, no one would have had to die.'' Cliff slapped his hand on the arm of the sofa. ''I just can't believe we all went along with you.''

''Well, to be fair,'' Eric said, ''none of you knew very much until it was time to hide the stuff. Celia even kept the details of Moonshadow from the three of us for quite a while. Talon was a former Marine; he was used to following orders without question. Boston didn't like it, but he was more interested in solving the problem of how to hide the toxin than he was with the morality of the project. But you and McDonald raised bloody hell, you worse than he was. We figured if anybody gave us trouble, it would be you.''

Cliff snorted, his stare so hard and cold that Eric involuntarily pressed himself deeper into his chair. ''So you decided to hypnotize the four of us and give us new identities. Why didn't you just kill us?''

Hawkins cleared his throat. ''The possibility was discussed.''

''Hey, what kind of talk is this?'' Celia laughed. ''Naturally we considered all alternatives before deciding on the memory treatment. But it wasn't just hypnosis, Cliff, it was a three-week daily process that included drugs and conditioning and a whole lot of psycho-this and psycho-that mumbo jumbo. We created new identities for you and detailed memories. We avoided giving you close friends or relatives. It was kind of an experiment and we've since used it with defectors. Unfortunately, however, the treatment wears off after a few years.''

Cliff shook his head. ''Yeah, it wore off with Felix and several years' worth of sublimated guilt came crashing down on him.''

''Look, I'm not going to argue moral issues, Cliff,'' Celia said. ''We don't have time for that. We have to get you on a jet to Miami as soon as possible.''

''Why me?''

''Two reasons. One, Felix knows you, so he might allow you to get close enough to stop him. And two, you both went through the same memory treatment, so you might be able to figure out his pattern. For example, why did he choose to hit Pittsburgh first, then fly across the country to strike in Seattle? And why Miami now?''

Cliff snapped his fingers. ''Right! You were the one who gave the list of Moonshadow operatives to Lieutenant Bagg and told him to make sure I got it. You thought I might unknowingly locate Felix for you.''

''We were a little disappointed when you went to Boulder. By the time you made it to San Francisco we'd already gotten the telegram from Felix. Our agents had his place staked for days before you arrived.''

Cliff leaned forward, grabbed Celia's wrist, and hauled her closer to him. The men shifted in their seats but made no move. They knew that if Cliff wanted to kill her, he could do so before they could stop him. "How could you be so goddamn sure I was innocent right from the beginning?" He squeezed her wrist hard.

Celia gasped at the pressure, but gave no other sign of distress. "You were the only one we could positively clear in the amount of time we had. Unfortunately we were able to do so only after our first attempt on your life. But I remind you that we were under a great pressure. Thousands of lives were at stake."

"They still are," Cliff reminded her as he released her.

She pulled away from him and rubbed the red finger marks around her wrist. "Will you help?"

"What's to prevent you from hypnotizing me again, or even from killing me when this is all over? I know a hell of a lot now."

"I could say you have my word."

"Somehow that just doesn't comfort me."

"Then I'll be more practical. It's obvious now that there'll be a federal investigation into the outbreaks of Brotherhood Disease. Someone's bound to come snooping around us sooner or later. The only way we can protect ourselves is to destroy all of the caches of Moonshadow and pretend that they've been gone for years. Once the toxin is all gone, we'll have no reason to harm you. Even if you told everything you knew, there'd be no proof."

Cliff nodded. "Makes sense."

"Then you'll help?"

"Bring me the files on the four of us. I want to know everything I can about all of us. Then bring me some breakfast. Pancakes with maple syrup. Real maple syrup, not that fake shit; fresh-squeezed orange juice, a whole pitcher; and a pot of hot coffee. I'll also need a phone."

"One that's not bugged, I suppose?"

"I don't want the impossible. There's probably not a

phone within two blocks of here that isn't tapped. I don't care if you hear what I have to say. Eavesdropping is your perversion, not mine."

"Cliff, where are you?" Ginger asked.

"Washington."

"The state?"

"D.C."

"What are you doing there?"

"It's a long story."

"I've got time."

"Sorry, Ginger, but I don't. Don't worry, I'll fill you in soon."

There was a pause. Her voice quivered. "When are you coming home?"

"A couple of days at most."

"Have you found out who you are?" She laughed. "Christ, that sounds like a line left over from the sixties, like 'I'm having an identity crisis' or 'Share my space.'"

He laughed. "It sounds just fine. I found a few things out, nothing much yet."

"Like what?"

"I had a pet beagle named Sparky. That's it so far."

"That's cute, but hardly worth flying all over the country for. What about Colorado and Moonshadow and all that?"

"You were right. That was a big misunderstanding. Moonshadow is an association of orphans. I just had things mixed up in my memory. I'll explain it all later, and you can rub it in and say I told you so."

"I told you so."

"At least wait until I explain, huh? Look, Ginger, I have to go now. I have one more lead to chase down."

"What kind of lead?"

"A third cousin or something. Just a long shot."

"I love you." She said it so unexpectedly it stunned him.

"What's your blood type?" he asked.

She laughed. "Why? You want to bring me a pint as a coming-home gift?"

"Just curious."

"B-negative, like the kids."

He sighed and felt his hands begin to shake slightly. "I love you, too," he said, and knew this time that he really meant it. "I'll be home soon. Gotta go."

"Where are you staying? In case something comes up."

"Uh, the Ambassador."

"Sounds expensive." She kissed into the phone. "Take care, babe."

"Right. Say hi to the kids."

There was a pause; neither wanted to hang up. Finally Cliff did, but he held on to the receiver a few extra seconds, not wanting to break the tie between them.

Stripped to the waist, Felix McDonald leaned over the bathroom sink and stared at the green and yellow bruise over his eye. He touched it gently with his fingertips, wincing at the stab of pain. Then he pressed harder and harder until the pain seemed to circle his head. He felt his knees buckle, and he stopped pressing.

The bruise would probably have been gone by now if he didn't perform this daily ritual of irritating it. But he didn't want it to go away. Ever. It was his badge, like a sheriff's, the reminder of his duty. It was the bruise he got the day he brought Moonshadow into their apartment. The day he came back from a quick trip to Woolworth's to buy the stationery on which he and Susan would write to the newspapers, the TV stations, the President, and anyone else who'd listen and perhaps try to stop this madness. But when he came through the door, he found them dead, their bodies virtually floating in their own blood. A detached foot. A hanging leg. He muffled a scream and turned to run, banging into the door, almost knocking himself unconscious. That blow to the head had been a sign. Not from God, whom he'd never believed in. But some power had told him that he couldn't run away. He had to carry through with their plan. Save the other wives and children of the world even if he had to destroy a few of them in the process.

As long as he had the bruise, he knew his duty.

He walked across the hotel room to the bed and pulled open the canvas tennis bag again. Inside were six cylindrical canisters the size of tennis ball cans, made of a special combination of plastic and aluminum. Inside each canister was enough Moonshadow to kill a thousand people. Under the cans was the rest of the equipment he would need, every item ready and waiting for the right time.

He reached for the phone and dialed the long-distance operator.

"May I help you?" she asked.

"Yes, operator. I'd like to place a long-distance call to Miami."

He gave her the number and waited. After a few rings, the phone was answered.

"Yeah?"

"Benny?"

"Right."

"This is Felix."

"I figured."

"You did fine, Benny. You can break the connection any time now."

"Okay, Felix. But that makes us square, okay?"

"Even-Steven, pal. How's the weather?"

Benny moaned. "Fuckin' ninety-eight degrees; you can slice it with a knife. How can they expect human beings to live in this shit?"

"Better get used to it, Benny. If you try to go back to New York, you'll be resting where the sun don't shine."

"Thanks for the good cheer," Benny said and hung up.

It had taken a little blackmail. Along with his memory of who he was came a lot of juicy bits of information about all kinds of people, like Benny Fields. He had helped Felix finger a minor mob figure in New York who'd been stealing army weapons years ago when Felix was still with military intelligence. Not many people knew where Benny was hiding out, and that knowledge gave Felix just enough leverage to ensure Benny's help. The mob figure was still in jail, but he had friends on the outside. And they would love to know Benny's address.

Felix's simple telephone scam involved using certain classified phone numbers. He had been able to place the calls, but he needed someone to set up a connection in the city that he wanted to be traced to. Benny had worked out just fine. By now Celia Bedford and her three little pigs would be hotfooting it down to Miami to look for him. They'd have the FBI, the CIA, and the National Guard combing the streets for him. But they wouldn't find him, because he was nowhere near Miami.

He walked over to the window and pulled open the curtain. The sky was a little overcast, but he could still see the Washington Monument poking over the rooftops in the distance. A few blocks east of the hotel was the White House. And a few blocks from that was the Smithsonian Institution. He chuckled. Maybe he would take a sight-seeing tour this afternoon. After all, it had been years since he'd been in Washington. And he had twenty-four hours to kill.

Ginger listened to the dead silence of the phone before hanging up. There wasn't a lonelier sound than three thousand miles of dead telephone wire.

She looked at the pile of dirty dishes on the counter near the sink and thought about washing them. She even considered doing a whole housecleaning trip from ceiling to floor so that Cliff could come home to an orderly house. He'd probably need some order now. So would she.

God, she missed him. Sleeping the last two nights had been almost impossible. She'd watched television in bed until her eyes burned; then she just lay there with her eyes closed listening to it. Even the kids were cranky without him.

Now he was crisscrossing the country trying to track down some obscure cousin in a desperate need to find his identity. Part of her resented that. It was as if he didn't want what he'd had with her. Their life together wasn't good enough for him, or full enough, or just enough. If she could only be with him now, help him, then maybe she wouldn't have this gnawing at her stomach that warned her he was never coming back again.

She drifted over to the sink, put the stopper in, and started running the hot water. She squeezed too much Joy into the water, and the suds billowed wildly, spilling over into the rinse sink.

"Shit!" she said and turned off the water. She wiped her wet hands on her jeans and shouted, "Bogie! Liza! On the double!"

Liza and Beau ran down the hall.

"What'd we do now?" Liza asked.

"Is that the only reason I ever call you?"

Beau shrugged. "Mostly."

"Traitor," she said. "That's not the reason now. I want you to pack one suitcase between you. Warm clothes and a change of underwear. Liza, you help Bogie pack. We're going on a trip."

Liza looked skeptical. "Where to?"

"To surprise Cliff. In Washington."

"The state?"

"D.C."

"Yeaaa!" Bogie yelled.

"Hurry up. I have to make plane reservations. And don't forget your toothbrushes."

"Have you flipped out, Mom?" Liza asked.

"No, sweetheart," Ginger laughed. "I'm just in love."

"Same thing," Beau said.

Liza lead Beau out of the kitchen, muttering, "I haven't got a thing to wear."

Ginger pulled out the Yellow Pages, A through L, and began flipping through the A's. "Oh, Cliff, don't worry. We'll be there soon." She couldn't stop smiling.

22

"WHAT KIND OF gun do you want?"

"How about the one I was carrying?"

Celia shook her head. "They didn't send it with you from San Francisco. How about a Walther PPK Lightweight? You always liked that one."

Cliff shrugged. "It doesn't matter."

"That doesn't sound like the Cliff I once knew."

He turned slowly and stared at her. "It isn't."

She picked up the car phone and punched some numbers. "Hello, Pete? Have a Walther PPK Lightweight waiting for us in the jet. . . . I don't care. We'll be there in fifteen minutes. The gun and a box of cartridges had better be there in ten." She hung up.

Eric Morley pulled the car into the left lane and rocketed past a pizza delivery van. The driver of the van looked over at the passing limousine and gave them the finger.

"Asshole," Eric muttered.

Celia and Cliff sat in the back seat as far from each other as possible. Between them was a leather attaché case that still smelled new.

Celia patted the case. "Everything you'll need is in here. The files on Talon, McDonald, Boston, and you. A thousand dollars in cash. Street maps, phone numbers, your old ID papers from the CIA, updated, of course."

"What about the Miami authorities?"

"Everyone from the governor on down has been alerted to cooperate."

"Do they know what's going on?"

She laughed. "I didn't tell the governor that a madman was about to release a deadly chemical poison that will kill several thousand people in his state."

"What did you tell him?"

"That it was a good time to visit his sister in Atlanta."

Cliff shook his head. "Subtle."

"What can I say? He's an influential member of the President's party, and if you screw this operation up, I'll need some brownie points later."

"One for all and all for number one, huh?"

She patted his knee. "Don't be self-righteous, Cliff. I remember you from the old days, even if you don't."

"Well, then you'll understand me when I tell you this." He twisted in his seat and faced her, his lips stretched in a thin, tight smile. "I'll give it some time down there for the sake of all those people. But if I haven't found anything in *eight hours*, I'll pull out and head back to California. I don't intend to become one of the victims."

"But you don't have B-negative or AB-negative blood."

"You said it sometimes affects people with other blood types."

"Hell, Cliff, one in a million."

Eric spoke over his shoulder, "Actually, one in 1,033,920. Hell of a long shot, Cliff."

"I don't see either of you going with me."

Celia tapped Eric on the shoulder. "Give."

Eric flipped open the glove compartment, grabbed a cigar-shaped cylinder and handed it to Celia.

"The antidote," she smiled and put the cylinder on top of the attaché case.

"What!" Cliff spun around to face her. "You mean there's an antidote for this thing?"

"Relax, Cliff. They managed to manufacture a few gallons before the project was canceled. Not nearly enough to help those people down in Miami—"

"But enough so that you have a personal supply stashed somewhere."

Her smile broadened. "You know how I like my after-dinner drink."

"Don't count too much on the antidote," Eric warned. "There's only enough there for one dose, and it has to be ingested within one minute of contact with Moonshadow."

"What about side effects?"

"The cure is almost as bad as the disease, in this instance: nausea, cramps, dizziness. But it only lasts a few minutes. And it's not fatal."

"Things could have been worse," Celia said. "Felix could have stolen the batch from our New Jersey cache; that one kills all infants under a year old. Or he could have hit the batch in Alaska; that toxin kills only blacks. We'd have had a hell of a time explaining that one."

Cliff looked out the window and shook his head. "Christ."

They drove in silence for a few minutes. Cliff was dying to get a look at the files in the briefcase, anxious to find out more about himself. But he didn't want to read the files in front of Celia and Eric. That information was too personal, too intimate. He'd have to wait until he was on the plane.

A few minutes later they pulled into a military airport in a remote section of Maryland and drove up to a waiting jet. Its engines were already racing loudly. Eric held the car door and offered Celia his hand. She swept gracefully out of the limousine.

"Good luck," she shouted over the roar of the jet.

Cliff ignored her and climbed up the narrow metal boarding ramp. It was a fourteen-seater the CIA reserved for members of Congress as a gesture of friendship, particularly around budget allocation time.

"There's one more thing I want," he hollered down from the top of the steps. "A reservation in my name at the Ambassador Hotel."

"That's going to be tough," Eric shouted back.

"Everything's booked solid because of the commotion tomorrow."

"Consider it done," Celia yelled.

The copilot pulled the door closed behind Cliff, and the small jet, which apparently had been given top priority clearance, began to taxi down the runway.

Celia clutched her camel's-hair coat closed at the throat and shielded her eyes from the wind. When the plane was airborne she climbed back into the limousine and smoothed down her hair. "Let's get out of here."

Eric drove past the guards with a nod. They waved him through the gate.

Celia stretched her arms and rolled her neck. "Christ, I hate it when I have to skip my trampoline workout. My whole body gets so tense. It's this damn job. You're lucky you don't have it, Eric." She rolled her neck a few more times until a bone cracked, and she sighed with relief. "What was in that vial we gave him anyway?"

"The mysterious 'antidote'?"

"Yeah."

"Just a little something the lab boys threw together this morning. Mostly tabasco sauce, I think, and a lot of harmless but sour tasting chemicals for authenticity."

"Good. He's no damn fool. I knew he wouldn't stay around there even at a million-to-one risk. He's been trained in survival too well for that. Now his conscience will give him an excuse to stay."

"What about a real antidote?"

She leaned forward and patted his shoulder. "No such animal, Eric. That's why this stuff is so scary." She reached for the phone and pushed some buttons. "Pete? I want a room at the Ambassador in Clifford Remington's name. I don't care who gets bumped. If he gets any messages, make sure we get them, too." She hung up and dialed another number. "He there yet? . . . Fine. . . . No. Tell him to wait right there until he gets my call. We have another assignment for him." She hung up.

"Edge Connors?" Eric asked.

"Yup. He's already in Miami. When we get back to

the office I want you to phone him his orders. He's to follow Cliff from the moment that jet lands. If Cliff doesn't stop McDonald before he sets Moonshadow loose, I want Edge to make sure neither Cliff nor McDonald leaves the city alive.''

"And if Cliff stops Felix in time?"

She shrugged. "Same order."

"But you told Cliff he was safe now. We have no reason to kill him."

"Come off it, Eric. However this thing goes, I-COOP could be in for some big trouble. There's still a chance we can cover our asses, but if too many people know our little secret, we could be in for some hot times." She rubbed the back of her neck. "You know how fond I always was of Cliff, almost as fond as I am of you. But this is business."

Eric smiled, flicking off the hidden switch in his lapel. "Whatever you say, Celia. You're the boss."

23

CLIFF THREW THE file folder across the aisle of the jet. Neatly typed papers and glossy photographs flew free and fluttered to the seats and floor.

The copilot turned around and looked back from the cockpit. "Everything okay, Mr. Remington?" he asked.

Cliff gave a short, barking laugh, then waved a dismissing hand. The copilot whispered something to the pilot, who nodded.

Cliff reached into the open attaché case on the seat next to him and wrapped his hand around the Walther PPK. Right now he was angry and eager to shoot somebody. He'd prefer to shoot Celia Bedford and her bunch, but anybody would do.

"Damn!" he hissed, thumping his fist on the armrest, rattling the metal ashtray lid. He closed his eyes and recalled every page of the file.

That file had told him everything. How I-COOP had taken four promising career agents from different branches, arranged a fake death for each, then given them new identities and enough "inheritance" money to start over. Their new careers had been based on aptitude tests they'd taken years earlier when each man joined his branch of service. The skills and knowledge for each career had been fed to the men while they were in drug-induced hypnotic states. Hence, Talon and McDonald, from military intelligence, had become a restauranteur and a photographer; Boston, of the FBI, had become a professor; and CIA agent Remington had become a landscaper. Apparently, I-COOP had even used its influence to make sure each man had enough work thrown his way until he was able to make it on his own.

And there was more. Much more.

Cliff's own career in the CIA had been distinguished by numerous successes in various parts of the world, from China to Moscow to East Berlin. He'd engineered kidnappings, blackmail, and mole operations against friends and enemies alike, all with enormous success. But during his last two years in the CIA, despite glowing progress reports, Cliff's superiors had repeatedly expressed doubts: His enthusiasm was deteriorating, they said, and his morale was low; burnout was imminent. That was why he'd been assigned to I-COOP, and Celia Bedford.

Cliff leaned back in the contoured seat and stared at the ocean below. Except for a few gulls, he could see no life. But he knew that just beneath the surface were millions of fish, most of them trying to eat the others just to survive. "Water is hell," he said to the ocean as he closed his eyes again.

And tried to picture his wife.

The file had given few details. He'd had a wife named Katarina, called Katie by her friends and husband. The only daughter of Russian immigrants, she was born and raised in New York City. She attended City College, where she met and married fellow student Clifford Quill (his real name). She had played field hockey and ragtime piano. She'd also had eight years of ballet training, though she was never very good. She had suffered two miscarriages and was four months pregnant at the time of Clifford Quill's memory adjustment.

Memory adjustment!

The file contained endless data: height, weight, birthdate, grades from kindergarten through college. Early romances and love affairs. But it all stopped three years ago, the day they turned Clifford Quill, undercover troubleshooter, into Clifford Remington, underbrush fertilizer.

Ironically, Cliff really was an orphan, the only one of the four men. Maybe that's where I-COOP got the idea. His parents had died in a car crash on their way home from a friend's wedding. Cliff had been raised by an Irish uncle who owned a pub on Long Island and took bets across the bar.

Cliff was suddenly grateful for the bureaucratic tendency to keep record of every detail, including how I-COOP chose new names for the men. This was crucial stuff, insight into the workings of brilliant government minds. Albert Adams had become Albert Boston because Boston was the brand name of a stapler that stood on a nearby desk during the naming session. Talon was the author of a book that was sitting on one of the shelves. The name McDonald was printed in bright colors on the paper bag the psychologist was eating his lunch from as he worked on their identities. Remington was the brand name of the typewriter he'd used to type up the reports. It had all been very scientific.

Cliff shut his eyes even tighter, trying to remember what Katie looked like. She was his wife, for chrissake; he should be able to remember her! He conjured up a composite from all the details in the file, like a police artist sketching a suspect from witnesses' descriptions. Dark hair, tall, slender, dancer's legs, small breasts, blue eyes, a tiny scar under her chin from a playground accident when she was ten. But nothing was clear; she was just a hazy shape, like someone walking toward him through a thick fog. Then the shape walked closer and closer until it became clearer. Suddenly he could make out the face.

Only it was Ginger.

He shook his head and opened his eyes. He didn't know what he was going to do with this information, or how he would tell Ginger. *Darling, let's postpone the wedding until I've located my wife.* Should he tell Ginger anything at all? Or should he just disappear and never go back? Should he find Katie and try to start a new life with her? After all, she was still his wife. They must have been in love once. And there were other considerations. She'd been pregnant. Had she given birth to his baby or suffered another miscarriage? Did he have a child he didn't even know about?

And what about Ginger? He could not deny the way he felt about her. When he'd asked her about her blood type and she'd told him it was B-negative, he'd felt a pulsing wave of protectiveness for her that was so strong it had made him dizzy. His stomach had turned cold with alarm, then warm with relief that she and the kids were three thousand miles away from danger. Thousands of others might die, but he had to know *they* would be safe.

"Approaching Miami, Mr. Remington," the copilot said over his shoulder. "Make sure you're fastened in now."

"Thanks," Cliff said, realizing that he had been holding the gun for the past five minutes. He released the wooden grip, now slick with a film of sweat, and buckled his seat belt.

He concentrated on the glistening city below, banishing all thoughts of Ginger and Katie and himself. This wasn't the time to think about the future. It was a time to return to the past, to the man he once had been and to the job he had done best. For the first time in three years he had an assignment: Find the maniac who had killed over a dozen people already, and stop him before he caused thousands more to die the same agonizing death. Simple enough.

Edge leaned across the hood of the blue Toyota and watched the small jet approach the runway. His stomach was still queasy from his own flight, but he'd popped a few Maalox tablets and felt a little better.

He was one of the best trackers in the business, so he wasn't worried about tailing Remington. Sure, it would have been easier if they'd told him why Remington was here and where the bastard might be expected to go. All Edge knew for sure was that Remington was going to lead him to McDonald and that he was to terminate both of them. But if Remington didn't find McDonald by morning, Edge had orders to introduce Remington's throat to Howdy Doody.

The jet screamed down the runway, bouncing once or twice. Edge's stomach twisted as he remembered his own plane's bumpy landing. God, he hated flying. He popped another Maalox tablet into his mouth and began chewing. Maybe when this was over he would take a bus home. Besides, that would give him some more time to study the Impressionists.

24

FELIX MCDONALD WASHED down the last bite of pastrami on an onion roll with the rest of his Dr. Brown's cream soda. The ice splashed against his lip, and he tilted the glass away with a loud "Ahhh."

"Anything else?" the waiter asked.

Felix smiled. "Nice place. Yours?"

The man shrugged modestly, but smiled with pride. "Sure. It's called Sam's Full-Belly Deli, and I'm Sam."

It was a small place, half a dozen tiny tables and a couple of refrigerated showcases for meats, salads, and fish. A wooden tray piled high with onion bagels still steaming from the oven sat on top of the showcase. A short, stocky customer wearing bifocals and carrying a large shopping bag read the price of lox aloud, shook his head in dismay, and stomped out. At the next table a boy of about thirteen was carefully lettering a sign with a black felt marker.

"How about a nice piece of cheesecake, mister?" Sam said, gathering up Felix's dishes. "Homemade."

Felix patted his stomach. "Too fattening."

"Pardon me for saying so, but you could use a little fattening up. My God, listen to me. I sound just like my father, the one thing I promised myself I wouldn't do." He sighed. "My father was born in Poland; I was born in Chicago. Yet sometimes I sound like I just stepped off of the boat."

215

Felix hooked a thumb over his shoulder. "Your son?"

"Yes. Mitzi and I started late with kids, too busy getting our business going. He was bar mitzvahed two months ago. Now he doesn't want to go back to the synagogue. Tells me he doesn't believe in all that mumbo jumbo. His exact word, 'mumbo-jumbo.' "

"Kids have a mind of their own. At least he's giving you a hand around here."

"Sure, but to get a hand I have to twist an arm." Sam laughed at his Yiddish syntax. "I have to watch myself or soon I'll be muttering *oy veh*! You want to know the truth, mister? I'm not even sure what *oy vey* means." He shrugged again. "What can you do? My kid makes this sign for me and I let him run in the marathon tomorrow."

"You expecting a lot of business?"

"Are you kidding? They expect at least a thousand runners, and five hundred times that many spectators. I hear even the President is supposed to be there."

"The President? That would be nice."

"Sure would. First annual Washington, D.C., ten-kilometer run for international human rights. He'd better show up. You interested in marathons?"

"Only this one. It's special."

"You bet it's special. In fact, part of the course will be two blocks over on Independence Avenue. Bound to bring in some early breakfast customers. Michael is over there making out a special Jogger's Brunch menu. Same old omelets, but with catchy names like Frontrunner's Bagel-and-Lox Combo. Stuff like that."

"And Michael here is going to run in it?"

"That's all he talks about."

Felix paid his bill, left a decent-sized tip, and carried his canvas tennis bag out of the restaurant. He looked at his watch and smiled. It was time to put it all together. He would just make a couple of stops to pick up some things he needed, and then he'd sneak or bluff his way past the guards, as he'd done a hundred times before, back when he was still active. In a few hours it would be finished. Done. And he'd have guaranteed that tomorrow's marathon would indeed be special. No one would ever forget it.

25

ERIC MORLEY RUSHED through the front door of his apartment, locked and bolted it behind him, and jumped excitedly into the air. "Hot damn!"

He laid the briefcase on the coffee table and flipped it open. With a flourish, he scooped up the handful of Memorex tape cassettes and kissed them. He wished he liked wine, because this was the kind of special occasion that called for an expensive bottle of something as old as sin.

His refrigerator contained nothing more sinful than Pepsi, which he drank straight from the can as he carried his treasure to his study. He plopped down at his desk, dragged the telephone in front of him, and began punching buttons.

The line was busy.

"Damn." He hung up and punched the number again. He *had* to get through. It was fourth down in the rain with a wounded quarterback who was about to get blind-sided. Even punting wouldn't save Celia now.

The line was still busy.

He punched the same number once more. He had to get the tapes to someone who could act on the evidence they contained. Never underestimate Celia, he told himself. She might just pull out of this whole thing smelling sweeter than ever. Timing was everything. There was almost no chance that Clifford Remington could stop Moonshadow from wiping out a large part of the population of Miami. And the way Celia had it arranged, Cliff wouldn't be around to bring any charges against I-COOP. But if these tapes were heard by the right people immediately after the Miami massacre, well, Celia would be out, and Eric would be in.

"Hello?"

Eric had grown so used to hearing the busy signal that he was momentarily startled by the sound of a human voice.

"Hello?" the voice repeated.

"Jack, this is Eric."

"Hey, buddy, how're you doing?"

"Terrific. How about you?"

"Are you kidding? Brilliant young executive on the rise. I'm practically indispensable at the White House." He raised his voice and spoke clearly for the benefit of eavesdroppers. *"Do you hear that, whoever might be bugging my phone? Indispensable!"* he chuckled.

"Relax, Jack. I checked it out, and your phone is clean."

"Thanks for the reassurance. What's up?"

"How would you like to be more than indispensable to the White House? How'd you like to be canonized and crowned king of your own state? How'd you like to have women of all ages throwing themselves at your feet?"

"You've got my attention, pilgrim."

"Good. However, despite my confidence in the integrity of your phone, I think we should meet."

"Fine. How does an hour from now sound?"

"No. Tomorrow, Jack, it's got to be tomorrow."

"Sorry, Eric," Jack said. "I've been planning an early weekend for months. The press secretary's niece and I are heading up to Connecticut for some Yankee Doodle diddling. We're celebrating her twentieth birthday in bed. And anyplace else we can do it. Fortunately, the prez got coerced into attending that run tomorrow, so that leaves me free until Monday."

Eric interrupted. "Forget the long weekend, Jack. I guarantee that something big will happen that will cancel your little party. *Nobody* will be leaving town tomorrow.''

''What the fuck does *that* mean?''

''Can't tell you. I don't have all the information yet; I'm still gathering facts. But I've been able to figure out that something dirty is going down tomorrow. That's all I know right now.''

Jack's voice became hard and official. ''Is the President in danger?''

''Only politically. But don't worry, with the stuff I'm going to give you tomorrow, you can make sure he'll be okay.''

There was a pause. ''Christ, maybe I should advise him to skip the closing ceremony tomorrow morning.''

''No, he's got to act as if he doesn't know anything. He's in no danger here in Washington.''

''Good,'' Jack sighed with relief. ''Hell, I'm the one who advised him to go to the damn marathon in the first place. A group of businessmen asked him to give the trophy to the winning runner. But you know how things are. He's in the middle of arms-limitation talks with the Soviets. If he's seen standing in front of a banner reading 'International Human Rights Marathon,' probably with another one nearby saying, 'Save Soviet Jews,' well, shit, that's not going to help our bargaining position. But these guys said if he didn't come they'd bring in Fish Lips from the Senate to do it. And he'd mouth off to the press for twenty minutes, angling for his party's presidential nomination next year. I mean, shit, I'd like to keep this job for more than four lousy years. Christ, what a mess.''

''Don't worry, Jack. Just go ahead with everything as planned. I just want to make sure the President knows where the information came from when the time is right. Credit where credit is due, that sort of thing.''

''You got it, buddy.'' There was another pause as Jack lowered his voice. ''How bad we talking here?''

''I can't be sure yet. But at least treason.''

Jack let out a low whistle. ''Who?''

"Tomorrow, Jack."

After he hung up, Eric toasted himself and took a swig of Pepsi. After this whole thing was over, he would take a trip and relax for a while. Maybe he'd do some backpacking in the Sierras or mountainclimbing in the Rockies. Two weeks alone in the wilderness shouldn't be too hard to arrange for the new director of I-COOP.

He gathered up the tapes, took a screwdriver from his desk drawer, and got down on his hands and knees. In a few seconds he had unscrewed the plastic plate that covered the electrical outlet, but when it came free, the whole plate and outlet fell out in one piece. Behind it was a built-in metal box about six inches deep. Eric slid the tapes inside, closed the lid of the box, and attached the hidden wires that would deliver a severe—perhaps even fatal—electrical shock to anyone who tampered with the outlet. Then he reattached the wall plate.

He stood up, brushed off the knees of his pants, and checked the time. Almost eight o'clock. He could throw a Stouffer's chicken pot pie into the oven, along with some Mrs. Paul's fried zucchini, and be done eating in time to watch the nine o'clock movie on TV. After tomorrow things would never be the same for him.

He drained his Pepsi, walked into the kitchen, and tossed the empty can over his head into the trash bag. "Two points," he laughed.

"How much longer, Mom?"

Ginger squinted at her watch. It was almost seven. She set the watch three hours ahead—Washington time. "We'll be landing in about an hour, Liza."

"What time will it be when we get to the hotel?" Beau asked.

"How many times are you going to ask me that question?"

He shrugged. "I don't know."

She reached over and ruffled his hair. "Wise guy. We'll be at the Ambassador by midnight."

"Funny, I don't feel tired."

"That's because your body's on California time,"
Liza explained.

"I don't get it."

Liza sighed. "What a pimp."

"Mom!"

"Liza."

"What'd I say?"

Ginger smiled. The kids were excited by the trip,
though Liza was careful not to show it too much. She
was doing her imitation of a sophisticated woman
again. Ginger remembered going through that stage herself at fifteen or sixteen; she'd always insisted on clink-
ing glasses with her dates before drinking, something
she'd seen in an old movie. Unfortunately, the glasses
at Ralph's Burger Emporium were barely up to holding
liquid, let alone being clinked. Once, when she finally
got a date with Ed Barnes, the school hunk, she'd tilted
her head and stretched her neck into a pose that she
hoped made her look like Audrey Hepburn. Then she'd
said, "Here's to a lovely evening," and clinked glasses.
Hers shattered instantly, cutting her hand and spilling
coke down the front of her new dress. Her hand needed
eight stitches.

She loved watching her kids grow up, and she felt
tears well up in her eyes as she once again realized how
quickly it happened, how soon they'd be gone. Too
damn soon. She took a deep breath and wiped her eyes.

"Is Cliff gonna meet us at the airport?" Beau asked.

"God," Liza moaned. "How many times do we have
to tell you? This is a *surprise*. What a pim—uh, jerk."

"Thank you, Liza," Ginger said. "That's better. I
think."

"Do you think Cliff'll be happy to see us?" Beau
asked.

Liza didn't answer this time. Instead she looked at
Ginger as if it were her question, too.

"Are you kidding? He'll be thrilled. You want to see
him, don't you?"

Beau nodded. "I miss him. Even when he's acting weird with that memory jazz."

"Yeah," Liza said. "I love Daddy a lot, too, you know. Really a lot. I mean, he's our real father and all. It's just that Cliff seems to have more time for us, and it's not like he's *making* time for us, but like he's enjoying us. You know?"

Ginger nodded, feeling the tears again. Maybe it was crazy to pop the kids in a jet and haul them across the country, but she'd been called crazy before. Like when she'd divorced Darren. She'd done what she'd had to then, and damn it, she was doing what she had to now. Some things were worth acting crazy for.

Cliff kicked the vending machine, pulled the handle, then kicked it again. This time the orange package of Reese's Peanut Butter Cups slid into view. He tore open the wrapper and shoved the first cup into his mouth, ignoring the fact that he didn't like chocolate. All he cared about was that it was his first taste of food since his breakfast fourteen hours ago in Washington. If you could call what came out of an FBI vending machine food.

"What now, sir?" the young FBI agent at his elbow asked.

"Now, Agent Phelps," Cliff said, "I intend to sit down on this hard bench in this cold hall and finish eating this stale food. Alone."

"Yes, sir." Agent Phelps walked away.

Cliff dropped onto the wooden bench and felt his wallet shift beneath him. The $1,000 in cash Celia had given him had dwindled to $167, plus $25 of his own. He'd spread cash in every sleazy joint in Miami, trying to buy a lead to Felix McDonald, real name Felix Boyer, but he still had nothing. There were hundreds of men searching this city, helicopters checking rooftops, uniformed police tromping through the tunnels and back alleys of Miami. No sign of Felix.

Cliff shoved the second peanut butter cup into his mouth. One problem was to determine where there would be enough people gathered for Moonshadow to affect them all at once. The second challenge was to figure out how Felix intended to expose them. The FBI and CIA were checking out all small planes, balloons, anything that could fly. Extra guards were posted around the reservoir and all open produce. They could have done all that without him.

But Cliff had the toughest job—trying to outthink Felix, attempting to predict how and where he would strike again. But Cliff wasn't having any success. He'd gone through all of their files over and over again, but he found no connection between a Pittsburgh hotel, a Seattle movie theater, and anything in Miami. Yet there had to be a link. Felix was daring them to find him. Why else would he have warned them this time? Why hadn't he just released Moonshadow without telling anybody?

Cliff suspected that Felix was basically a decent man fighting for a cause, at least in his own mind. Perhaps his actions were more than a challenge to I-COOP; maybe they were a cry for help. Maybe he didn't really want to kill all those people, and if I-COOP caught him in time, he wouldn't have to. But what if they didn't catch him? Then none of that psychological crap meant anything, because Cliff had no doubt that Felix would carry out his plans.

Cliff licked the chocolate from his fingers.

Thinking he could predict Felix's reasoning was stupid. How could I-COOP assume that Cliff could read Felix's mind just because they'd both gone through the same memory treatment? That was like believing two people would think alike just because they were born in the same city. If Cliff had come out of the conditioning first and remembered his part in Moonshadow, would he have done anything about it? Probably not. He would have shaken his head cynically and just gone on with his life. Maybe in some way that made Felix a better man than him.

Or maybe Cliff just wasn't the superagent he thought he was. After all, he still couldn't really remember his earlier life. Maybe the files were false and he'd been just a klutz that I-COOP had been relieved to get rid of. Why else couldn't he come up with anything?

Yet, he and Felix did have certain things in common. Felix had lost a wife and child; so had Cliff. He wasn't sure about the child, but that only made it worse. And I-COOP had put Ginger and the kids in danger the night they tried to kill him. How would he have struck back if those men had killed Ginger?

He licked the ridge of chocolate from the inside of the candy wrapper.

"My God!" he shouted, jumping to his feet. "Of course!" He ran down the hall and burst through the door of the communications office. Three men and two women, all wearing headphones, looked up with the same annoyed expression. Cliff ran to the severe-looking woman at the scrambler. "Tell them to immediately send us all the files on McDonald, Remington, Talon, and Boston. Not the hard files, I already have them. I want the manufactured case histories of each, the blueprints they used for programming them."

She patted the bun at the back of her head. "I don't understand what—"

"They will. Do it."

The others in the room exchanged puzzled glances and returned to what they were doing. Cliff marched over to the matrix printer and waited. A satisfied grin spread across his face as it occurred to him he might have been one hell of an agent after all.

Felix McDonald walked into his hotel room and tossed the canvas tennis bag onto the bed. The bag was now empty.

With a weary sigh he shuffled into the bathroom and turned on a faucet. While hot water steamed into the tub behind him, he washed the black powder from his hands. His clothes smelled of sulfur, but he couldn't tell anymore whether the smell came from the sodium ox-ylate, the barium chlorate, or the copper oxide. He winced when the soap touched his right thumb. One of the copper wires he'd used in the timing device had slid under his thumbnail, penetrating the skin. So much discomfort for such a small wound.

Slowly he peeled off all his clothes. He'd been careful not to wear anything synthetic. A spark from the built-up static electricity in the fabric could have set the whole thing off accidentally. Then the only one dead in Washington would have been him.

He leaned over the sink, lathered his face with the shaving brush, and carelessly began scraping his face with the razor. As usual, he nicked himself a few times with the new blade and tiny blood spots began to bloom through the white foam. He'd never been good at shaving, maybe because he hadn't started until he was in his midtwenties. When he was done, he rinsed his face off with cold water.

He climbed into the steaming tub without testing the water. It was hotter than he liked it, but right now his body needed the heat. All that climbing and sneaking and crawling had taken its toll. He looked down through the water at his long, pale body. He could count his ribs where the skin stretched across his chest. His appendix scar looked wrinkled and shriveled, like a fossil of some extinct sea worm. He'd lost at least fifteen pounds in the past week from all the traveling and eating airline food, or not eating at all. He didn't always remember to eat.

He dipped his head back until the hot water covered his ears. At first it burned a little, but the sudden and total quiet was worth a little pain.

With his eyes closed he remembered his visit to Monaco the previous year. The Guccis had once again won the International Fireworks Competition with a dazzling aerial display. He'd taken some of his best photographs there. Great fiery dandelions blossoming in the sky in endless color combinations like a giant, flaming garden. He'd sold photos from that night to half a dozen different magazines. He had used the money to buy Susan a loom.

But he'd been fascinated by more than the visual display of fireworks; he'd wanted to know how it was all done. He'd interviewed one pyrotechnician after another, asking them about their special techniques. Each country had its own trademark. The French were known for low-to-the-ground, slow-burning Roman-candle effects; Italian shells were famous for their especially loud noise; Brazilians were noted for their use of blue, the color most difficult to achieve in fireworks displays.

And he also learned how to combine the sulfur, resin, metal powders, and various salts to achieve colorful fireworks of his own. He knew how to form the paste and slice it into tiny cubes, not with the star-making machine used by some pyrotechnicians, but by hand. The oil in a machine could combine with chlorates to form an explosive gas, so the handmade devices were safer. He had mastered the five or six complicated steps required to produce sound charges. He had learned to use timing devices attached to the smaller shells to create multiple bursts. It had been easy for him. Only later, as his memory started to come back, did he realize that it had been easy because of his demolitions training in the army.

But none of that mattered now. All that counted was tomorrow. Everything was set. According to newspaper reports, a single rocket would be fired to mark the start of the ten kilometer race. Later, when the first runner crossed the finish line, a full-blown colored smoke and fireworks display was scheduled to go off while the rest of the runners trickled in. Afterward, the President would present the trophy to the winner. But of course by then it would all be over.

Felix lifted his head out of the water and lathered his black hair with the tiny bar of Ivory soap provided by the hotel. He turned on the hot water until the tub was steaming again, then slid back down to listen to the waterfall underwater.

He had arranged a little colored smoke and fireworks

display of his own, wired to go off automatically when
the main display began. The combinations of sound
charges would trip the programmed timing device, and
ten seconds later six smoke rockets would flare into the
sky, explode in a dazzling array of colors, then explode
again, this time spreading Moonshadow particles over
the crowd, like Peter Pan throwing fairy dust over
Wendy and the boys. And if there was a breeze, some of
the Moonshadow would make its way through the rest
of the city.

Felix stood up and toweled himself dry, then wrapped
the towel around his waist and splashed Old Spice on his
face. It stung where he'd cut himself shaving, but he inhaled deeply and smiled. Susan's grandmother had
given it to him two Christmases ago, and the bottle was
still almost full. Quickly, he peeled the cellophane wrapper off one of the drinking glasses and filled the glass
with water. He reached into his pants pocket, pulled out
a small metal Anacin box, and snapped the lid open.
The large red pills inside the box were not aspirin.

He went into the bedroom and threw the damp towel
on a chair, then climbed between the cool sheets. His
body was still damp, and he shivered slightly.

Everything was set. The rockets would fire automatically, and everybody who knew what was going to happen was in Miami checking sewers and flophouses. No
one could stop what would happen tomorrow. No one
except him.

He checked the small travel alarm he had set on the
bedside table. It was almost midnight. He picked the
nine red tablets out of the Anacin box and swallowed
each one with a sip of water. He'd never liked to take
pills; he'd been afraid they'd get stuck in his throat and
choke him. Well, this was the last time he'd have to
worry about that. These were slow acting but absolutely
painless. He'd be dead by morning.

26

CLIFF STUCK HIS head out the door of the communications office and shouted, "Agent Phelps!"

Twenty feet down the corridor another door popped open, and Agent Phelps stepped into view. "Yes, sir?"

"On the double."

Agent Phelps ran down the hall and stood in front of Cliff. For the first time, Cliff noticed that Agent Phelps was in his mid-twenties and still had a slight case of adolescent acne. His black-rimmed glasses added to the youthful effect, making him look like the kid in algebra class who always knew the right answers but whom no one would sit with at lunch.

"Phelps, call the airfield and tell them to have the plane fueled and ready to take off in half an hour." Cliff checked his watch. "That'll be two-thirty A.M. Got it?"

"Yes, sir."

"Also, get me a car with a phone and a driver who knows how to haul ass."

"Right, sir," Phelps said without a smile. "I believe I can haul ass for you, sir."

Cliff grinned. "Okay, but make that call first."

"Yes, sir."

"Phelps?"

"Yes, sir?"

"Do you know what this is all about?"

"Only what everyone else around here knows. We're

229

searching for a fugitive named Felix McDonald.''

"Do you know why?"

"No, sir."

"Are you married?"

Phelps blushed. "Almost."

"After you drop me off at the airfield, go straight to your girlfriend's place and stay there all day. Don't leave the house for any reason. If the Bureau wants to send you somewhere, tell them you're sick."

Agent Phelps nodded slowly. "Okay. Sir?"

"What?"

"You know something, don't you? I mean about what's really going on."

Cliff looked down at the stack of teletype paper in his hands. "Too much, Phelps. Much too much."

PART FIVE

Thursday

27

GENERAL GERRARD SLAMMED his fist on the table in the I-COOP office. "This is ridiculous."

Hawkins cleared his throat. "I have to agree with Steve. None of this is, uh, hard evidence."

Eric rubbed the sleep out of his eyes and sighed. "Damn."

Celia said nothing. Dressed in a white pants suit with a ruffled pink blouse, she was the only one in the room who didn't look as if she'd been dragged out of bed in the middle of the night to be told that in three hours the nation's capital would suffer the worst holocaust since Hiroshima. Her face was meticulously made up, and her fingernails flashed crimson.

Cliff sat on the sofa where only hours earlier he'd escaped from handcuffs. The others sat in their usual places and, except for Celia, looked the worse for wear, with puffy eyes and unkempt hair.

"I don't really care what you decide," Cliff said, standing up. "I've been running around for long enough. You brought me in because you thought I could help capture Felix. Well, now you know as much as I do."

"It just doesn't make sense," General Gerrard said, tugging on his sparse mustache. "Why would he choose Washington?"

Cliff sighed and explained once more. "I told you, General, because it fits with his pattern. You were looking in the wrong file. You assumed that because Felix had regained his memory, he would again behave like

Felix Boyer, but that was a mistake. Part of him is still Felix McDonald, the man you created." He hefted the papers he'd brought with him from Miami. "These are the details you programmed into each of us. Our replacement identities. All the little quirks and habits and memories that changed us into the men you wanted us to be. You trained us to remember friends who never existed, jobs we never held, places we'd never been to. And that's the key to Felix's behavior. To Felix Boyer, Pittsburgh and Seattle wouldn't mean anything, but Pittsburgh is the city where Felix McDonald was supposed to have been born. His father was supposed to have worked as a desk clerk at the Commodore Hotel, where Felix first released Moonshadow. Felix McDonald was supposed to have been raised by his grandparents in Seattle, and his first job was supposed to have been in the movie theater he attacked."

"But what about Miami?" the general insisted.

"For God's sake, Steve," Eric sighed, "he already *explained* that."

"Miami doesn't fit in at all," Cliff said patiently. "That was a trick. Felix allowed you to trace him to Miami to divert you."

"And you think Washington is his real target?" Tom Hawkins asked.

"That's an educated guess. Washington was the city where Felix Boyer ceased to exist. This is where you put us through the memory process." Cliff shook his head. "Hell, I don't know for sure, but it makes sense. If I were him, and if I hated you as much as he does, this is where I'd come. This is where he can hurt you the most. The people he wants to expose you to are here. Suppose a few senators die tomorrow, or the First Lady. What's the President's blood type?"

No one answered.

Cliff grinned. "Maybe you should find out. You could warn him or make up some story to get him out of town. But after tomorrow, that would only prove to him that you knew all about it. He'd bury you."

"I still don't see . . ." General Gerrard protested.

"Shut up, Steve," Celia said quietly. "Tom, I want

you to keep the operation in Miami going, but I want you to activate as much manpower as you can to start sweeping through Washington. It's four thirty-seven right now, and Felix will probably set the toxin loose between seven and eight this morning. On the phone he said we had twenty-four hours.''

''That doesn't give me much time.''

''Not if you sit around here bitching.''

Tom Hawkins stood up, pulled his sweater in place, and walked out of the room fighting a yawn.

Celia continued. ''Steve, I want you to get as many men as possible into civilian clothing. Have them line the route of the marathon from start to finish. They are to haul in every man in the crowd who vaguely resembles Felix.''

The general nodded and waited for more orders. When Celia merely stared blandly at him, he stood up and left the room.

''The marathon?'' Cliff asked.

''Yes. It's the kickoff of International Human Rights Weekend. A ten kilometer race starting at Washington Circle near the university, across Pennsylvania Avenue, past the White House, along Constitution, through Lincoln Park, ending up at Hubert Humphrey Memorial Stadium.''

''Where the President will be waiting like a sitting duck to award the trophy to the winner,'' Eric added with a moan.

''Right. They're expecting anywhere from five hundred thousand to a million people. Maybe more. Anyway, that crowd is the most likely target I can think of or Moonshadow.''

Cliff nodded. ''It's perfect. Good luck.'' He walked to the door and opened it.

Celia jumped up from the sofa. ''Where do you think you're going?''

''I intend to be on a flight to California long before Felix pulls the plug.''

''But we still need you here, Cliff.''

''Forget it. I won't risk my life again. You've already taken it from me once.''

"You don't even have the vulnerable blood type."

Cliff snorted. "I'm not willing to take your word on who's vulnerable."

"The antidote would protect you."

Cliff walked over to the briefcase he'd left next to the sofa, opened it, and removed the vial. "There's no antidote, Celia. One look at the way your friends were sweating told me that." He unclipped the cap and poured the liquid on the carpet. "So much for Dr. Bedford's magic bullet." He walked to the door. "Bye."

"Oh, I forgot to tell you, Cliff," Celia said, sitting back down and crossing her legs. "I received a message from Ginger."

Cliff paused at the door, his stomach twisting painfully. "Yes?"

"She's here."

He swung around quickly and snarled, "Where?"

"In Washington."

Cliff started toward her, his hand reaching for his gun.

"I wouldn't," Eric warned, aiming his own gun at Cliff's head.

"You're a lucky man, Cliff," Celia continued as if nothing had happened. "Ginger's a terribly attractive woman, with two lovely children. The three of them arrived several hours ago and checked into your room at the Ambassador. The people at the hotel gave her an argument about that, but she's quite a forceful woman. Naturally, we got word of their arrival and sent someone over to keep an eye on them. For their own protection, of course. I also learned that they were up all night watching TV, so I had our man go in and introduce himself as a friend of a friend of yours. Seems they all had quite enough sleep on the plane, so he took them out for an early breakfast. He has orders to drive them anywhere they want to go."

"But they're in danger here. Their blood—"

"Yes, well I didn't know that when I sent them out did I?"

"Where are they now?" he demanded.

"I don't know."

"But you can reach him by car phone?"

She shrugged. "I suppose so. But I won't."

Cliff took another menacing step toward her, and Eric steadied his gun and shook his head.

Celia went on, "Cliff, there's very little chance of your finding them in time. I suggest you concentrate your efforts on stopping Felix. That's the surest way to save them." She looked him straight in the eye. "The *only* way, Cliff."

Cliff returned her stare with a sneer. "I'll need a phone with several outside lines."

She nodded. "Down the hall, two doors on the left. That's Eric's office. You want any special help?"

He made a harsh sound that might have been a laugh and walked out of the room.

Eric let out a loud sigh and tucked his gun back under his sweater. "He's got a tough job."

"He's a tough man. Besides we've given him a little incentive." She rolled her neck until it cracked. "Looks like another day without Donna Summer and my trampoline. By the way, is Edge back from Miami yet?"

"He arrived an hour after Cliff. He's waiting in Tom's office. I thought they could talk over old CIA times together."

"There won't be any old times if we don't get cracking. Tell him to wait downstairs and pick up Cliff's tail when he leaves. His assignment is the same."

"Right." Eric stood up and paced behind the sofa.

She glanced at him over his shoulder. "You look nervous, Eric dear. Don't worry, you're not the right blood type. I checked."

"What about you?"

She laughed. "Haven't you heard? I don't have any blood."

28

CLIFF CONSIDERED MURDER.

He sat at Eric Morley's desk with the telephone lodged between neck and shoulder, releasing the ammunition clip of his Walther PPK repeatedly, then slapping it back in place. Murder wouldn't be difficult. He could slip back down the hall, burst into the conference room where he'd left them, and pump three bullets into Celia Bedford's sweet face before her shadow had time to move.

Finally the woman came back on the line. "Sorry, sir, no one by either of those names is registered here."

"Thank you," he said and hung up.

There was only one thing wrong with his plan to murder Celia. It would waste time he needed to save Ginger and the kids. Part of him was furious with Ginger for doing something so irresponsible as flying across the country to surprise him. But part of him felt pleased, wanted to smile at such a rare act of faith and love.

He decided to stick to this plan: calling every hotel in Washington to see if a Felix McDonald was registered there. Thinking that everyone was in Miami looking for him, Felix wouldn't have bothered to use an alias. In fact, he'd probably thought it amusing to be so open. Just another little detail to rub I-COOP's nose in when an investigation of the tragedy took place. Something the press would use to make I-COOP look foolish.

Considering how slowly he was moving through the Yellow Pages, Cliff considered asking for some help. Eric Morley could have fifty FBI operatives make these calls. But then I-COOP would know what Cliff knew. And if they knew where Felix was, they'd burst in and probably kill him before he told them how he planned to disperse Moonshadow. Celia had been right about one thing, Felix knew Cliff and just might let him get close enough to take him alive.

He punched another number on the phone.

"Royal Inn. May I help you?"

"Registration desk, please."

"One moment." Tiny clicking noises.

Cliff stared at his watch. He'd wasted almost a minute on this call so far.

"Registration desk. May I help you?"

"Do you have a Felix Boyer or a Felix McDonald registered?"

Five seconds passed. "No, sir. Neither name."

"That was fast. Are you sure you checked thoroughly? He might have checked in a few days ago."

She laughed. "Yes, sir. You were just lucky I had the computer checking on another name when you called. I just punched in your names, too. But there's no one by either of those names here."

"Thanks," Cliff said excitedly and hung up. "Of course! This is Washington!" In any other city, the names of people registered at hotels would be recorded only at those hotels. But in Washington, with its constant flow of world leaders and diplomats, security was tight. The name of anybody registering at any hotel, motel, or inn would be fed into the various computers of the security agencies. If Felix McDonald was registered under either of his names, one of those computers would have it.

But how could he gain access to those data banks without letting I-COOP know what he was up to?

Cliff looked at his watch again. It was 5:45 A.M. The race was supposed to start at 7:00, and within the hour Felix had promised to release Moonshadow.

He hunched over Eric's desk and punched the number for the I-COOP operator. "Get me the FBI office in Miami. Agent Timothy Phelps."

"Open line?"

"Whatever's fastest."

Buttons were pushed, electronic notes sounded.

"Agent Phelps here. May I help you?"

"Phelps, this is Cliff Remington. I see you didn't take my advice about sitting this day out at home."

"Sorry, sir, but I've never called in sick since I've been with the Bureau. And we're in the middle of a fugitive search. I couldn't let my buddies down. Besides, there's some talk of sending a few of us up to Washington today. That assignment could lead to a promotion. And what with me getting married soon and everything . . ."

"I'm glad to hear you haven't left yet, because I need your help."

"Yes, sir?"

"I want you to call the FBI office in Washington and have them run two names through their computer to see if their name is currently registered at a Washington area hotel, motel, inn, or guest house."

"Can't you just do that direct from where you are, sir?"

"Of course, but—" Cliff lowered his voice—"we're trying to avoid a security leak here."

"I'll get on it right away, sir. Do you want me to call you back?"

"I'll hold."

The line hummed with that dead space sound of hold and Cliff stared at his watch. He imagined the second hand as a long sword slicing away the rest of Ginger's life.

"Aren't you kids tired yet?"

Beau shook his head and looked around the all-night coffee shop in search of their waitress. "I'm still hungry."

"Hungry? You've already had juice, pancakes, sausage, English muffins, and strawberries. You'll make yourself sick."

"No, I won't. Traveling makes me hungry, that's all."

Ginger smiled. "Well, you'll just have to struggle on in your present famished state. After all, I'm sure Mr. Elliott here has better things to do than chauffeur us around all day."

Ronnie Elliott smiled. "No, ma'am. I'm at your service for the whole day."

"I don't get it," Liza said. "You work for Cliff?"

"No, Liza," Ginger said. "He works for a relative of Cliff's. Some kind of distant uncle."

"Aunt," Ronnie corrected.

"That's right. Sorry."

He shrugged. "No problem."

"Anyway, Cliff had to go out of town to visit another relative he'd never met and asked his aunt to respond to any messages we left at the hotel." Ginger turned to Ronnie. "I'm really sorry about just popping in like this. I just wanted to, well, surprise Cliff." She blushed slightly.

"No problem," Ronnie said again. "Mr. Remington's aunt is tied up for most of the day, but I'm to take you anyplace you want to go. I'm sorry about knocking on your door so early, but I heard the TV playing and all."

"I'm glad you did. After sleeping on the plane for so long, the kids were restless. And TV at five in the morning doesn't offer much entertainment."

Liza pushed her half-eaten waffle away and started tearing little pieces of her paper napkin. "How come Cliff has relatives he doesn't know about?"

"Cliff's parents were killed when he was very young, and he was raised by his grandparents. Then they died. Sometimes in a situation like that people lose touch with their families."

"That's right," Ronnie added. "Me, I got a sister lives not fifty miles from here, and I haven't seen her in three years."

"What time is it back home?" Beau asked.

"Who cares, drip?" Liza said.

"I do."

Ginger checked her watch, subtracted three hours. "It's, um, fifteen past three in the morning in California. It's still dark there and everybody's still asleep.''

"Hey, let's call Freddy and wake him up!''

"Let's not, drip.''

Ginger shook her head. "Do you have any kids, Ronnie?''

"No, ma'am. I've got a dachshund.''

"Oh.'' Ginger sipped her coffee. The waitress drifted by and asked if they wanted anything else. Over Beau's protests, Ginger said no. The waitress slapped the check on the table, and Ginger reached for it.

"No,'' Ronnie said, snatching it away from her. "Ms. Bedford insists that you accept her hospitality while you're staying here.''

"Thank you,'' Ginger smiled. "Kids?''

"Thank you,'' they mumbled dutifully.

Outside it was significantly brighter than it had been when they'd gone into the coffee shop. Ginger had been about to ask Ronnie to drive them back to the Ambassador for a nap, but the bright sunlight melted away her weariness, and she felt suddenly energized. She stretched her arms, stood on tiptoe, and took a deep breath.

"Since Cliff isn't expected back until this afternoon, and since this may be the last time we'll ever ride in a chauffeured limousine, I suggest that we see the city. How about it, kids?''

"Yeah,'' Beau agreed.

Liza nodded. "Sounds reasonable.''

"Okay,'' Ronnie said. "Some streets are already blocked off 'cause of the marathon this morning, but we can see most of the town.''

"What run?'' Ginger asked.

"Ten kilometers through the middle of town. Kicks off some kind of Human Rights Weekend or something. Anything to make a buck, right?''

"I read something about that last week in *People* magazine. The President's going to be there, isn't he?''

"Right. He'll give the winner some kind of trophy. There'll be a colored smoke display and food and music. A whole big deal.''

"Can we meet the President?'' Beau asked.

Ronnie laughed. "You can't *meet* him, but you can *see* him. I'll drive you over to the Humphrey Stadium where the runners will be finishing up."

"That would be wonderful," Ginger said. "Can we get in?"

"No sweat. This limo can get in anywhere."

They all climbed into the car. Ronnie pulled away from the curb and headed for the stadium.

Cliff ran through the lobby of the Regency Hills Hotel as if chased by a tribe of headhunters. Several guests shook their heads disapprovingly as Cliff bolted across the plush carpet and bounded up the stairs three at a time.

He didn't have to look at his watch anymore; a built-in timepiece ticked loudly inside his head. It had taken Agent Timothy Phelps fifteen minutes to come up with the name of this hotel and the room number. Cliff had spent another ten minutes persuading the switchboard operator to let him borrow her car, a beat-up gray Honda that seemed to run on one cylinder. Fighting his way to the hotel through the detours and crowds ate up another fifteen minutes.

That made it almost 6:30.

Cliff lurched up the stairs, one hand gripping the railing, the other steadying him against the opposite wall. On the sixth-floor landing he took the corner so fast that his gun fell out of the waistband of his pants and bounced to the floor. He was already half a flight up when he realized it had fallen. He wondered briefly if it was worth the time to go back for it.

He decided it was.

With the gun clutched in his hand, he panted up the remaining two flights. He was gulping air as he rushed down the dimly lit corridor in search of Felix's room.

When he found it, he stood in front of the door and realized that he had no specific plan. How could he get inside? Knock on the door and claim to be room service? Say that he had a telegram? Claim to be hotel maintenance come to fix a leak?

"The hell with it," he grumbled, gripping the gun tightly in his hand, and kicking open the door.

He went in on a roll, almost as if his body had decided what to do without consulting him. When he came up again his gun was sweeping the room in search of a target. It zeroed in on the figure in the bed.

"Get up, Felix," he said.

The figure did not move.

"Get up, Felix!"

No response. The man lay with arms sprawled, mouth slightly open.

"Oh, my God, no!" Cliff shouted and ran to the bed. If Felix was dead, there was no way to stop Moonshadow. No way to stop the thousands who would die. No way to save Ginger and the kids.

He lifted Felix's wrist and felt for a pulse. Then he put his head to Felix's chest and listened.

He whipped the covers off the bed and dragged Felix's naked body out. The flesh was clammy and cold.

"Come on, you son of a bitch. You're not dead yet." With one arm around Felix, he began walking him around the room. But Felix's head merely rolled against his chest, and his toes scuffed across the carpet. "Come on! Come on!" Cliff yelled.

An elderly couple in matching jogging suits walked past the room, looked at the shattered door, the naked man being carried around the room by another man with a gun, and quickly walked away.

Cliff looked at his watch.

A quarter to seven.

The race would begin in fifteen minutes. At some point during the race, Moonshadow would be released. If Felix had tried to kill himself, then the toxin must be set to go off automatically. But when? And how?

He stopped pacing and threw Felix back onto the bed, propping his head up with one hand. "Felix! Felix, wake up."

Felix's eyes fluttered slightly, fought to open, but could only manage a tiny squint. "Cliff." There was a funny kind of joy mixed with relief in his voice.

"Yeah, it's Cliff."

"Come . . . to help, huh?" He squeezed the words out with slow deliberation, like a drunk trying to pass a sobriety test. "Knew you'd . . . join us. You hated . . . it, too."

"Moonshadow."

"Yeah. Bad medicine." Felix tried to laugh, but started to cough instead.

Cliff tried to think. He didn't recognize this man, except from the photos in his file. Yet Felix knew him, even seemed glad to see him. Somehow Cliff had to use Felix's apparent trust in him to find out what he needed to know.

"It's over, Felix," Cliff said. "You did it. Moonshadow went off and spread through the crowd lining the streets to watch the marathon." He laughed. "The President's wife is dead, and he's organized an investigation that's going to put an end to this kind of thing forever. He's already got Celia and her bunch put away. He's even promised public hearings."

Felix's eyes opened wider, and his voice became clearer. "I knew it would work."

"It was a good plan."

Felix shook his head and closed his eyes. "Didn't want innocent people to die. No choice. They'll understand."

Cliff said, "They're still trying to figure out how you spread the toxin so quickly over so many people."

"Sometimes the race . . . to the . . . swiftest." A phlegmy chuckle rumbled in Felix's chest. "But the prize . . . for everyone." A terrible coughing shook his body. Cliff could smell death on his sour breath.

"Yeah," he said, "but you fooled them, Felix. They never knew what hit them."

"Fooled them, I—" A high-pitched whistle followed by an explosion interrupted Felix, and he raised his head, looking confused. "You said . . . it was over. They're supposed to be . . . dead."

Cliff ran to the window and saw a puff of red smoke where a rocket had exploded. He looked at his watch: seven o'clock. The start of the race. Felix was confused. He had believed the race was over and everyone was dead. But he'd said something else, too, about the race to the swiftest. Cliff looked back at Felix. "Damn! It's the fireworks. You've got the display rigged somehow, or you've rigged your own. Which is it?"

Felix moaned softly and shook his head.

Cliff looked at his gun, but realized it would do no good to threaten him with it. Felix knew he was dying, probably had only minutes to live. He'd have to try something else. He went to the bed and held Felix's head, forcing him to look straight up into Cliff's face.

"Listen to me, Felix. My wife and kids are somewhere in this town. If Moonshadow goes off, they could die too."

"To save . . . many lives," Felix mumbled.

"Felix, my wife and kids are out there. Isn't that who you want to protect?" Cliff mentally rifled Felix's file for a name. "Susan," he said, bending closer. "My wife's name is Susan, Felix, just like yours."

Felix mouthed the name, but no sound came out. Finally he said, "Stadium . . . VIP Lounge . . . roof."

Then there was a popping sound, and Felix's neck exploded.

Blood and bits of flesh sprayed up into Cliff's face, but he was already moving, somersaulting over the side of the bed and into the wall. He came up with his Walther in his hand and managed to squeeze off one shot at the doorway.

But Edge Connors had already ducked around the door frame and Cliff's bullet thudded into the corridor wall. Edge's shot had almost severed Felix's head, and Cliff could hear the faint gurgling of blood pumping out of the neck. He kept his head down and crawled to the corner of the bed.

Suddenly Edge leaned around the corner again and fired off two quick rounds. The first bullet kicked into Felix's chest, causing the body to bounce on the bed. The second one dug into the wall behind the bed, where Cliff had stood a moment earlier.

"You're not supposed to kill me, you moron!" Cliff yelled. "Didn't you get your new orders? Call Colonel Bedford or Morley."

Edge chuckled. "I got my orders. And I also know what Felix told you. So we don't need either of you anymore. When I'm done with you, I'll phone the information in. Then it'll be hero time for me."

"You don't understand. There's a time factor."

Another shot shredded the corner of the bed. Cliff dropped flat on his stomach. "Damn waste of time," he muttered, then leaped out from behind the bed and fired four bullets at the doorway just as Edge showed himself.

Edge Connors pitched forward with a groan, his hands clutching his side. His gun tumbled across the carpet out of his reach. Only one of the bullets had hit him, but it had shattered a rib. He writhed on the floor cursing.

Cliff kicked the gun into the bathroom and checked his watch: 7:06. Ten kilometers was a little over six miles. How long would it take a good runner to cover that distance? People ran the mile in less than four minutes, but that race was a sprint. A longer race would take at least five minutes a mile. Figure at least thirty minutes. The race had started at seven. That left Cliff with twenty-four minutes in which to get to the stadium VIP Lounge, find the rockets, and disable them. The police would have heard the shots; they'd be here any minute. Cliff had no time to explain anything to them. He ran for the door.

But as he passed Edge Connor's hunched form, he felt the iron grip of Edge's hand around his ankle. When he turned to kick free, he saw the flash of Edge's pocket knife as it plunged into his calf. He let out a cry, pivoted, and with his good leg kicked Edge in the face. Edge's head snapped back and thudded into the carpeted floor. He lay motionless.

Cliff stooped down, plucked the knife out of his leg, and threw it on the bed. Gritting his teeth, he shoved his gun back into the waistband of his pants and limped down the hall.

Edge stirred on the floor.

29

"IT'S ALMOST LIKE the Olympics," Ginger said, nudging Beau with her elbow.

"I'm hungry," he complained.

"Ronnie went to get you something, so don't forget to thank him when he gets back."

"I will."

"Mom?"

"What, Liza?"

"Is Cliff's aunt rich?"

Ginger shrugged. "She must be if she can afford a limo and a chauffeur."

"Does that mean Cliff is going to be rich?"

Ginger laughed. "I wouldn't count on it."

The Hubert Humphrey Memorial Stadium was almost filled to capacity, and more people were pouring in. A rumor was going through the crowd that Willie Nelson was going to sing, but a counterrumor said it was Rickie Nelson. Occasionally a voice over the loudspeaker would announce that a New Zealander named Billy Gleeson was leading the men's race, while a New Yorker named Tina Fedlow was leading the women.

Ginger wished she were in that race. She imagined the thrill of running into this crowded stadium with all eyes staring at her, everyone cheering and shouting her name. She often used a similar fantasy to get her through her daily three-mile run. She promised herself to increase her distance to four miles a day starting Monday. After that she would work her way up and enter one of the ten kilometer runs at home.

"Here you go, sport," Ronnie Elliott said, squeezing down the aisle with his arms full of food cartons. He handed something in wax paper to Beau.

"What's that?" the boy asked.

"A blintz." Elliott shrugged an apology.

"Looks like a burrito," Liza said.

"Yeah, well, they have those, too. In fact, all they got down there is ethnic food. Foods from all the countries where they want better human rights. Lots of South American foods down there." He handed Liza a Coke. "I asked them, 'Don't you have hot dogs in Poland?' But the closest they had was bratwurst from East Germany. What can I tell you?"

Ginger glared at Liza and Beau.

"Thank you, Mr. Elliott," they chorused.

"You're welcome. Hey, look! There's the President's limo."

A long black car surrounded by Secret Service men rolled slowly toward the elaborate platform in the middle of the field. Loud cheers sprinkled with boos rocked the stadium.

"Gee," Beau said. "It looks just like our limo."

"Yeah," Ronnie said proudly. "Almost."

"What's that?" Liza asked, pointing at a long wooden trough at the far end of the stadium. The trough was filled with sand and there were dozens of thick pipes sticking out of it. Two men and two women were walking back and forth inspecting each pipe.

"That's the fireworks," Ronnie explained. "In Washington they shoot off fireworks every chance they get. Somebody dies, they shoot off fireworks; somebody gets elected, they shoot off fireworks; somebody sneezes, they shoot off fireworks. This time it's daylight, so they add red, white, and blue smoke and shoot off fireworks anyway."

Ginger watched them check the fuses, then looked over at the limo as the President climbed out, flanked on all sides by serious-looking Secret Service men. The Marine band struck up "Hail to the Chief" as the President's entourage moved up the platform's wooden stairs. The loudspeaker boomed out that the New Zealander, Billy Gleeson, had dropped behind England's Thomas Flower, but that Tina Fedlow still led the women.

"Boy," Ginger said, squeezing Liza's hand. "This is exciting after all."

Cliff's leg burned as he made his way toward the VIP Lounge in Humphrey Stadium. He'd found a dirty scarf in the car and tied it around his calf to stop the bleeding. But the pain was getting worse. And so was his limp.

The drive to the stadium had been a series of near tragedies as he ran red lights and stop signs, nearly broadsiding a cab at one intersection and barely missing a young, helmetless couple on a motorcycle at another. But considering the way the day had gone so far, he figured he deserved a little luck.

His updated CIA card and a few mumbled words about presidential security had taken him past the gate guards, and he had managed to get directions to the VIP Lounge on the top floor.

Cliff checked his watch just as the loudspeaker announced that the runners were in sight at the far end of Independence Avenue.

"It's just a matter of minutes now, folks," the voice on the loudspeaker said.

Cliff found the elevator, flashed his card at the security guard posted there, and waited while the guard used his key to summon the elevator.

"Come on, come on," Cliff growled at the metal door.

The guard laughed. "Slowest damn elevator in kingdom come."

Outside the Marine band finished playing "Hail to the Chief," and another roar greeted the President as he stood at the lectern, awaiting the appearance of the first runner through the stadium gates.

The elevator door slid open and Cliff lunged inside. He punched the top button and tried to will the elevator up the shaft, but it chugged and rattled along at its own tired pace.

When the door finally squeaked open, Cliff bolted through it. A dozen young Cuban waiters in white jackets were placing linen napkins neatly on the elegant refreshment tables; others hovered over a long serving table laden with metal trays of steaming food. One waiter was telling a joke in Spanish. He stopped in the middle of his joke and looked up at Cliff. "Private," he said, waving his hands. "Private party."

Cliff ignored him as his eyes searched the room. It was basically a large box that hung out over the side of the stadium. The three exposed walls were solid glass, providing a magnificent view not only of the field but also of the Anacostia River and the park beyond. The VIP Lounge was the perfect place for the President and the rest of the VIPs to retreat to after the opening ceremonies, while the other 66,000 spectators poured out of the stadium and wrestled their cars out of the lot and into traffic that would be backed up for hours.

If Cliff didn't find the Moonshadow soon, the exodus from the stadium would be tragic.

He had to force himself not to press his face against the glass and search the crowd for Ginger and the kids. There was no reason to believe they were here, and even if they were, he couldn't get them out in time.

"The roof," Cliff said in Spanish. "How do I get to the roof."

The waiter who had been telling the joke stared. "The roof?"

"*The goddamn roof!*"

One of the other Cubans stepped forward and pointed to a closet at the back of the room. "A trapdoor in there takes you to the roof.''

Cliff limped to the closet, pulled open the door, and positioned the ladder under the trapdoor. He climbed up a few steps, unfastened the latches, and opened the trapdoor. The sudden flood of bright sunlight forced Cliff to squint as he climbed the ladder. He banged his wounded calf as he hoisted himself to the roof, and let out a curse.

Then he saw a small wooden box with six metal mortars packed in sand. Black fuses stuck out the top of each mortar, and Cliff could see the tan paper around the shells. Attached to each fuse was a filament that led to a thicker cable. The six cables led to a red metal tool box, next to which stood a sound amplifier and a microphone, also with wires running into the tool box.

The voice on the loudspeaker was providing a continual commentary of the race now. ''Billy Gleeson is back in the lead, ladies and gentlemen. Pulling several meters ahead of the others. Just another minute now . . . ''

Cliff looked over the edge of the roof and saw the churning crowd waving and shouting. The Marine band launched into a brassy version of the theme from *Rocky*. One section of the crowd was shouting ''Gonna fly now'' with the music, and the loudspeaker was blaring: ''And here comes Gleeson through the parking lot, heading for the stadium gate. The President is standing, waiting to congratulate this outstanding athlete . . . ''

Cliff stared at the tool box. He could feel the blood running down his calf, taste the sweat dripping into his mouth. He was certain that a particular sound or sequence of sounds would trigger the timer and send the electricity across the filaments to the rockets. He could break the filaments right now and stop it.

Unless the box was booby-trapped. Unless Felix had added one final precaution, one last little trick for the bastards at I-COOP.

''And there he is now,'' the loudspeaker blasted, ''Billy Gleeson of New Zealand, passing through the

stadium gate, his arms raised in victory. And what an
enthusiastic crowd it is . . . ''

Cliff reached out toward the box, then hesitated. If he
was wrong, he could detonate the whole thing himself.
Then he'd be responsible for all those deaths. But if he
did nothing . . .

"It's official, Billy Gleason is the winner. Let the fireworks officially begin this Human Rights Weekend!"

Cliff plucked the feed wires out of the tool box,
breaking the connection.

The first rocket of the smoke display screamed out of
the stadium and burst into red, white, and blue columns
a thousand feet above the crowd. The crowd roared approval.

It took Cliff less than ten minutes to dismantle the six
shells. In the middle of the roof he made one pile of all
the stuffings that were part of the fireworks, and another pile of canisters containing Moonshadow. Each
canister had a special charge attached that would have
caused it to explode in the air, spreading Moonshadow
over the crowd.

Cliff handled the shells just as carefully as he handled
the Moonshadow canister, for those shells contained
enough black powder and chemicals to send him
rocketing off the roof if he allowed one spark to ignite
them.

The colorful display overhead must have been
magnificent, though Cliff never looked up at it. The
crowd alternately gasped and applauded as the colors
splashed against the sky. When it was all over, the President began his speech.

"When we talk of human rights, we aren't pointing a
finger at any individual country. Rather, we're taking a
universal approach . . . ''

Cliff stood up and let out a deep sigh. He suddenly
realized he had hardly breathed for ten minutes. He
took several long, shaky breaths.

He heard a noise in the closet below and felt relief.
Finally someone was coming up to give him a hand. The
busboys must have reported his behavior to the security
guards. It was just as well. His leg hurt like hell, and he
was so exhausted he didn't think he'd be able to climb
back down without help. He heard footsteps on the ladder and walked toward the trapdoor to lend a hand.

A head and gun popped through the opening.

Edge Connors grinned.

Edge's jaw was obviously broken where Cliff had
kicked him. It hung at an awkward angle and there was
a long, splotchy bruise along the chin.

He continued up the ladder, pointing his gun at Cliff
and favoring his side where he'd been shot. Large drops
of sweat were beaded along his forehead. Occasionally
one would shake loose and splash down his cheek.

He appeared to be smiling, but Cliff couldn't be sure
that wasn't because of the broken jaw. Cliff backed up,
his hands away from his body.

Edge stood on the roof now weaving slightly. Half of
his face seemed to have caved in, and he leaned to his
right, still favoring his wounded side. He walked with a
lurch, like the Frankenstein monster. His magnum
gleamed silver under the bright morning sun.

The President continued his speech. "My administration will be known throughout the world as the one that
stood up for what was right, regardless of . . . "

"You're making a mistake," Cliff said quietly. He
had backed up to the edge of the roof, and there was
nowhere else to go. Edge stood near the dismantled explosive device; the Moonshadow was on his left. Cliff
knew there was no mistake. Celia had planned to have
him killed all along. That was the practical solution, and
Celia was a practical woman. Always had been. He
could remember the first time they'd met and . . .

The first time!

He could remember!

Teetering there on the edge of the stadium roof, Cliff
could suddenly recall many things. He remembered high
school, and being called into the principal's office for

flushing Karen Benson's lunch down the toilet. And college, where he met Katie. Sweet, lovely Katie and her collection of pornographic postcards. There were more memories, all crowding into his head at once. They vanished when Edge spoke.

"Jump," he said simply. "At least that way you'll have a chance."

"That's a two hundred-foot drop," Cliff reminded him.

"Beats a slug in the head. I'd hate to fire now while the President's speaking. Makes all them Secret Service men nervous and spoils the festive mood." He managed to grin wickedly. "Don't you care about Human Rights Weekend?"

"Look, pal, there's been a mistake. Just take me in, and you'll be clear. But if I die, they're going to be peeved at you."

"That's possible. But if you die from a fall, I can claim you slipped. You see, I don't really care right now whether they want you alive or not. I've got my own plan for you. And what's good for Comaplan is good for the country."

"What's Comaplan?"

"Never mind. Are you going to jump or take your chances with the magnum?"

Cliff looked over his shoulder at the drop below him. "I guess I'll take the jump."

"I thought you would," Edge chuckled. "Like Sir Francis Bacon said, 'The desire of power in excess caused the angels to fall; the desire of knowledge in excess caused man to fall.' "

"Clever," Cliff said, "only in my case it's a magnum that's causing me to fall."

Edge shrugged and pointed his gun. "Whatever."

Cliff leaped into the air.

The first shot came as soon as Edge realized Cliff had not leaped off the roof, but rather had dived for the cover behind a wooden structure that looked like a storage shed. The second shot was for good measure.

Both hit Cliff.

The first chipped his shoulderblade as it skimmed across his back like a stone skipping over a pond. The second removed the first joint of his left thumb.

Suddenly 66,000 people screamed. Someone shoved the President to the floor behind the bulletproof lectern, and Secret Service agents began scanning the stadium and yelling into their walkie-talkies.

"Up there!" people under the protruding VIP box yelled.

Cliff had his gun out, but was still pinned behind the wooden structure. His Walther had a seven-shot magazine, but he'd fired only four in the hotel. He had to make these count, and there wasn't much time. Fifty Secret Service agents would be pouring up here any minute, and he knew Edge would try to kill him before they got here.

"I'm going to kill you, Remington," Edge chuckled. "Just for the damn paperwork this is going to cause me."

Cliff pressed what was left of his thumb against his chest. He started to lift himself to his knees so he could pop up for a shot of his own, but he couldn't move. The bullet that had chipped his shoulderblade had also numbed his whole back. He heard Edge shuffling closer.

He had no choice. He'd have to shoot blindly, just raise his gun and fire in Edge's general direction. Even if he didn't hit him, the shot might hold him off until the others arrived. On the other hand, if he missed, the bullet would just sail off into the crowd.

The loudspeaker boomed with a calm voice, "Please stay calm and remain in your seats. You will be in greater danger if you try to run. Everything is under control . . ."

Edge fired another shot, and the lip of the wooden structure broke off near Cliff's head.

It was now or never, Cliff told himself. He had to do something to save his own life.

He dragged himself to the corner of the structure and peeked out. Another bullet whizzed past his head and punched through the wood. He raised his right hand and fired at the one target that wasn't moving.

The pile of disemboweled fireworks.

But Edge had fired as soon as Cliff had, chopping off another section of wooden structure, spraying splinters into Cliff's face. Cliff's eyes felt the sting just as the fireworks exploded.

He heard Edge's horrible screams while he frantically rubbed his eyes, trying to get the shards of wood and dust out so he could see what was going on. A series of loud booms sounded, and Edge's helpless cries clawed up Cliff's spine. Finally he managed to open one eye far enough to see what was happening.

Edge stood in the middle of the roof, his whole body glowing with bright red, white, and blue flames, his screams now nothing more than hoarse gasps. His hair flared up suddenly, then died out. His face was already charred black as he tried to slap the fire out with his burning hands. A strip of flaming skin peeled off his neck and spun to the ground. Another of the shells exploded, and Edge was quickly engulfed in a green flame. He spun convulsively in a pitiful dance before plunging off the edge of the roof into the screaming crowd.

30

CELIA RAISED HER glass of champagne. "Success."

The three men raised their glasses and drank.

She was wearing a lavender wool dress with a plunging neckline. Around her neck was a gold chain given to her by a grateful Middle Eastern sheikh whose assassination she'd once prevented. Months later, without his knowledge, she'd funneled funds to his opposition, financing his overthrow. His execution had followed shortly thereafter.

Tom Hawkins cleared his throat. "Well, I-COOP is saved."

"And our asses as well," Eric added.

General Gerrard tugged on his mustache. "Certainly, we were doing only what was best for this country and . . . " He let the rest of the sentence drift away, and polished off his champagne. "Good stuff," he said, refilling his glass.

"What did you tell the President?" Tom Hawkins asked.

"That we uncovered and foiled an assassination plot."

Eric laughed. "Did you really say 'foiled'?"

"He expects that kind of language from us," Celia smiled.

"I hate to prod a sore spot," Hawkins said, "but what about the Moonshadow?"

258

"Gone," Celia answered. "Those six cylinders were the last of Moonshadow, and they've been destroyed."

"Well," General Gerrard said, finishing his fourth glass of champagne. "All's well that ends well, eh?"

"Hold that thought, Steve," Celia said. "In the meantime, it's back to work. Chop chop."

Eric snickered as Tom Hawkins and General Gerrard refilled their champagne glasses and wandered out of the room. "Chop chop?"

"I heard that in a Doris Day movie." She leaned forward, caught Eric glancing down her dress, and smiled broadly. "Naughty, naughty. You have a reputation, remember."

Eric smiled.

"You're in a terribly good mood today, Eric my dear."

He raised his glass of champagne. "Success, remember?"

"Well, I wouldn't call it a hundred percent success. I lied to the others."

"What do you mean?"

"I guess I can trust you, Eric," she sighed. "But there is still one canister of Moonshadow left."

"What?"

She handed him a sheet of paper. "This came an hour ago."

Eric read the hand-written note: "You must have noticed that there were six canisters of Moonshadow on the stadium roof. However, after making his rockets, Felix had a little left over in his hotel room. Just enough to kill a few dozen people. Don't worry, it's safe with me. However, if any harm comes to me or to Ginger or to her kids, it will automatically be sent to the President, with a detailed report of what happened. For your sake, we'd better remain one very healthy family."

"Think he's bluffing?"

Celia shrugged. "Hard to say. I'd hate to take the chance, though."

"Then it looks like he's out of it."

"For now," she smiled. "He'd just better hope this President gets reelected."

Eric tapped his apartment key impatiently against the elevator door as it carried him to his floor. He couldn't remember being this happy before. He'd barely been able to contain himself at work. Even Celia had noticed his good mood, though he'd cleverly attributed it to their recent success.

In thirty minutes he was scheduled to meet Jack, the President's bright-eyed boy. After he handed over the tapes, Celia Bedford would flash those capped teeth no more. Come Monday morning, Eric would be the new head of I-COOP. "What a nice way to end Human Rights Weekend," he said to himself as he unlocked his apartment door.

He unscrewed the electrical outlet plate and disconnected the hidden security wires. Then he held in his hands the four one-hour tapes he'd compiled during this crisis, when Celia's usually impenetrable defenses were down.

" 'Is it live or is it Memorex?' " he chuckled as he popped the first tape into his portable cassette player. At first there was nothing but static, so he turned up the volume. Then Donna Summer sang "On the Radio." His stomach turned sour, then growled as he put the machine on fast forward and pressed the play button. Donna Summer and Barbra Streisand sang "Enough is Enough." Frantically he played each of the other tapes. But they were all music. The Village People singing "YMCA." The Bee Gees doing "Stayin' Alive." And in the background, not a part of the music, was some kind of noise, a thump, thump, thump.

Like someone jumping on a trampoline.

PART SIX

Friday

31

CLIFF TAPPED HIS bandaged thumb on the steering wheel. He tried to take a deep breath, but the gauze around his chest and shoulderblade was too tight. Amid the confusion at the stadium, the Secret Service had taken one look at his CIA card and had their own medics do a superficial patch-up job on him. There'd been some talk of a hospital, and at that point Cliff had ducked out and found his own "doctor."

He'd needed the time to send the note to Celia. He didn't know whether or not she'd buy his story, but she was a practical woman, and she had nothing to gain by calling his bluff. So he was safe. For now.

He looked out the window of the car at the house across the street. He'd been parked here for three hours now, waiting for the woman to come out. He wasn't sure what he would do when she did.

It was a big house, in an affluent neighborhood with clean streets.

He'd done some checking up on them. David Turner was a dentist with a steady practice. He played tennis and squash, though he excelled at neither, which somehow made Cliff feel better. Turner drove a ten-year-old Mercedes that cost him more in repairs than it was worth, but he fancied himself a fair mechanic and liked to work on the engine whenever he got the chance.

Katie Turner worked as a court reporter and was, by all accounts, good at her job. She also played tennis,

usually beating Dave. Apparently he wasn't a very good
sport about that. Otherwise, they were the perfect couple.

Katie Turner had once been Katie Quill, Cliff's wife.

The Turners had two sons. The older boy had been
born a month prematurely following her first husband's
unexpected death. Two years later she had married
Turner. The second son was only two months old, and
Katie was still on maternity leave.

The house stood among spreading trees, piles of
raked leaves, well-kept lawns. What was a man with
half a thumb and a bullet groove down his back doing
here?

Cliff slammed his hand against the steering wheel
again. She was *his* wife, and the older boy was *his* child.
He'd come to claim them. He remembered their life together now. Every detail. It had been a good life, filled
with love and caring and laughter and anger and making
up. Sure, there had been problems. Long periods of
being apart while he traveled. And missing her. And
deep depressions because he couldn't tell her the truth
about where he'd been or what he'd done.

But, damn it, she was still *his*!

Then Ginger's face filled his head, and he gave a sudden sigh. Last night he had called her at the hotel and
told her everything, the whole truth, including Katie.
The hell with open lines and codes. He had to tell somebody. He needed to. No, not just somebody—Ginger.
She had listened quietly, and when he was all through
she'd said only, "When are you coming home?"

"I don't know," he'd said, and made her promise to
take the next plane back to California. Later he'd called
the airline, and they confirmed she had flown back.

The front door across the street opened, and a tall
woman with short dark hair eased a baby carriage down
the front step. At her side was a little boy with Cliff's
sandy hair.

Cliff opened the car door and got out.

32

GINGER RAN THE hot water in the sink until the steam stung her eyes. It had to be good and hot. Antiseptic. This house was going to get the kind of cleaning it never had. She swept a pile of dishes into the sudsy water with her arm.

"Where do you want this?" Liza asked with a frown. She held the dried-out sponge mop as if it were a dead snake. "I don't think this mop is going to get anything clean. There's more dirt on it than there is on the floor."

"Well, then, we'll buy a new one tomorrow," Ginger replied. "In the meantime start folding the clean laundry."

"Jeez, Mom, we just got home this morning. I'm tired. We hardly slept in two days."

"You slept on the plane."

"That's not the same thing."

Beau shuffled into the kitchen with a watering can. "I did all the plants. Can we take a break now?"

"Not yet. I want this place in order. Things are going to be different around here from now on. We're going to keep everything neat. Everything has its place. Got it?"

"Boy, what'd we do now?" Beau mumbled.

"Search me. She must be having her period."

Ginger spun around, her face contorted with anger, her hands dripping with hot suds.

"Her period?" Beau asked. "What's that?"

"You dumb pimp," Liza replied.

Ginger had meant to yell, maybe even cry, but it came out as a laugh. Not a hysterical laugh, but the loud, booming laugh that always caused heads to turn and strangers to smile. She laughed and laughed until the kids joined in, not even knowing what they were laughing at.

"Ah, the hell with it," she said, drying her hands on her jeans. "Let's run out for pizza and watch TV."

"Yea," Beau shouted.

But the shouts were interrupted by a new voice. "All right, who left the front door unlocked?"

Cliff walked into the kitchen.

Ginger gasped when she saw his bruises and bandage.

"Cliff!" Liza shouted, grabbing his arm.

"Hey, watch it," he laughed with a wince, holding up his bandaged thumb.

"Wow," Beau whistled. "What happened?"

"It was shot off."

"Neat!"

Cliff laughed again. "I thought I heard something about pizza."

"Go grab your sweaters," Ginger said, and the kids ran out of the kitchen, chattering happily.

She looked at him from across the kitchen for a long time. When she spoke, her voice was low but firm. "What happened on Long Island. With Katie?"

He shrugged. "Nothing. I almost talked to her. Decided at the last moment not to. Instead I jumped back into my car and drove like hell to the airport."

"Why, Cliff?"

"There was no point to it. She has a good life now. And so do I." He walked toward her. "Here with you and the kids and the fertilizer."

A tear slid down her cheek. "You sure?"

He wrapped his arms around her waist. "Positive."

She flung her arms around him and hugged tightly.

"Owww. Be careful of the walking wounded." He

leaned over and kissed her softly on the eyes, then the lips.

The kids ran back into the kitchen carrying sweaters.

"Come on, they close early," Liza urged.

"When I told you to get sweaters, I didn't mean to carry them. Put them on."

They struggled into them as they ran out the front door.

Cliff stopped and turned to face Ginger. "I love you."

She smiled and kissed him lightly on the cheek. "I love you, too. And don't forget it."

"Don't worry," he said, slipping his arm around her as they walked out of the house. "That was the one thing I didn't forget."

**An American-Russian face-off
from the author of
topselling SHOW OF FORCE and
THE SUNSET PATRIOTS**

FIRST SALVO

by Charles D. Taylor

The Soviets have a plan — and the Americans
are in for their ultimate test at sea.
Rear Admiral David Pratt pits a hand-picked
team of naval mavericks against
the Soviet's top military strategists in
a thriller that follows real-life
global intrigue to its inevitable climax.

__ **FIRST SALVO** 0-441-23982-X/$3.50
On Sale in February '85

Prices may be slightly higher in Canada.

Available at your local bookstore or return this form to:

 CHARTER
*Book Mailing Service
P.O. Box 690, Rockville Centre, NY 11571*

Please send me the titles checked above. I enclose _____. Include 75¢ for postage
and handling if one book is ordered; 25¢ per book for two or more not to exceed
$1.75. California, Illinois, New York and Tennessee residents please add sales tax.

NAME_____

ADDRESS_____

CITY_____ STATE/ZIP_____

(Allow six weeks for delivery.)   **(FS)**